War of the Dremrel
(Book One)

Fat Man Walking

Jackson Tuwcroze

Published by Tuwcroze Books

Book Cover Image Copyright © Nejron Photo, 2013

Used under license from Shutterstock.com

ISBN-13: 978-0-9576190-0-5
ISBN-10: 0-9576190-0-6

DEDICATION

To the one who makes all things possible, including the
power to dream.

ACKNOWLEDGMENTS

No one person can create on his own. We are products of the best and worst in us and in those around us. I was privileged to receive the best of my friends in creating this work and seeing into some of the worst in myself. The journey continues for all of us.
My wife is the one I lean on and without whom this wouldn't exist.

1 THE JOURNEY BEGINS

Darjoon sat staring at a wasp buzzing against the window pane. It was a typical hot, drowsy afternoon in class, like so many he'd endured over the last four years. The teacher was droning on about the application of fourth year magic, but the wasp was much more interesting. In the back of his mind he knew this would be over soon, like a bad dream that had to end eventually, and he found it hard to pay attention now. The wasp landed on the window and started exploring the crumbling plaster. He wondered if it was looking for a new home, then idly slipped into a day-dream about how it would crawl through the window and sting his teacher. He chuckled to himself, then looked around the old room with its sleepy students and peeling walls. Various charts on different types of magic hung next to old, yellowed maps and drawings of exotic, far-away places. He wished he could be walking down the streets in one of those ancient cities, or exploring the desert with its many strange tribes, or riding across the green plains under a big, blue sky. Anything instead of this awful place. With typical teenage angst, he'd hated his years at college, always feeling that he was out of place and out of time, loathing the endless messing around with books and spells and especially the unending physical exercise. He was sick of the over-protective teachers who lectured on all kinds of interesting magic, only to warn you of the dangers and never let you experience any of the benefits. Those same teachers who heartlessly banged on your bedroom door every morning before sunrise and then drove you mercilessly through the mind-numbing, choreographed fight drills. Darjoon sighed and then smiled to himself, remembering that graduation wasn't far away and soon he'd be lying in and waiting for the smell of grandma's pancakes to waft up the stairs. An irresistible siren-song of syrupy sweetness that invariably lured him down to breakfast. He shook his head to clear the delectable image as it didn't compare well with the red-faced anger he currently endured every morning from old Kromnak, his form teacher. The big man may have been old, but he was still every bit as formidable a warrior mage as he must have been during the Freedom Wars and he remained an imposing figure to the young boys. For some reason Kromnak had disliked him instantly when they met, and pretty much been angry with him ever since. The old teacher was still determined to mould him into a decent mage, in spite of Darjoon's best efforts to avoid that happening.

The wasp tried another listless prod of some loose plaster on the hot window-sill, then gave up and flew off into the heat haze surrounding the college buildings. Oh how wonderful it would be to just fly off right now, drifting over the college and away.

"Sweet Zukar", he thought to himself, "will I make it to the end?"

He'd no idea how he'd managed to survive these last four years of hell. Every young raven-born was forced to attend college at the age of fourteen for four intensive years of training. There'd always been the hope that he'd wash out early in disgrace and get assigned to manual labour on the farms in Lower Srinth. Not that he cared much about disgrace, after all honour and valour were still foreign concepts to him. This was in spite of Kromnak's fierce, relentless tutelage. Besides, the thought of endless supplies of food and ale sounded like an ideal lifestyle. It wasn't that working with livestock would be appealing but he was certain there would be other ways to make himself useful, like keeping bees and making honeyed ale. Hmm, licking his lips, he thought of himself in a bee-keepers outfit surrounded by buzzing insects and delicious pots of honey. Longingly, he glanced out the window at the sky outside and then sighed again. If only he, Darjoon, could actually fly away. A boy in front glanced back at him and shook his head slightly, frowning as he did so. The students had all been put to work transcribing notes from old scrolls and, as usual, he was far behind, the tell-tale stack of scrolls on his desk a mute testimony to his lazy day-dreaming.

Yes, he thought to himself, he knew he didn't measure up, after all it wasn't as if the teachers and students hadn't tried to beat honour and valour into him countless times. As Kromnak often put it, "To forge a half-decent weapon out of low-grade metal, you have to burn it hotter and strike it harder" and he'd been determined to prove that with Darjoon.

But it seemed he had a surprising capacity for enduring punishment that was only matched by his strange and powerful magic. He knew that's why they made him stay on at college, so they could see how his strange magic would finally develop. Not that he hadn't thought of leaving many times, but running away from the raven-born hierarchy was like flying without wings. There was nowhere you could hide, either from them or their agents, and you wouldn't know who was after you until it was too late. If they decided to send one of those Spidralites on your trail, well, he shivered involuntarily and glanced at the boys in the class around him. Not a single Spidralite assassin had ever failed a mission in thousands of years. He could just imagine an assassin silently creeping up on him right now, ready to blow a poisoned dart into his neck and end his life.

Thwack! The small ball of elastic hit him just behind the ear and right on the sensitive tip. He jumped up in surprise, jolting his desk and knocking over his inkwell, which rolled to the edge and dripped its contents over the side. The floor around his desk was already dotted with previous ink-stains, and now this one just spread out and joined up with them, slowly oozing into the wooden boards. Quickly stepping back to get away from the dripping ink, he barged into his chair which sent it crashing into the desk behind. Turning, he stared, transfixed, as on that desk, an ink bottle wobbled, wobbled some more, held, then slowly toppled and oozed its dark contents all over the meticulous writings of the perfectly proportioned, muscular and good-looking Soodram.

Darjoon froze, knowing this was going to be bad. To all outward appearances, Soodram was the raven-born ideal of an athletic young man with impeccable manners to match. Yet inside that perfect young man was a festering pit of darkness that Darjoon had thankfully only witnessed a few times. Which is why he did his best to avoid him at all costs, and why originally he'd made a point of sitting on the far side of the class where he was well away from the evil boy. Of course the teacher had called him over at the start of the year and told him to sit at the desk directly in front of Soodram. This had been in the vain hope that he would absorb some real raven-born qualities by just being near the star pupil.

So now with growing horror he watched as the familiar, evil anger appeared and spread across Soodram's face like a red rash. Instinctively Darjoon started to back away but suddenly strong, thick fingers grasped his sideburn and lifted, causing him to freeze in position. The teacher had stealthily ambushed him from behind. He waited for the now familiar roar, but nothing came, and although the grip didn't let go and he couldn't actually see the teacher standing behind him, he saw a look of shared understanding pass across Soodram's face, followed by a smirk and then a subtle nod. He gulped. This did not look good for his future well-being, not good at all.

"Well, oh great fat one, can you cast a spell to clean up your mess this time? If you even think about using one in my classroom I'll make sure your form teacher knows all about it. You know what that means for you, don't you Darjoon, lots of running and no food. The one you always avoid and the other is your passion, isn't it! Isn't it, you fat slug!", the teacher roared, then abruptly sighed in dramatic fashion.

"I suppose I shouldn't complain as you won't be here much longer, thank Zukar. I've never understood why they bothered keeping you at our fine college. If those in charge had thought you'd amount to anything, then surely by now they've realised what a mistake they made? I mean, isn't it obvious you've eaten up what little promise you ever had, fat and clumsy as you are."

The teacher turned around to the rest of the class, raising his shaggy eyebrows, "Careful everyone, fat boy walking!"

The other students laughed at the familiar phrase and then, as the bell rang, jumped up and stood to rigid attention. All except Soodram, who stood glaring at Darjoon as he painfully dangled from the teachers firm grasp.

"Very well, class dismissed, all except for this fat worm. He has to lick up the ink he's spilt on our beloved Soodram's desk. Maybe, if we're lucky, he'll absorb some understanding and come close to being a real raven-born like Soodram", the teacher sniffed, then waved the class out with his free hand.

Darjoon groaned inside as this meant he'd not only be late for the next class, he'd be dirty as well. Meaning he'd have to endure even more tongue-lashing from the other teachers. Oh well, another day at college, why should it be any different to all the other days. Zukar, how he really, really hated this place. Soodram glowered at him one final time, then joined the other sniggering students that were slowly filing out of class. Darjoon sighed and went to get a mop, a bucket and the dirty old towel from the small room behind the teachers desk. He was used to these grand threats of serious harm, but the teacher would never force Darjoon to actually lick up the ink. That would be against the code of conduct for a raven-born because it would not be honourable. The teacher glared at him as he started wiping the stain, then walked to the front of the class and sat behind his desk, marking papers and giving him the occasional hate-filled scowl. Once he'd finished, he headed off for his other classes, getting scowls and growls from all his teachers due to the ink that had inevitably dirtied his shirtsleeves and smudged his hands.

Later that day, after the final bell of the afternoon rang and the last class of the day was dismissed, Darjoon waited patiently at his desk and pretended to be busy until the usual, perennial bullies had filed out the classroom. Radnort and his gang glanced over at Darjoon as they walked past, then carried on talking among themselves as they exited the door. He sighed. If he could just avoid them until the year was out then he'd be away and finally rid of them forever. Every school had bullies and these were the usual, relatively harmless kind, happy to hand out an odd beating or embarrassment but nothing more. At least not when compared to the dark, inner evil of Soodram, who Darjoon had ominously not seen for the rest of the day. He sighed again and sidled out of class, his instincts working overtime as his eyes flickered everywhere, desperately trying to spot any danger. He couldn't see any of the bully boys down any of the corridors, and they didn't seem to be waiting in the grassy quadrangle under the big tree like they usually did, so he quickened his pace.

"Fine, Darjoon, all clear", he mumbled to himself, "Now just slide round the corner, ease across the quad and get to the study hall."

It was a fact that once he was studying they tended to leave him alone, not wanting to make too much fuss. This was mainly because the teachers would occasionally pop in to make sure everyone had their heads in their books. Not that any of the students would directly interfere, oh no, all the young raven-born lived by their precious code. One of the precepts of the code was that only the strong should survive, which is why the students were surprised every year that Darjoon was still with them. He would typically be greeted with a mixture of hilarity and disgust whenever he wandered into the first class of the new year. He eased past the grassy quad, then headed swiftly towards the corridor that led to the study hall.

He felt the tingling on his skin long before he heard the slight crackling and saw the blue haze in the air. Without blinking he deftly countered the containment spell with his own defensive magic and shredded it easily. Glancing around guiltily, he tried to see if a teacher was nearby, knowing that unsupervised magic was theoretically taboo, especially for fourth years. The teachers didn't even allow a tiny fire spell for lighting your candle, although that didn't stop the students from trying. Thankfully, the minor spells were easy to get away with but anything more powerful and the wards in the college grounds would be triggered. The duty teacher, who was always linked to the wards, would then know a strong spell had been used. They'd also know who the offender was, so it wouldn't be long before a pair of teachers arrived to escort the student off to their punishment, usually extra chores or writing out.

But spells used in combat were dealt with very severely. Most of the time the offending student was never seen or heard from again. In fact, some of the stories said the student was set loose in the Darken Hills, the massive mountains that bordered the raven-born lands, and then they were slowly hunted for sport by the elder mages or by terrible monsters. Others said they were set adrift on the Salacian Sea in a small boat, slowly gyrating on the random, looping, maddening currents for eternity and never seeing land again.

In typical raven-born machismo however, physical fighting was actively encouraged by the staff. Everyone knew that matters between students were meant to be settled in traditional ways to preserve honour and balance. This meant privately with fists, or using borrkilli in duels that were arranged and supervised by the teachers. Borrkilli were wooden training swords with blunt edges and a rounded tip, and although not fatal could still be wielded with painful effect. He'd never been on the receiving end of a borrkilli, simply because he preferred to let the bullies beat and kick him while he pretended to suffer. It was easier and a lot less painful, especially as for some reason he almost never felt their beatings. When he did feel anything he could quickly heal himself afterwards. But the borrkilli could break bones and those were a lot harder to repair, besides which he was meant to be a coward and had a reputation to uphold.

Darjoon watched carefully as Radnort and his gang sauntered out from under the tree. He'd known it was him because he was the only student audacious enough to use such strong combat magic right out in the open. Radnort's father, Mokdor, was the High Sorcerer and so it meant his son had a degree of immunity. Mokdor was a man of great courage and valour, a true raven-born, but if he had one weakness then it was his wife, a conniving woman of no real ability, some beauty and great aspiration. She had pushed Mokdor into training their eldest son, Radnort, long before he ever came to college, thereby making sure he arrived with a head start on the other students. It was no secret that she was grooming Radnort to take over his father's position one day and consequently the young apprentice mage was a spoilt brat, only moderately powerful in both physique and magic, and average in every other way. He had learnt to bully his way to the top from his mother and also chose his alliances carefully, mainly by including in his inner circle those gang-members who only listened to him, and then bullying any who dared show any signs of weakness or opposition. He made sure that he flattered any of the students who were truly powerful and influential, including Soodram who followed Radnort out from behind the tree. He was smiling a nasty smile and holding a borrkilli loosely in one hand. Darjoon's heart sank. The presence of Soodram meant this was not going to be just another regular bout of bullying that was soon over.

"Well, well", Radnort said as he sauntered over to Darjoon, looking him up and down and grinning back at his gang who smirked and grinned in response, "we couldn't let you leave here without a taste of the borrkilli, could we, Darjoon? You've never been man enough to face one before. Oh, you remember how many times we tried to call you out? Those times that we took your manhood from you, beating you like a girl until you snivelled and cried. Somehow it was never very satisfying, not until today that is. You see, Darjoon, our beloved Soodram here tells me his favourite magic teacher wants us to especially punish you on his behalf. Something to remember him by before he leaves, to try and make up for all those years you made him, Soodram, and the rest of us look so bad. Oh, of course, you wouldn't have heard? He's leaving tomorrow to investigate a silly rumour about a new Dremrel outbreak in the Darken Hills, apparently there's a lot more of those evil things. So consider this his parting gift as it were, a last chance to redeem yourself. Of course, Soodram is also rather annoyed because now he has to write out his copy again, seeing how you stupidly spilt ink all over it."

Darjoon cringed and looked around frantically. The teachers had seemed pretty distracted lately, holding lots of meetings, and so it meant they'd not be around until much later in the evening. And all the other students were now in the study hall, frantically cramming for final exams. Also, although Radnort had used strong magic, he knew the duty teacher would know who it was and so probably ignore it. As usual he was entirely on his own and about to get another beating. If the physical pain wasn't always that bad, the shame that flooded him afterwards was. Darjoon resorted to his usual tactic of cajoling and wheedling, something that normally incited a quick reprisal and a short beating.

"Please, Radnort, I, I'm really very sorry. You're so right, that was just stupid of me. I'll write it out for you, Soodram, every word of it. I will! I promise. It was all my fault, all of it. Please, please just let me go, I, I've got a lot of studying to do", he cowered in front of the boys, hoping they'd take the bait.

Soodram looked at him, stony-faced, then walked over and without saying a word slapped him hard, rocking him back on his heels. Darjoon put a hand up to his face, and with his ears still ringing, saw the gang looking at each other in stunned surprise. Students who wanted to settle things honourably would usually go to a teacher who would then set a day for battle. The duel was supervised by that teacher, a few students attended as witnesses and there were strict rules of engagement. Each student was given the borrkilli and was told there were to be no head or groin blows and no stamping, biting, gouging or kicking of any kind. Then the students fought until the teacher was satisfied the matter was settled, which was usually when one or both of the students were lying on the ground rolling in pain.

But what Soodram had just done was an adult act and called for an immediate duel to the death. The gang of bullies looked nervously at their leader and one of them cleared his throat meaningfully. Radnort glanced across at Soodram, whose face was mottled red with rage. This did not look like a casual afternoon's drubbing of Darjoon but appeared to be turning into something a lot more serious. Radnort frowned and stepped forward.

"Uh, Soodram, are you okay? I mean, we just want to scare him and mess him around a bit, right, big guy? We're not actually going to use the, uh…", Radnort's voice trailed off as he saw Soodram's face redden further with rage. The flashing eyes swivelled to focus on him, piercing him like daggers and he involuntarily stepped back a pace.

"Shut up, you half-wit! Can't you see what a mockery he is? How he makes us all look bad? The fat, snivelling coward! You should have done this long ago, Radnort. You should have run him out of here with his tail between his legs. I can't believe my final year of graduation is going to be marred by this ingrate. This incompetent sack of…"

Soodram's rapid, angry barks turned into a low, incoherent growl. He turned from Radnort and advanced menacingly on Darjoon with the borrkilli raised over his head. Suddenly he lunged forward while his right arm swept down and drew the borrkilli in towards his chest. At the same time, he snapped out his left arm and grabbed Darjoon's shirt to pull him close.

With a real sword this action would have pulled Darjoon onto the blade, effectively driving it into his chest and through his heart. But before the borrkilli could touch him, Darjoon lifted his right arm with his fist clenched and slid Soodram's left hand away, forcing him to let go. In the same fluid movement his left foot flowed forward, shifting his weight, and his left palm connected with the blunt tip of the borrkilli, thrusting the other end through Soodram's right hand and hard into his chest with Darjoon's weight fully behind it. Soodram gasped with pain, then staggered back and sat down hard, dropping the borrkilli and clutching his chest.

As Radnort and the others stared in disbelief, Darjoon realised it had now gone from bad to really, really, very bad. For as long as he could remember, he had hidden both his fighting and magical abilities and practised by himself whenever he got the chance, to make sure no-one could see what he was capable of. The gang, however, had just witnessed his real fighting skill and he saw a glimmer of understanding as they looked at him and then each other in awe. The move he'd just made was a smooth, well-executed, defense strategy that was taught only in the fourth year and was quite difficult to master effectively. He'd repeatedly got it wrong in class, much to their amusement and the teachers disgust, but he'd now performed it smoothly and flawlessly and to very good effect.

Radnort was thinking furiously, knowing that Soodram didn't have an off-switch, especially if he thought he was being shown up or about to be bested by someone. This was why he always won, because others would just give up and let him win, rather than fight on endlessly. Radnort quickly stepped in front of Soodram and picked up the borrkilli where it had fallen on the ground. He didn't offer his hand to the stricken boy, who was battling to catch his breath, knowing full well that any help like that would be rejected, but instead he laughed out loud to try and ease the tension.

"What a lucky break for Darjoon, he must've gotten his inky fingers on the borrkilli causing it to slip". Turning the wooden sword over in his hand, he glanced down at Soodram, hoping against hope to see any sign that he'd give this up.

His gang laughed and shuffled nervously, smiling with him in agreement. Soodram stood up, a studied frown on his face, then calmly and deliberately taking control of his breathing silently held out his hand for the borrkilli while glaring at Radnort.

"Uh, I think we should be studying, don't you Soodram? I mean there's a lot we need to review for the tests tomorrow, don't you agree?", Radnort kept hold of the borrkilli, holding it in front of him like a shield. He knew he had to get Soodram away from here before it got ugly. Some of his gang started to drift off in a vain attempt to encourage Soodram to leave.

In hindsight, if Soodram had just used simple magic the outcome may have been different, but he performed two unusual acts of magic that caused Darjoon to react instinctively and immediately. First, Soodram grabbed the borrkilli from Radnort, and then before anyone could react he spelled a shield barrier around Radnort's gang. Second, he swung the borrkilli overhead at Radnort with real, violent intent, accentuating the blow with a force spell. Darjoon gasped. The large shield spell alone required highly skilled mastery of fourth year magic, but the combined use of that and an acceleration spell that meshed with physical attack, well that was not something you could ever learn in college. Soodram must have had a private tutor, or else he'd been doing some late night studying and practice of what were strictly forbidden techniques.

Darjoon countered without thinking, raising his hands to send out a tendril of reactive force that deflected the borrkilli and saved Radnort's skull from certain crushing. Simultaneously, he reversed the polarity of the shield spell so that it rebounded on the caster, effectively wrapping Soodram in his own shield. This used the combined might of both Darjoon and Soodram's power to at least double the original efficiency of the spell. Darjoon had been doing some late night studying of his own, however he had not had a tutor nor any combat experience to help him measure the strength of the magic he was using. This meant that instead of simply deflecting the borrkilli away from Radnort, it reversed direction with such tremendous force that it shattered the bones in Soodram's arm and continued, smashing into his face where it pulverised his nose and broke his jaw. Darjoon's magic also augmented the rebounding shield spell so that it blocked all physical aspects. This meant that no-one in the quad other than

Darjoon himself could see or hear what was going on inside. Not that it mattered, as the result of the spell soon became very obvious. Due to the power of the magic that was unleashed, the shield spell constricted far beyond the original instruction. It compressed Soodram's body into a small, spherical ball of flesh and bone and then disappeared, dropping the soggy ball onto the lawn with a sickening squelch for everyone to see.

There was dead silence in the quad for what seemed like ages, and then a few of the boys, including Radnort, turned away to the shrubbery behind them and retched. For Darjoon it had seemed to happen incredibly slowly, as if time had just stood still around him, whereas for the others the exchange of spells was over in the blink of an eye. The sickening wet thud of the grisly ball hitting the turf had stunned them. The boys who hadn't eaten lunch or had stronger stomachs all turned from staring at Soodram's grisly remains to see Darjoon's bulk disappearing at a surprisingly rapid rate. For all his apparent size, he could move like the wind at times, and, recovering faster than the other boys, he realised this was definitely one of those times.

He was now moving very, very quickly indeed.

It was only when he was some distance from the college that he become aware of an important fact. Not only was the scenery a blur rushing past him but this blurred scenery was actually some distance below him. He'd heard other students talk about senior mages who could move themselves through the air, having mastered a form of levitation, but he didn't know of any young raven-born apprentice who could actually fly as he was doing now. The only problem was that now he'd started flying, he really had no idea how to stop. He closed his eyes as the wind whistled past his ears, letting his mind drift in search of an answer, a habit he used when studying. Instead, as was often the way with him, his mind drifted to memories of his past.

Darjoon had grown up without a father, never knowing him or anything about him or even who his father's family had been. His mother had simply mentioned that he'd gone off to hunt Dremrel and never returned and given him no more information than that. She'd tried to surround Darjoon with other father figures, but despite her best intentions he'd remained a quiet, sensitive and aloof youngster. The naturally boisterous rough-housing of the average raven-born meant that he had to change who he was and pretend to be like them, or stand out like a sore thumb. Darjoon chose the latter, as even from an early age he didn't really care what people thought of him. Besides, there'd been that incident when he was much younger. He had joined in some rough-housing, after much cajoling from his mother, and had accidentally broken bones. All he'd done was instinctively grab a boy's arm to make him stop hurting another child, and without much effort on his part the arm had snapped like a twig. He'd been scared all day, thinking that he was going to be severely punished. However raven-born didn't squeal and neither did the boy at the time, saying instead that he'd broken it in a fall. Apparently honour also meant you could lie to protect someone which he'd thought strange. After the incident he'd just avoided that kind of play, not caring if they thought he was a coward and so that pattern of behaviour had been set.

His mother became recognised as one of the few great warrior mages of the raven-born nation, and consequently very busy, especially when she was elected to the High Council. So he lived what seemed to others to be a painful, lonely, isolated existence in his own world. To Darjoon however, it was bliss just being with himself. There was one person he could tolerate aside from his mother, and that was his maternal grandfather. Grandpa was a grumpy, gnarled old man who was known as something of a rebel, especially as he was prone to correcting everyone regardless of rank or title. Even the other five great mages of the High Council, who occasionally stopped by to see his mother, were not exempt from grandpa's criticism and grumpiness.

And then one day, while Darjoon was still quite young, his grandfather sat him down and looked at him seriously. He'd been vaguely aware that his mother was engaged on raven-born business, but not what it was or where. As he'd sat looking up into grandpa's face he'd known with the certainty of youth that she wasn't coming back again. Grandpa told him, with tears in his eyes, that she'd been killed in a fight with a Dremrel coven, and that they'd found her dead body in the mountains. The funeral had been a simple, understated affair with only himself, his grandparents and the five great mages in attendance. The body had been placed on a large bier that was lit by mage-fire and the last he'd seen of his mother was an image of leaping flames reaching up into the late afternoon twilight.

As for his maternal grandmother, she was a typical old raven-born woman with no fine feelings, just hard muscle and sinew and a no-nonsense approach to child-rearing. If she was considerate, sometimes making him pancakes for breakfast, then she was also removed, paying him no more attention than her ruugyam which she doted on. This was a small, furry, six-legged cat-like creature with a long tail that had a bushy tip. In fact, she'd been known to mix up the things feeding bowl with Darjoon's own plate and once he'd been halfway through his meal before he realised what the food was. She'd told him it was to test his awareness, although in truth she could often be forgetful and absent-minded. According to her, he'd failed the test, and when he said that he liked the ruugyam's food anyway, she'd just frowned at him and shaken her head in disapproval.

One thing that grandpa did well was teaching. Despite all his cantankerous years of correcting people and his early years growing up on a farm without any training of his own, he'd been pretty good at patiently instructing

Darjoon in the arts of fighting and magic. Even with his grandfather, Darjoon had been very careful to conceal his true abilities. During grandpa's training, Darjoon discovered that despite his own apparent bulk, his reflexes were lightning fast and his body could move with fluidity. One particular day he'd been a little too eager, getting caught up in the exercises and forgetting to hold back as he allowed himself to become one with what he was doing. He'd stopped immediately when he saw his grandpa standing and staring at him with his mouth open.

"Even fat worms become dragons", he'd heard grandpa mutter to himself, shaking his head in disbelief and unaware that Darjoon could hear him.

After that he'd been extra careful to keep within his self-imposed limits. Something that had quickly become obvious to him was how his magic was different to others, and then he discovered just how different. Fooling around one day when he was still young, he'd accidentally set the ruugyam's tail on fire with just a stray thought. The truth was that for almost all raven-born magic to work, it involved real discipline and concentration, with specific waving of hands in the air according to predefined patterns and exact chanting. But it seemed he didn't always need the chanting or hand-waving and in fact his power seemed to thrum through his bones, bursting out of him with just a carefully constructed and controlled thought.

Well, he'd always thought it was controlled, until today that is. He opened his eyes and blinked, realising that without knowing what he'd been doing, he'd drifted down to stand in front of his grandparent's house. The cottage they lived in now was a lot smaller than the large farm house they used to have. It was set on a small lane that led up to the farm proper and there were no other cottages in the lane so it was unlikely anyone had seen him arrive. He started trembling as the reality of what he'd done set in. Closing his eyes, he could see the grisly wet ball lying on the quad and the blood seeping into the grass. That ball was all that remained of Soodram. The reality that the boy was actually dead and that he'd been the one to kill him hit home and he staggered and went down on one knee, retching emptily as the bile flew up his throat. As he began to panic, his training asserted itself and he went through a calming exercise, reaching for that elusive, much-needed balance inside himself. He needed to think clearly about his next steps. Unfortunately his grandparents were old and infirm, his grandfather confined to bed and slowly fading away and his grandmother as like to turn him in as help him. No, they wouldn't be any help now.

As he stood up slowly, thinking furiously about the best plan of action, he felt the hair on the back of his neck lift and suddenly he was thrown forward and down. His limbs were immobilised and it actually felt like he was physically tied up, even though he instinctively knew it was just a rope spell. Without thought he immediately used his magic to cut through the spell as if it were tissue paper. Hearing the gasps behind him, he threw himself three paces to the right, somersaulting in mid-air and landing on the balls of his feet, facing the enemy. A part of his brain was screaming at him to stop, to cower on the floor, to just give in and not fight, but some long-dormant instincts inside him came to life and he felt himself fill with raw power.

The shield spell that he'd thrown while somersaulting through the air had immobilised two senior mages. Their mouths were working but he couldn't hear any sound and so he immediately collapsed the spell, afraid of the same effect he'd witnessed earlier with Soodram. That turned out to be a mistake, as they had been busy chanting spells of their own and the new containment field that now trapped him was much, much stronger. Even though he felt he could still shred it with relative ease, the calm, rational part of his mind had come up with a plan. It was one that his instincts were screaming at him to reject, but it was simple. He was just going to surrender, because no matter what he did or where he went, the raven-born would never stop hunting him. As powerful as he seemed to be against the two senior mages in front of him, a High Council mage would easily destroy him, let alone a Spidralite assassin who never failed. He believed they would definitely send one if not both after him, especially if he reacted with any more violence. So there really was no point in resisting or running away. Darjoon clasped his hands in front of him and returned to his calming exercise, slowing down his breathing and heart-rate and battling to achieve an internal balance in his thoughts. He had no idea how long he might be in this containment spell and although he could open a hole to let in some air, he didn't want to reveal any more of his power. The two mages conferred, then one put a palm to his head while waving his free hand in the air and chanting a communication spell. It wasn't long before a carriage arrived and Darjoon was bundled in, still wrapped inside the containment spell they'd trapped him in. One of the mages climbed up next to the driver, while the other got in next to Darjoon to keep an eye on him as the carriage trundled off. The mage just sat beside him and stared at him in silence as the carriage took them directly to the college. Once they arrived outside the gates, instead of entering in the normal manner, they bundled Darjoon out of the carriage and took him along the high wall and dry moat to some steps that led down into the moat itself. He started as a small door in the wall suddenly appeared in front of them. One of the mages waved his hands and invoked a quick spell to gain access, and as the door swung open they entered and hurried down a dank passage and up into the private wings of the college. Proceeding along some narrow, faintly musty corridors, they took him straight into the Headmaster's study without encountering anyone else. Although neither of the mages spoke a word, it was clear to Darjoon that he was here to wait for his judgement. Occasionally they glanced at him as if he was some exotic animal and then exchanged knowing looks with each other. From what he knew of raven-born history, there hadn't been an incident like this in over a thousand years, not since Kostero, a young, crippled apprentice that had gone insane and killed five students. That had started what people would later call "The Great Purge", the eradication of any weak, strange or even just erratic raven-born. They simply disappeared overnight and soon it became part of the raven-born way, part of the balance, that only the strong, the normal, the healthy and the well-balanced should survive and non-conformists were removed. Now they were obsessed with everything around them being in order, and requiring perfection from everyone, both physically, mentally and magically. Any deviation was treated with suspicion and distrust and dealt with swiftly and terminally.

Darjoon looked around at the room he was in. The Headmasters private study was long and narrow but cosy, with only a few dimly flickering lamps behind sturdy glass lanterns. A desk stood at one end on a raised dais, and there were large bookshelves lining the walls groaning with weighty tomes and scrolls and interspersed with the occasional wooden table on which were strange artefacts, some in clear glass cases accompanied by reading lanterns that were presently unlit. A large, red, stuffed leather chair peppered with gold buttons was positioned behind the desk and Darjoon had been placed in a clear space before the raised dais with the mages to either side of him, almost hidden against the bookshelves. The Headmaster, Orthad, walked in and sat down. He was a tall, thin man whose very presence would command respect, and his pinched, grim face, overshadowed by a large, hooked nose, stared down at Darjoon. He was known to be a disciplinarian who encouraged bullying in order to weed out the undesirables, an unyielding man who lived strictly by the raven-born code. He adjusted his long black robes and then rested his arms on the desk, leaning forward slightly to get a better look at Darjoon in the dim light. Seeing the mages to either side, he waved them away and they walked out, closing the door behind them. Taking up a position to the headmaster's left was Kromnak, Darjoon's form teacher, his huge figure towering over Orthad as he stood there, his face mottled with age and his present high emotion. The rasping, heavy breathing of his form teacher, as he fidgeted and shuffled, sounded very loud to Darjoon. Kromnak had never been able to stand still. He was a large, well-built man whose every muscle seemed to move of its own accord. He'd spent some time up in the mountains and the cold, crisp air had given him a permanent wheeze which is why he breathed so loudly. He did his best to turn his students into the raven-born ideal, to impress on them that courage, honour and valour were their birthright, and their responsibility to the code and the raven-born way must be placed above all other loyalties. For all his bluff and blustering demeanour however, at times he could be surprisingly gentle, although no-one dared to take advantage of it. But when enraged, he was truly awe-inspiring, as his face reddened and he would start to wheeze as if he were about to breathe fire. To the right of Orthad stood the still, silent figure of Mokdor, the High Sorcerer of the Council whose very presence showed just how serious this was. The High Council seldom got involved in College affairs, having far too many other important matters to deal with. Mokdor's long blue robes had fine gold thread worked into intricate patterns that glittered and seemed to writhe in the candlelight. Darjoon wondered why Radnort and his gang weren't here as witnesses, knowing they'd be eager to blame it all on him in order to absolve themselves. Radnort especially didn't care for the code as much as his own skin.

The silence lengthened and deepened through the room, broken only by Kromnak's breathing and the creaking of floorboards as they moved under his angry, fidgety weight.

"Well, it has been a long time since the Stream of Life coughed up a young raven-born with so much potential", Orthad addressed the two mages standing next to him. He looked at Darjoon while he was speaking, but in an abstract way, as if Darjoon wasn't there. Kromnak shuffled angrily and opened his mouth to speak, but the Headmaster raised his hand to quiet him and continued.

"If those brats are right about what happened, then the possibility exists that this fat worm in front of us is the hope we're waiting for. But please tell me, both of you, that this is not some sick joke of Zukar's? The dark goddess of war must be highly amused if this cowardly, overgrown whelp is the fulfilment of prophecy that we've been waiting for."

"Ha, that's impossible, Headmaster! Huuuuh", Kromnak's rasping, angry voice boomed in the close confines as he continued, wheezing on every breath, "He's practically useless at physical training, huuuh, academically weak, huuuh, and only marginal at magic. He, huuuh, has no talents that I can see! Not, huuuh, unless you count eating as an especial talent."

"There is no chance this, huuuh, cowardly maggot has the abilities to become the one from the prophecy. He's fat, huuuh, lazy, undisciplined and his mother refused to tell us who the father was, huuuh, if you can believe that? Unless it was you that she was protecting, Mokdor? We all know, huuuh, that you had a thing for her in the past. If he had your magic, huuuh, combined with the mother's, then maybe it is true?", Kromnak peered round at Mokdor, leering.

Mokdor turned slowly to face Kromnak, his black eyes glittering in the candle-light. Those eyes were set in a handsome, noble face and the hooked nose so common to the raven-born sat above a wide, full, sensual mouth that at the moment was pinched as the brows ominously lowered, the right one slowly lifting. There was a still calm in the study, the kind you get just before a thunderstorm, when the very air holds its breath and the earth waits with dread for lightning to strike. His utter stillness contrasted distinctly with the fidgeting Kromnak, whose movements slowly ceased and then became rigid as Mokdor addressed him.

"Kromnak, do you remember the last time you made a comment like that? I thought we'd already handled that once before, or is the scar no longer visible among the wrinkles on your thick, old face? Oh no, wait, there it is, I see it now. The one I gave you back in college. You remember what I said? The bigger they are the further they fly, I think it was. And oh, how you flew that day, straight into the tree in the quad. Head-first as I recall? Would you care to relive that experience? You look like you've put on a little weight, so I'm sure I can make you go even further now. The tree's right outside, if you're interested?"

It would've been funny, seeing two older men behaving like schoolboys, but the cold, twisted smile on Mokdor's face, and the sudden pallor in Kromnak's removed any humour from the moment. Mokdor's smile deepened at the sight of the fearful Kromnak, then he turned to the Headmaster and addressed him briskly, "Orthad, this is the one, I'm certain of it. I don't know how he's done it, but he's fooled all of you. For Zukar's sake, the boy frankly reeks of power. How you blundering idiots missed that I don't know, but it is definitely there."

Darjoon stared at them. He'd never seen Kromnak or Orthad humbled before. If he wasn't so terrified he might have enjoyed the experience.

"Mokdor, yes, but he... well... even so. How were we to know that the power of his magic would mask the, well, the power of it? This is not a type of magic we are familiar with. In any event, whoever he is, there has been death and death must be paid for. The raven-born can only survive if there is balance!", Orthad fairly spat the word out.

Mokdor folded his arms, looked straight at Darjoon, sighed, and then said, "I agree. Harmony and peace are important for the balance and death must be repaid. He must leave here immediately and must be banished until the Garduin moon. Three years from now he may return, and at that time, we shall test his restraint, and his effect on the balance. If he is truly the one the prophecy spoke of, then he will need no teacher and he will learn for himself and be in harmony. If he is not, then he will either die out there or when he returns we will make sure that he disappears. Permanently! Agreed?"

Orthad and Kromnak simply nodded their heads.

"Very well then, it is decided. Kromnak, would you please release the shield so he can hear what Orthad has to say. I doubt he will try anything with the three of us here. Even though he can't hear us, he still looks like he's going to wet himself. Oh, and another thing, for all our sakes we must not let him learn about the prophecy or any of its details. Who knows what the knowledge of that will do to him or to the balance."

The two mages grunted in acknowledgement and Kromnak raised his hands and muttered an incantation. Darjoon suddenly realised the light had become brighter and sounds were now clearer. His mind was whirling with what he'd just heard and with what he'd done. How did they not know that he'd made a small hole in the shield spell, in the mistaken belief that it would let him breathe easier? It had also meant that he could comfortably hear their conversation. He thought they must have known because it had been so easy to do. He looked around the study in wonder at the difference now the shield was gone, the colours brighter and sounds clearer, then turned as he realised Orthad was addressing him.

"Young man, I'm talking to you! Are you paying attention? You will look at us now", Orthad waited ostentatiously until he was sure Darjoon was listening, "Raven-born, you are here today because of your betrayal of the code we all live by and your danger to the balance. We expect you to honour the egg we emerged from and bring glory to the Great Raven who is mother to us all."

Orthad used his thumb and forefinger to draw the shape of a feather on his forehead in the traditional genuflection, then continued, "Instead, you have shamed your people, defiled this college and dishonoured the memory of your own faithful mother, she who was our worthy companion. You are a threat to the balance, and so you are banished from your nest and from all lands of the raven-born. If you are found within our borders after nightfall you will be summarily executed. You must return at the time of the Garduin moon which is some three years from now. At your return, we will judge if you are in balance and whether you are worthy to earn your place among the people again. That is all. May Zukar and the Great Raven herself protect you on your journey."

Orthad stood up stiffly and together with Kromnak they left the study. Mokdor looked down at Darjoon in silence for a moment, then walked over to him, his glittering black eyes boring all the way into his soul. Darjoon shivered as the High Sorcerer leant over and spoke softly into his ear.

"I'm only going to say this once, Darjoon, so you better listen carefully. Remember your mother as you travel from this place. Even though she is gone, she will still be of help. Look for the sign of the wolf to guide you. You must discover the truth about your father if you ever want to return in peace and harmony. Oh, and, Darjoon, don't even think about running off somewhere and hiding, because I myself will come and find you. I've got eyes on you now, so there is nowhere that you can hide from me. Pay close attention to those you meet, learn all you can, and then come back so you may bring honour to your mother and her memory. The balance requires that you return and make no mistake, I will make sure you do, one way or another."

Mokdor straightened, stalked out of the room and soon the two senior mages that were his captors came back to escort him home. Looking at his slumped shoulders, they glanced at each other and didn't bother raising a new shield around him.

Once home, Darjoon gathered everything he thought would be useful for his travels. His grandmother had already known about the verdict and so before he arrived she'd set aside some chranth, a form of travel-bread as well as a few other odds and ends he would need for a lengthy trip in the mountains. He'd thought about engaging her in conversation, but her silence and stiff back told him that was pointless. He finished stuffing an extra cloak into his pack and then made his way to his grandparents bedroom. His grandfather was old and sick and looked small and frail, lying still in his bed. Darjoon walked over to say goodbye, taking the old man's hand in his. Seeing his lips moving, he leaned in closer to hear what he was saying.

"Darjoon, the magic in your blood isn't only from your mother", his grandfather wheezed, "You need to travel to the desert to discover its true source. You must beware the wolf, it lies in wait in the dark and used to visit your mother too. Never forget that even when it looks friendly, it has long, sharp teeth and will easily and quickly draw blood. You are not what you seem, my boy and you don't fool me, nor can you fool yourself. You will need to let go of all your power before you can truly hold on to it. Oh Darjoon, may Zukar protect you, my son. I know you have it in you, Darjoon, you always have. I believe in you, my boy. We'll be together in the end. Always together. When the Great Raven comes for me, I will look for you on the River of Life."

Exhausted from getting the words out, his grandfather's eyes closed as his head slumped back on the pillow.

Darjoon wiped away the tear that trickled down his cheek and slowly left his grandfather's sick-room. He endured a tentative hug from his grandmother, whose eyes were suspiciously wet, and then, escorted by a mage on either side he walked out the house, down the familiar lane and finally arrived at the border on the trail heading towards the forbidding Darken Hills. The mages looked at him silently, one scornfully and the other with pity in his eyes, and then left quietly, leaving him fully alone with the wind and his thoughts.

He took a deep breath and looked across the valley to the dark mountains, knowing he would need all that hidden strength his grandfather had mentioned to cross them and make his way through Spidral to the Desert of Thoth. So many questions whirled in his head and he knew the answers were out there in the night, lying in wait for him in the desert and beyond. As he stood there, he thought he could hear a wolf howling from somewhere deep in the Hills. Time to grow up, it seemed to say, time for the fat boy to fly away and for the fat man to start walking. He turned and looked back towards the sun that was setting on the only land he'd ever known, the darkness slowly flooding in. It wasn't as if he felt much regret, after all he'd never been particularly happy there but it was his home.

"Well, fat boy, you've got your wish", he thought to himself, "No more college for you, but then, no more pancakes either. This time you really are alone. Watch out world, here comes the fat man walking."

2 INTO THE HILLS

Darjoon turned from his homeland, shivered, then lifted his eyes and looked despairingly up at the large, black mountains in front of him, the misnamed Darken Hills. It wasn't just the late afternoon chill nor the ever present cool night breeze blowing in from those dark and jagged peaks, no, it was the simple fact he'd never been this far from home. Having only a vague idea of where he was headed, he tried to piece together the jumbled facts he'd been told. Something to do with his father in particular, and some secret society his mother may have been involved in. He'd heard rumours at college of a sinister organisation that had a wolf as its emblem and so assumed they were the ones that Mokdor and grandpa had been talking about.

"The problem with a secret society", he muttered, "is that it is exactly that, a secret! So how am I supposed to find it?"

He shook his head in frustration. Why couldn't they have given him more information? The High Sorcerer had seemed to think this wolf society could help him, but grandpa had warned him about them. So what were they, good or bad? As for finding out about his father, well he'd been told nothing at all about him while he'd been growing up. Not by his mother or his grandparents even though he'd begged them all. In fact his grandparents had always been unwilling to share information about his past, especially after his mother had died. He knew he'd inherited some magical abilities from his father and these abilities were supposedly powerful and in a way different to what the raven-born were used to, but that was it.

Grandpa had mumbled something to him about the answers being in the desert. Well, that could only mean the Desert of Thoth, a strange place he'd heard about that lay to the north-west, beyond the Plains of Breath that were in turn way beyond the Great Forest inside Spidral. This was the neighbouring country to the raven-born lands and lay beyond the Darken Hills looming directly in front of him. He shivered again, remembering from college the stories about the desert being inhabited by strange, secretive tribes, and, if it could be believed, by lizards as big as a man that walked on their hind legs. The students had always laughed about that, making crude jokes as to how they mated, and whether they laid eggs or not. Well none of it had seemed real at the time, yet now he was going to have to go and find out for himself. He pulled the cloak tighter and decided there was no point standing still and thinking while he froze.

Taking a deep breath, he started humming quietly, feeling the magic rise in his blood as he began to chant the incantation that would provide him with direction. Closing his eyes and calming his mind, he attempted to focus on the desert and his intended goal. Seconds later he shook his head in exasperation. This was all a little difficult as he didn't really know where or what that goal was and he'd never been to the desert. Thoughts of his enigmatic father kept intruding and his mind whirled with thoughts. Eventually he managed to calm himself, completed the spell and opened his eyes.

"Yes, that's more like it", he said and grinned in delight.

A faint, luminous trail appeared in front of him, leading off through the barren, rough moorland, typical of the highlands of the raven-born, and then heading towards the Darken Hills that rose up between him and the Spidral forest. These were in fact really large mountains, not hills, and most were jagged and forbidding with some snowy peaks. According to what he'd read in the books that he'd managed to smuggle out from the forbidden section of the library, they were populated by strange beasts, renegade mages, and runaway thugs who lived in caves that riddled the sheer cliffs. In addition there were stray Dremrel that roved the trails. These were fierce, magical, bat-like creatures with large fangs and a paralysing venom that allowed them to eat their prey alive. He had been told by his mother that the Dremrel were magically created or altered during the Great War, and that the raven-born considered them dangerous abominations which had to be destroyed. What little was known about them included the fact that they hunted in small groups or covens of not more than three or four individuals. Regarded as intelligent creatures, one of them would often pretend to be injured or use some other means of distraction while the others waited in ambush. Their magic was undeniably strong and seemed to appear in different forms and strengths among the different Dremrel covens, making it hard to formulate a standard plan of attack. Many had become victims to these foul creatures, and for an apprentice like himself to encounter one would surely mean a painfully slow death.

As he walked, he sent up a quick prayer to Zukar asking her to help him avoid the evil beasts while he travelled through the Hills. Zukar was one of the few gods the raven-born deigned to acknowledge. A warrior goddess, she was often depicted with limited clothing, providing many young raven-born adolescents with sweet dreams of combat and sex. In raven-born culture, the two were often interlinked, and some maidens would only marry a man who could actually beat them in battle, often testing him directly. These were truly dangerous, passionate fights that took place in secret and after a fierce battle the relationship was often consummated, unless either combatant had died or the male had lost. A raven-born wore his early scars with pride as they were far better than any ring on a finger or a white lace dress.

The raven-born had always been a fierce, proud, warrior nation who valued independence, passion and skill in both magic and fighting. In recent history their strong beliefs about balance had evolved from several terrible disasters that ended with many deaths. For some reason, the raven-born did not have many children and because of that they had a strong desire to protect themselves from themselves. This meant their beliefs now included those in which only the strong and normal survived, and any weakness or difference was not easily accepted. Most, if not all of the handicapped or impaired youth were sent away into the Darken Hills to die alone. Although that was just a rumour, it was certainly true that they disappeared and were never heard from again. Darjoon himself had really only ever been on trial at the college. This was because of his large, round figure that was so unlike the raven-born's lean and wiry build, as well as his strange magic.

As he followed the glowing path, Darjoon continued mulling over what he'd been told. Ahead of him lay three years of lonely wandering far away from home, being forced to wait until the rising of the next Garduin moon. The Old Lands had two moons: a blue one called Tregora which appeared every fortnight, rising and setting over four days; and a red moon called Garduin that appeared only every three years, sailing through the night sky for a year and even now barely visible just above the horizon. On his return he would be judged by the Council and then either accepted or killed, depending on what he'd learnt regarding self-restraint, power and balance.

He snorted and kicked at a clump of weeds next to the

path as he walked past. A wasp darted up and flew straight at him, following him while he ducked and ran down the path, finally stopping and panting heavily only when he was sure he'd really left it behind.

"Blasted wasp, you're the cause of all this, you know!", he shook his fist back down the trail. Catching his breath, he shifted the pack across his shoulders and started walking toward the Hills again, following the luminous trail.

This time his thoughts drifted to his mother. She'd been cold and forbidding just like any self-respecting raven-born mother should be, but there had been moments where they'd connected. For the umpteenth time he wondered how a powerful mage like her could've died. There was just the little his grandparents had told him, that she'd been ambushed by a Dremrel coven and it was sheer chance that her body had been found by two mages out on patrol. There wasn't a mark on her when they found her and it appeared that during the struggle she'd killed two Dremrel and badly wounded a third. The mages had to finish off the injured beast, but not before it mentally crippled one of them with a vicious blast of magic. They believed his mother's brain had also been damaged or destroyed by this Dremrel, but she'd wounded it before it could bite her. This would explain her unmarked body. It had all seemed a bit unusual to him. Part of what they had been taught in college was that Dremrel were not supposed to use magic that much, nor have such powerful magic in the wild. Which didn't explain why only the strongest mages were sent to hunt them. Darjoon's mother herself had been a senior, experienced mage with both great combat skill and superior magical ability. It was precisely for this reason that she'd been chosen to exterminate Dremrel covens.

"As opposed to tame Dremrel in a chicken coop", one of the students had sniggered when the teacher had used the "in the wild" phrase, promptly receiving a rap on the skull for being so cheeky. It had been suggested that Dremrel in captivity seemed to improve their magic somehow. In any event, they were supposed to be easier to kill during winter, when they were slower because of the cold. A typical coven would consist of three to four siblings who would have weaned off their mother at the same time and been taught basic hunting techniques. They would then find a cave together and refine their hunting as a pack, with one of them naturally assuming command. Any large mammal was fair prey for them, and this included the many species of deer and goat that were found in the Hills. Occasionally they would venture into the neighbouring country of Spidral, as the deers were large and juicy in the Great Forest. Sometimes they would even venture down into the populated Empire farmlands of Lower Srinth, where they would catch the domestic animals, occaisnally even a bront, a large, shaggy, bovine creature the Lower Srinthians used for tilling their fields and pulling their carts. Although docile, the bront could be a fierce creature when aroused and had large forward-facing horns, so it was usually only a target if the Dremrel were desperately hungry.

It was these dangerous Dremrel covens near the farms that his mother and other mages like her were hunting, particularly those that had begun to prey on human children. Normally they would be sent out in pairs for safety but his mother always did like working alone. Given his grandfather's dubious background and poor standing among the raven-born, as well as his father's mysterious and unknown identity, it was hardly surprising that no-one clamoured to partner her or that the Council kept silent about it. She was considered more than borderline eccentric. It was one of the many reasons why the other students picked on him, not that he cared as he hadn't wanted to fit in with them anyway. It did mean his mother was always going to be vulnerable when she was hunting though. So why had they allowed it? Maybe the Council had always wanted something to happen to her? She had begun to question the precious raven-born code before her death, and that was never healthy. No, that sounded paranoid, why would they go to such extremes?

While he'd been musing, he'd kept following the luminous trail but now he realised it was veering off toward the south-west and heading away from the Hills and back into the raven-born lands. Sighing heavily, he took off his backpack and sat on a rock by the side of the trail. Taking out a small square of chranth, he munched thoughtfully while he considered the now fading trail. The magic was supposed to use your thoughts for its direction, so by concentrating on details of his destination it would map out a likely path for him. Admittedly his knowledge of any of his given destinations was sketchy, coming primarily from the geography and history lessons he'd had at college. Smiling, he remembered being bored as usual and didn't pay a lot of attention back then. He frowned though as he looked at the slowly fading glow of his spell. The direction it seemed to be going in was the south-west shore and beyond that was the Pristine Sea and not much else. Suddenly he smiled again then snapped his fingers as he remembered. The Glass Isle was actually somewhere across the Pristine Sea. It was a large island that used to be called the Sorcerer's Isle before the Great War. He stared in that direction. So why would the spell take him that way when he'd wanted to go to the desert?

What had he been thinking about when he cast the spell? It was his father and the knowledge he wanted about his father which he believed was in the Desert of Thoth, to the north-west beyond Spidral. So why would the spell head towards the Pristine Sea? He stood up and cleared his mind using the calming exercises he'd learnt at college, then, instead of focusing on his father, he focused on pictures of Spidral and the Great Forest that lay inside its vast borders. He knew that he had to walk into the Darken Hills to the north-west in order to get there. Slowly and deliberately he cast the direction spell and opened his eyes. The luminous trail now veered off to the left, down into a valley and headed in what he was sure was a north-westerly direction, in other words the right way. He wondered why thoughts of his father had led him towards the coast? He shrugged his shoulders, lifted his pack and trudged down into the valley towards the mountains looming up ahead and to the right of him.

The sun was starting to slip below the horizon when he realised the ground underfoot was becoming hard and rocky. The tufted grass and plains scrub he'd been walking through was slowly giving way to small clusters of blue mountain flowers and sparse evergreen trees. The air was also beginning to cool rapidly as the sun disappeared and he looked back, realising he'd left the raven-born lands far behind and was now moving into the foothills of the mountains.

"So", he said to himself wryly, "you've got out of there before sunset at least. Now your sentence really begins. You're an outcast and nothing but a wanderer doomed to travel the world and never return."

He smiled at his melancholic statement, "Well, okay, not quite, I've still got to be back in three years or Mokdor will come get me."

Ruefully, he realised that he could only return if by some miracle he managed to stay alive. A sudden wave of loneliness and fear washed over him as he realised he was heading out into the world with no family, particularly no grandfather, the one person he'd been closest to in his short life. Grandpa was old and infirm when he'd left, and was likely to be dead long before he'd return. Blinking away a tear he gritted his teeth. Now was the time to be a man and let the boy fly away for good. It was the only way to survive. He stopped, turned back and shouted down the trail, "I will return, raven-born! And when I do, I will return with power! You will rue the day that I come back!"

He looked around quickly and self-consciously blushed,

then turned and continued along the trail. Why had he reacted like that, getting all shy and embarrassed? It wasn't as if there was anyone to hear or even to laugh at him. He was finally alone, and after all, wasn't that what he always wanted? He realised that although he prided himself on being aloof and independent, he really did want someone to share the journey with.

Sighing, he shivered suddenly. The sun was almost gone and it was beginning to turn bitterly cold. His skin twitched as if some insect had landed there and he unconsciously brushed it off. Looking around and realising it was time to make camp while he could still see, he found a small alcove between two large rocks. After making sure there were no snakes or other dangerous reptiles or insects, he took out the small tent he'd grabbed from grandpa's shed while brushing away another insect that irritated his skin. He paused a moment, looking around for the insects that he was sure were buzzing around. "That's odd", he thought to himself, "it should be too cold for bloodsuckers or anything like that. Come out, come out, wherever you are!"

Seeing nothing, he shrugged and turned his attention back to the tent. He'd only put it up a few times before when grandpa had taken them camping and he had to wrestle the memory from his mind before he could lay it out properly. Seeing a long tear in one corner of the roof, he cursed and then cursed even louder when he realised that the last time he'd used the tent, he'd neglected to replace the small bag containing the tent pegs and guy ropes. Slumping back against a rock, he stared at the forlorn, shapeless tent flapping in the breeze.

"Way to go Darjoon, you fat lump", he grumbled to himself, "What a wonderful beginning and what a great explorer you've turned out to be. Thank Zukar that grandpa can't see you now."

Suddenly he remembered the time he'd sat with grandpa and they'd played with some iron ore, plants and magic. He'd made a knife with a rope handle which had pleased grandpa no end. Scouting around quickly using his magic sense, he found the type of stone he was looking for and collected some rocks. At the same time he gathered some long grass and reeds that he found next to a small stream that ran down from the hills. Just doing these simple tasks and filling his water skin made him feel a whole lot better, especially as he remembered to magic out the impurities in the water while he'd filled the skin. He smiled to himself. It seemed he could get the hang of this living rough after all.

He focused carefully on the rocks he'd collected in a pile and began chanting the spell he'd been taught. He wasn't sure he really needed to chant or wave his hands with any of his magic but it helped him focus. It wasn't long before he had a mound of rubble on one side and four glowing tent pegs cooling neatly on the large slab of stone that he'd used as a worktop. Then it was the turn of the plants and before long he had some sturdy coiled rope with loops on either end, perfect for guy ropes. Picking up the cooled tent pegs, he attached the guy ropes and lifted the tent into position one corner at a time, finally using magic to make sure the pegs were firmly anchored in the hard ground. In the growing darkness he used more magic to turn what remained of the plants into a patch across the long tear in the tent. Climbing inside, he fell into a deep, exhausted sleep with a satisfied smile on his face, smug in the knowledge he'd restored some balance to his world even if it had cost him magical energy.

Darjoon woke to the sound of raucous crowing and a steady pitter-patter of rain on the tent roof. Putting a hand to his face, he felt wetness and looked up in disgust, watching as a large, wet drop formed on the roof of the tent and then plopped onto his nose. Squinting up at the small chink of light, he realising his mending of the night before hadn't been as good as he thought. He groaned and rolled over, wondering what those silly crows were making such a fuss about. Stepping outside, there were three or four of the large black birds pecking away at what remained of the chranth they'd pulled out of his bag, which he'd handily left outside for them.

"Get off, you little thieves", he clapped his hands loudly to shoo them away and retrieved his pack before the cawing mob could return. Looking inside he saw they'd left him with only a few slices. He smiled ruefully and took a swig of water only to spew it out as the salty, rotten taste made him gag. Cursing, he realised he'd grabbed a newly cured skin from his grandfather's stores and it hadn't been washed out yet. The disgusting taste came from the salt used during the curing process. "Aaaaaahhhhh!", he screamed at the morning in frustration and was soon followed by a response from his new best friends, the crows, who cawed loudly in return.

A while later he stood with his hands on his hips, looking up at the mountains. He'd washed out the skin until he could tolerate the water inside and then taken down the tent after properly repairing the tear this time. Gathering up the newly-made pegs and guy ropes he carefully stowed them in his pack along with the tent. Feeling a strange tickling on his skin he crouched and looked around cautiously.

"Those aren't insects at all", he said to himself, "someone's using magic. You idiot! Why didn't you figure that out yesterday?"

Surely Dremrel wouldn't come this far down from the Hills, would they? Closing his eyes, he concentrated on what was making his skin tingle and soon detected a faint hint of magic drifting gently all around him. He knew what that was, it was a watching spell! Someone was watching him with very powerful, well-concealed magic and to anyone not having Darjoon's magical ability they'd have been completely unaware. The magic seemed strangely familiar and an image of Mokdor, the High Sorcerer popped into his mind. Not feeling any malicious intent, he was confident that now he'd sensed it, he could shield against it. Of course, as soon as he did that then whoever it was would be instantly alerted to his full potential. As it might be Mokdor, he decided to ignore it for now. Shrugging the pack into a better fit on his shoulders, he began to trudge up the trail.

"Well, young apprentice", he thought to himself, "Mokdor did say he'd have eyes on you. Turns out he really does."

After a long day walking up into the Hills, Darjoon decided to pitch camp a little earlier so he could give himself time to rest and relax. His feet were particularly sore as they were not used to all the constant walking and he realised his boots were a little tight, probably because he was still growing. Making new boots would have to wait until he got hold of some leather. Grimacing, he knew that meant he'd probably have to kill and skin some poor animal which wasn't something he looked forward to. Once he'd set up the tent, he ambled down to a small stream to refill his water-skin. Spotting a small bush with blue-green berries, he tried to remember what they'd learnt in college about edible plants. In his head, he could hear the teacher talking about colours and he was pretty sure that bright colours were poisonous, like red or yellow, while darker colours like blue or green weren't. He harvested a few of the plump, juicy berries. Not wanting to make a fire in the hills, he munched on the berries and some chranth, washing it down with the water he'd collected. After making sure there were no sticks or small stones under him, like that stupid sharp one that had dug into his side last night, he lay down inside the tent to sleep. Exhausted and helped by the fresh mountain air he soon fell into a deep sleep. Stars wheeled and danced over the little tent as the night wore on.

"Oooooaaahhhh!", the long drawn-out moaning floated through the still night air. Darjoon opened his eyes groggily, blinked, then stared at the orange mist that was hovering in the air in front of him. Wait, no, it was changing, coalescing into a purple something. Or was it bright blue? What were those little red stars blinking inside the mist, were they eyes? Wait, what? What was he looking at, and what was that mournful noise he kept hearing? A sudden cramp in his belly caused his whole body to convulse and he let out another groan, realising he was sweating profusely. For a moment he thought the tent was on fire. Why was it so hot? He rolled over and reached for the water-skin. Taking a swig, he suddenly and violently dry heaved and immediately felt his stomach ripple as the cramps redoubled. He moaned again and clenched his fists.

"You idiot, Darjoon! Those berries were poisonous", he heard a voice in his head, "what were you thinking? You know you shouldn't just eat anything you find, especially not in the Darken Hills."

Was that his voice? It didn't sound like his voice although it sounded strangely familiar. The mist was starting to fade into darkness, for which he was grateful. He had a pounding headache and his stomach was tied up in painful knots. He breathed slowly past the cramps and started to surrender to the darkness, desperately wanting the cool peace it offered him and an escape from those awful red stars that blinked slowly on and off like evil little eyes.

"Wake up fool, you're about to fall into a coma. Get a grip, boy, you're a mage for Zukar's sake!"

His eyes snapped open as he heard that strange voice again, the one that sounded like his but wasn't. The voice was right though, a mage does magic, doesn't he? He chuckled to himself. Just imagine being in pain when you could heal yourself? That would be so silly! He winced at the biting pain in his belly and closed his eyes again. A few more minutes to get his strength up and he'd be fine. This cool darkness was just so inviting.

"Wait, what am I doing", he thought, "It's true, I am a

mage!"

He struggled to shrug off the blackness, desperately trying to focus his thoughts and wake himself up. The darkness slowly receded and he struggled up onto an elbow. Calming his mind, he imagined the berries out of his system and began chanting a spell he'd learned at college related to healing. A little later, he felt a buzzing sensation in his stomach and a tingling on his skin. A wet, acrid, vomit smell filled the tent and the pain in his stomach died away. He saw a small pile of half-digested berries in the corner, and as he slumped back heard that voice in his head again, "You fool apprentice, could you not at least magic them outside the tent? You really are hopeless!"

The voice faded and darkness closed in as Darjoon fainted away.

Waking in the morning, he felt empty and wretched with the sweet and sour smell of sick strong in the tent. Gagging as he did so, he dragged himself out of the blankets and scraped up the mess he'd made, disposing of it outside.

As he stood in the early morning light, he took in a deep, deep breath of fresh mountain air and then another. Could he be more stupid? He'd almost killed himself last night. If it hadn't been for that voice in his head he'd probably be lying dead in his tent right now. He shook his head and took a deep swig of water, looking around with renewed interest at all the plants he could see. How could he tell which were poisonous and which were edible? Food would soon be a problem, thanks to his feathered little friends who had ransacked his supplies the day before, and the fact his stomach was now quite empty. Thinking back, he remembered a lesson in which they were taught to "know" the properties of plants by using magic. He closed his eyes and threw out his senses, trying to discern edible plants. Nothing happened. After a few more tries, he realised it would probably help if he actually focused on specific plants, rather than just trying to discern whatever was nearby. Returning to the berry bush that almost killed him, he focused on it and chanted the spell he'd learnt at college. Grimacing, he "saw" the poison inside the berries and knew it would be bad for him to eat. Looking around and spying a small tree with large, round, green seeds on it, he repeated the exercise. This time he "saw" that they were edible. Harvesting the seeds he took them back to his tent, munching on a few along the way. They were hard with a sharp, acid taste and he knew they would be good for his teeth, if not particularly tasty. Carefully folding and packing up the tent he lifted the pack onto his back, wondering whose voice he'd heard in his head last night. He'd been a bit spaced out by the berries, so was it his own, or the silent watcher who he thought was probably Mokdor? And why would that great mage, or any of the raven-born for that matter, take such an interest in his survival? Particularly as they'd seemed more interested in him surviving on his own. In fact, with some of them it seemed they'd prefer that he died out in the wilderness. Maybe there really was something to this prophecy, but what could that be? He knew his magic was different to anyone else's that he'd met. It seemed more powerful but he was under no illusions to how raw and ignorant he was. What possible help could he be to the raven-born nation? There were much stronger mages than himself, even among the apprentices. It was known that not all the senior mages were on the Council, some choosing to live relatively isolated lives with only occasional contact. Darjoon shook his head and set out on the trail, his mind churning with unanswered questions.

As he continued trudging into the Hills he began to sense a connection to the edible world around him including plants that were good or bad, insects that could be eaten or would bite, sting or otherwise poison him and other wildlife that was potential food. A particular caterpillar in a tree caught his attention, and he knew it would be a good source of protein to balance the berries and seeds he'd been collecting. As he stood under the tree looking up at them, he realised they were high up on a branch and too far for him to reach. Sitting down, he thought about the problem and wondered if there was magic he could use. Out of the corner of his eye he saw a small black creature with tiny elongated paws and delicate feathered ears jumping onto the trunk of the tree. It had a large bushy tail and two long, sharp front teeth like little spades. Common to the forested areas of the Darken Hills, they were known as guskorn. Fierce and territorial, they'd learnt to run away from human-shaped creatures, largely thanks to the Dremrel who happily gobbled them up as a little snack.

The guskorn ran up the tree and he looked at it intently, subconsciously focusing his magic on the little animal. For just a moment his vision blurred and overlapped, so that he was both looking up at the tree from where he sat, yet at the same time he was seeing the tree up close as he scampered up it. The blurred image suddenly faded and so he refocused his magic, commanding the guskorn to bring him the caterpillar. As he did this, he mumbled to himself, "Come on you horrible little beast. I don't want to eat you, just do what I want."

Frustratingly, nothing happened. Trying again, he remembered a lesson he'd endured in college and patiently nudged the guskorn, rather than commanding it directly. After what seemed like ages, the link to the animal reconnected and again he saw the world from his and the animal's perspective in that weird blurred vision. Focusing more on the creatures view, it got clearer and sharper. It was still odd to simultaneously watch the little creature as it balanced on a branch cautiously sniffing the air, while at the same time looking out across the valley from the animal's high vantage point. Smelling a strange, unfamiliar smell that made his nose wrinkle, he became very nervous.

He started with the realisation that it was his own smell the squirrel was smelling and that he could sense the little creatures emotion.

"Well, hang on", he mumbled, "I haven't washed for over two days, so no wonder I stink like that. Guess I'll have to make soap because I know I didn't pack any and neither did grandma. I think I remember..."

His vision suddenly cleared and he cursed, knowing that losing focus had made him lose contact with the animal. The guskorn jumped into trees further away and nothing he did was able to recreate the link they'd had.

"Just like a first year student, Darjoon", he sighed out loud, "getting easily distracted by the mundane."

Looking up, he tried to feel the caterpillars again. This time, he did so surprisingly quickly and with the link established, attempted to gently nudge them so that they crawled off the branch and fell out the tree. It was done without any real expectation, yet with a soft plop, first one, then another and soon seven of the caterpillar's were squirming on the ground in front of him. Picking them up and placing them in a pouch inside his bag to dry out, he looked at the last one squirming in his fingers, grimaced, and sent up a silent prayer, "Please Zukar, give me the courage to put these in my mouth later and eat them."

Darjoon stood up and brushed himself off, looking at the mountain ahead of him. He knew it was going to be a long, long climb. As his gaze swept the snow-covered peak, he spotted out of the corner of his eye some movement among the rocks and quickly enhanced his vision with magic. Gasping, he stared at the massive feline shape that seemed to rear up right in front of him. He remembered reading that the truktari, a type of highland cat with large eyes and ears, were particularly dangerous this time of year especially if they had youngsters in tow. It made them even more aggressive, which was saying a lot as normally they were a wild ball of energy. He watched, entranced as the beautiful, black and white striped animal bounded gracefully down the rocks on large paws, stopping every now and then to yawn and making a strange mewing noise as it did so. Realising that if the animal continued on its current path, it'd walk right into him, he calmed himself and focused his magic, nudging the large truktari to detour round him. With a quiet sigh of relief he turned, watching the large animal move around and away from him and then bound away gracefully among the rocks. Smiling to himself and feeling rather smug at his new-found means of control, he felt a soft bump against the back of his legs. It made him start and snapping around he saw three tiny purring little truktari sprawled at his feet, one of them rubbing its back against his legs.

"Well, and where did you cute ones come from?", he laughed with delight as they engaged in mock combat, chasing each other around his legs.

Suddenly, and with a dawning sense of impending doom, he realised this was the litter of the large animal he'd just nudged away.

"So that's why she was making that strange noise, she's been calling you to follow her!", he addressed the little cubs at his feet.

They stopped at the sound of his voice and stared up at him just for a moment, then sensing he wasn't going to do anything, began purring and playing again. Now that they'd found a new playmate they didn't want to go anywhere in a hurry. One of them found the straps dangling from his pack and was trying to jump up and grab it with its teeth. As he watched them play he forgot about the mother and laughed at their playfulness, then froze as from behind him came a low, menacing growl. Turning around slowly and already sensing the anger deep inside the giant truktari, he saw it staring down at him from the rocks, its amber eyes glowing with rage as it watched him and the cubs together. Realising that the anger she was feeling had overridden his control of her, he quickly took a deep, ragged breath and focused on her again, quietly muttering his incantation. This time through the link he could feel she was a coiled spring, ready to pounce at the slightest twitch. She refused to move as he tried to nudge her away and the resistance from her was palpable. She was fixated on the cubs and her strong concern was not going to let him move her easily. Trying again, but doing so slowly and with care, he reached out and calmed her, waiting and watching as the twitching of the great tail slowed down and then finally stopped as she began to relax. Reaching out again and sensing the three cubs still behind, he willed them to go around him and follow her. Initially all he got were chaotic, random pictures as they tumbled, playing and fighting with each other. Slowly and painfully they trotted over to join their mother, and eventually he nudged them all to retreat and move away. He was sweating and the air felt electric with tension as he struggled to keep the link between all of them. At first the great truktari resisted and then as the cubs gambolled around her she shook her large head and pushed them along with her nose, finally picking one up in her mouth and ambling off with the the rest. Darjoon gasped in relief as they slowly disappeared from view and then slumped to the ground, his body shaking from adrenaline and the expenditure of so much magic in such a short time. Reaching into his pack, he took a deep swig from his water-skin and then quickly grabbed a handful of berries to restore his energy before dragging himself to his feet again.

"Darjoon, that was too close for comfort. You need to wake up or you'll die out here!", he muttered to himself as he resumed his plodding into the Hills. The truktari's paws were easily as large as his head and with just one blow from her he'd have been a mangled mess on the mountainside and food for her kittens. He shivered as he entered the great shadow cast by the mountains and swung up the trail to the pass, remembering something his grandfather used to say: "Don't be surprised that having mastered a skill, you realise how much more you have to learn".

Realising that magic by itself was never going to see him through the years ahead, he knew he was going to have to learn fast to survive in the Hills. What was it his teacher had told the class?

"Remember young ones, magic is a finite resource and not inexhaustible. The more powerful you are, the greater the danger and the greater the harm you can do to yourself. Your magic should, I repeat, it should run out before you do but sometimes, if you are too focused on the task at hand, it won't. When that happens then you will simply die. So always remember this: magic used without wisdom means death."

3 FLYING INTO TROUBLE

Darjoon hauled out the extra cloak from his pack which was beginning to feel like it weighed a ton. Wrapping the cloak around himself he stamped his hands and feet to put some warmth into them. He'd been walking into the mountains for three days now, trudging up the trail through the pass, and as he got higher it was turning a lot colder. Last night had been a miserable affair as he realised that the thin tent, while perfectly adequate for the highlands of his home, was not really suited for the altitudes he'd climbed into. He'd shivered as the icy air breezed through the tent last night, belatedly remembering that a mage could use magic to warm himself, albeit at the cost of some energy and lack of sleep. In the last few days he was beginning to slim down a lot owing to the exercise and the almost continual use of magic. As he was so big-boned though, he doubted anyone from home would notice. To them he'd still just be the fat boy he'd always been.

Darjoon breathed in the icy air and sighed. His home was rapidly becoming a fading memory, even though he'd only been there such a short time back. It had been confusing anyway, because for the last four years he'd been at the college, living there and not at home whereas a lot of the other students simply came in daily. It meant that horrible college had become more like home than his grandparents house, although he'd never settled in, hating it and keeping nothing personal in his room. He'd always treated it as temporary, as if he was going to leave at any moment. One of his fantasies had been that his father would come marching in, demand he be released and then he would go and live with him in a black tower where they would create new spells and destroy all the Dremrel. So living rough wasn't really such a big deal, even though he did miss grandpa. Smiling to himself, he realised he was even beginning to miss that stupid ruugyam pet of his grandmother's. When he was younger it used to lie in wait to ambush him, then jump on the back of his legs, scratching him with horrible sharp claws and making him scream in fright. He swore that horrible thing could actually smile, if not laugh outright. But as he got older he'd retaliated with his magic and so they'd endured an uncomfortable truce. Then in later years, as the ruugyam aged and mellowed, they'd shared the same bed, the silly thing even purring when it kneaded his chest while it lay on him and dreamed. He'd gotten quite fond of it in the end and had been sad when it died.

He shook his head free of the memories and stared at the large rockfall in front of him. The magical, luminous line of his direction spell led straight through the great boulders that had tumbled down from the slopes above to fill the narrow ravine he'd been walking through. If his memory from his geography lessons served him right, the trail went up from here, between two peaks and then swerved sharply to the left and down on its way out of the mountains and west towards the forest. So what was he meant to do now? The cliffs beside him were almost sheer and didn't look climbable. He supposed he could use some magic to fly over the boulders to the other side of the trail, if he could remember how to fly, which was a big if. Even then, he'd still have the long hike up and around, travelling through the freezing cold pass. He shivered involuntarily at the thought of it. On the other hand, if he could just fly over the peak to his left it would probably cut almost two days off his journey and put him the other side the peaks, where it wouldn't be so bitterly cold. After all, the cliffs to his left didn't look that high from here. He chewed his lip as he thought on it. He'd need to meditate and calm himself as he was pretty sure that it would use up a lot of magic. In fact, he didn't really know how much it would use, but he knew his magic was pretty strong, surely strong enough for a quick flight. He grimaced as he knew it was time to start eating those worms he'd harvested previously off the tree. He'd dried them out in the sun one late afternoon and now they should be full of protein and fat which he would need. Lifting one gingerly out of the small bag he was using, he opened his mouth, dropped it in and quickly chewed and swallowed. Although the gritty, sandy texture wasn't great, it did taste vaguely like the nuts he snacked on back home. At least it didn't make him gag like he thought it would. He waited to see what effect it would have and swallowed some water to help it down. With nothing happening, he popped a few more in his mouth, although the last one wasn't as dry as he would've liked, still feeling a bit too slimy. He almost gagged as it slid down his throat and quickly washed it down with large gulps of water.

Looking up at the cliffs, he tried to remember how he'd been able to fly last time. He'd accidentally killed that stupid boy who'd used magic, and then, as he'd been so scared, he'd done what came naturally to him. He'd run away as fast as he could. Only much later when he looked down he'd realised that he'd actually been flying and not running at all. In the end, as he'd been thinking about his grandfather, he'd landed at his grandparents house where the mages had finally caught him. So really, it wasn't through any conscious thought that he'd started flying, it was accidental and related to the wanderings in his mind and his reaction to the circumstances. Back then it had been the danger he was in but he wasn't in any now. As he really didn't feel like stepping off a cliff to see if that triggered it, he'd have to figure this out while safely on the ground. He tried to visualise the other side of the mountain, but struggled to know what it looked like? He'd never been there before, had he.

"Come on, big boy, focus! You can do this!", Darjoon's own private pep rally wasn't helping him much.

Again, he focused on what he could see, on the snowy peaks in front of him, and then tried to let his unconscious slide into his conscious mind. This was a trick he'd studied in one of the books which they were supposedly not allowed to read at college. As he'd done so often, he'd sneaked it off the bookshelf one night when the librarian had been distracted. There'd been some references to a strange kind of magic, and a place filled with snow and ice and odd-looking people wearing long, furry skins. They had what looked like long whiskers on their faces and large, woolly canine creatures with sinuous, elongated bodies that walked next to them. He'd ignored that, as well as the part about blood-magic which had sounded disgusting to him, and focused on the chapter that talked about bringing your subconscious mind into your conscious world. Something to do with the fact that almost all of the powerful magic lay in the subconscious. There'd been exercises you could do, including one with a strange diagram. It had looked like a snowflake, and when you focused on it in the way they described, it jumped off the page and started spinning in mid-air. At least, that's what he saw. Everyone else who'd taken the book and looked at the diagram just saw some scribbling on a page and couldn't make it do anything. He'd had to scrub dishes every night for four weeks as part of his punishment for taking the book. One of those miserable students had told on him. He was sure they'd been jealous that he could make the diagrams jump up and spin in mid-air and they couldn't. Come to think of it, he'd just thought it was in his head, so how was it they'd also been able to see the diagrams jump up when he made them spin? He must have been doing something right. If only he could do it again though.

He relaxed, and rooted around in his memory, chanting the words he'd seen in the book while at the same time imagining himself flying toward the peaks. Screwing up his face, he waited and waited, but felt nothing at all. He was about to give up when a sudden cold breeze made him open his eyes. Now on reflection he realised that he would probably have been fine except for two important facts. First of all, he'd not been aware that his magical energy hadn't fully recharged, especially not after controlling the large feline and her kittens. Although it had been a few days ago, it had really taken it out of him. Secondly, he'd made the mistake of looking down, only to find himself flying high over a deep, dark ravine between two sharp peaks while the wind was whipping his cloak around his legs. Never look down, isn't that what they always say? Especially if you're such a long way up. In a heartbeat his control was gone, his subconscious running back to a safer place in his mind and his conscious frantically screaming at him as he hurtled toward the ground.

"I'm faaaaaaallllllliiiiiiiing..." was probably not the brightest thing he could think of, especially as it was followed by an eerie echo of "you foooooool!". He was sure the second cry wasn't actually his own voice.

As the wind whistled through his ears and the ground rushed up to meet him, he quickly threw out a shield barrier spell that wrapped itself around him. It was just in time for him to bounce off a ledge in the ravine, fall through a tree on the ledge below, bounce again and then finally land with a thud on another ledge as the shield barrier gave way. A few minutes later, he raised his head from his rocky pillow, only to immediately drop it again as the world started spinning. Lying for a while and breathing heavily he waited for the spinning to stop, then rolled over with a sigh and sat up, shuffling back until he was sitting against the stony wall of the ledge he'd landed on. Peering up, Darjoon looked at the top of the cliff some distance above him, way up above the two ledges he'd bounced on during his way down and cursed, long and loudly. The curses echoed down the valley, mocking him. He could feel his magic had drained away, what with the flying and the shield spell. No wonder the shield had failed at the end. Finite resource indeed. Feeling the chill breeze howling up from the ravine below him, he wrapped the cloak tighter around himself and slumped down. After a while there were faint echoes of his snoring whispering down the valley. Waking up much, much later, he stretched and groaned, feeling cold, hungry, stiff and sore. Grabbing his pack he munched on what little remained of the chranth bread, grimacing as he swallowed the dry food. He put his head back and stared up at the cliff above him.

"What to do, Darjoon, what to do?", he mumbled to himself, "You can't go down, and you can't fly up? Guess you've got to use those big bones you were born with and climb."

Hours later, panting, he hung onto the rock outcropping and felt his muscles burn with the strain of climbing. He looked down to see the dark ravine stretching out to either side. He could feel the wind whistling around him as it tried to pluck him from his perch. Not for the first time, he wished he'd taken off his extra cloak before climbing as it billowed out behind him in perverse pleasure, trying to help the wind rip him from the sheer cliff-side. It was also making him hot and he was now sweating profusely, the rivulets running down his face and then freezing into miniature icicles.

"If I could just get a boost of some kind", he thought tiredly, "If there was just someone else with me. If I was just back in that hateful classroom. If, if, if, if…

Aaaaaahhh!!", the ravine echoed back at him and the noise died away slowly to either side. He leant his forehead against the cool rock, feeling tired and dejected as his imagination idly drifted into what it would be like to fly again. With a start, he grabbed hold of the cliff and dug his feet into cracks in the wall. Looking down, he could see the outcropping where he had been hanging just seconds ago, now yards below him. How did that happen? He threw his senses inward to check the effect on his body, but found little or no magic loss. Repeating the act of leaning his head against the cool rock, he once again imagined himself flying up and had to suddenly grab hold of the wall as he moved yards up the cliff.

"Okay, Darjoon, that's more like it", he said to himself, "You can do this, just do it slowly, a bit at a time."

Continuing to climb up the cliff face, every now and then he used short bursts of magic to help him over the ledges and smooth sections. In this way he made good time up the side of the ravine until finally he hauled himself over the edge of the cliff. Flinging the extra cloak into his pack, he shivered slightly as he felt the cool wind blow away all the heat he'd generated. Grabbing a cloth out of the pack, he tried to wipe off most of the icy sweat that had been sliding down his face. He lifted his head and glared across the barren rock with its twisted scrub and scattered snow, seeing the mountains still lying in wait for him.

"No more flying for you my boy, no flying at all", he muttered, "this time you've just got to keep walking". Staggering to his feet, he stumbled away from the ravine behind him, carefully crossing the barren wasteland that was pockmarked with craters and strewn with large boulders that had fallen down from the mountain above. He headed for the trail he had spotted that looked to be heading through a gap in the mountain. His feet were throbbing with the pain of walking, particularly after he'd spent the day digging them into small cracks in the side of the ravine. Spying a small cave off to one side of the trail, he projected his senses into it, and, finding it empty, threw in his pack and clambered through the small entrance. Grabbing his extra cloak out of the pack, he wrapped it around himself and rolled over. Sheer exhaustion from the days climbing and walking and the overuse of magic meant that despite the bitter cold and sore feet, he drifted easily into a deep sleep. Darjoon moaned in his sleep as he dreamt that he was continually flying and falling, flying and falling until he landed on an exercise mat. A woman with blonde hair and no face helped him up and he started to exercise with her, sparring backwards and forwards across the mat. He tried talking to the girl but she had no face and no mouth and just nodded at him. They were spinning around as they fought and finally at the end, he fell into the arms of a tall man in a smart black coat, who had no eyes but gave him a big grin, showing off a mouth full of long, sharp white teeth.

Darjoon started awake, the dream fading quickly, while at the same time resolving itself into a grinning face in front of him. Staring in fascination at the long, sharp teeth, he could see they were not clean and white like they'd been in his dream. In fact, there was a bit of grisly old meat lodged between the sharp incisors. Above the teeth were two slits for a nose and above them a pair of cold, calculating, glittering black eyes that stared at him and drilled remorselessly into his mind. Staring back into the twin black pools, Darjoon began to relax, feeling drowsy and peaceful, secure in the knowledge that he was warm and cosy and among friends. Just as he started to become aware that his skin was tingling like crazy, a flicker in the black eyes of the thing in front of him betrayed the creatures interest in something going on behind it, almost as if there was a hidden conversation that it was listening to. It broke the spell and Darjoon stared up with new-found horror at his first Dremrel, the evil, magical, bat-like eater of men. In one of the smuggled library books he'd read that people thought there was a time when they were once human but an ancient civilisation had magically blended them with bats to create this obscene thing in front of him. Halfway through the entrance, he could see it was about the size of a man and was leaning on the knuckles of a large claw-tipped hand that in turn was linked to leathery wings that shrouded the creature like a dark cloak. The other hand was fastened on Darjoon's ankle in a vice-like grip, the talons cruelly biting into his soft flesh. As if the creature sensed a sudden lack of control, Darjoon felt it increasing the magic and inwardly he fought off the strange, sleepy feeling that started in his mind. He began to chant a fire spell to throw in the creature's face, but the response to that was a spell that sucked all the air out the cave and left him gasping for breath and unable to complete his incantation or create fire. The creature began to shuffle forward menacingly and this time Darjoon relaxed, feeling his subconscious bleed into his conscious. Imagining the creature expelled from the cave like a cork from a bottle he closed his eyes, fancying he could hear the popping noise it made as it blew out and the air rushed back into the cave. Sucking down lungfuls of air he opened his eyes to see that the creature was actually gone. With no time to waste he erected a shield barrier at the mouth of the cave just as a searing fireball smashed into it. A Dremrel! Oh sweet Zukar, a real, adult Dremrel and he was all alone. He had felt the beast's magic and it was really, really strong, not weak like the college had taught them.

"Think Darjoon, think! What kills Dremrels?", he muttered frantically to himself, dredging his memory for facts.

As far as he could remember, the only advice the college had ever given students about Dremrel was to run, or if that failed then they had been told to prepare to enter Khamoos, the eternal twilight of the after-life, where the Great Raven would pick them up and carry them to the

River of Life for rebirth. What use was the college, if it couldn't prepare someone for the real world? Those bungling teachers that prattled on about discipline and devotion, who prevented any real test of magic or strength and controlled every aspect of life from dawn to dusk. He'd been out on his own for three days and not much of what they'd taught him had been of any use. A lot more help had come from those books he'd read on his own. That can't be right, can it? Surely the raven-born would prepare their young for the world outside their lands? All that control, all those endless, meaningless exercises, what had they really been teaching them? To serve mindlessly as slaves doing whatever the ruling council dictated while it preached about balance? They'd certainly not learnt independence of thought and action.

Darjoon noticed it was quiet outside and he extended his senses beyond the shield barrier. An agonising pain immediately ripped across his temples and he collapsed, breathing hard. The pain had almost knocked out his hold on the shield and the Dremrel had obviously been waiting for him to expose himself. There was a scrabbling noise near the entrance, and he watched, transfixed, as dust started filtering in through that side of the cave. The Dremrel was now starting to dig him out, and, given the tingling he felt, was using powerful magic to do it. He couldn't hold a shield wall across the entire front of the cave, not at the strength needed and definitely not for that long.

"Come on, Darjoon, think, think! You need to find a way out or you'll be trapped in here", there was that voice in his head again. He still wasn't sure it was his own. He grabbed his pack and collapsed the shield wall without hesitation, flinging himself through the opening and using magic to propel his body forwards. Flying out at speed, he collided hard with a Dremrel standing outside. As he hit it, he could feel and hear bones breaking in its chest. Like the bats they were supposedly blended from, their bones felt small and fragile. It was bright outside after the dimness of the cave, and he blinked as he rolled to his feet and looked around. A Dremrel was lying on the floor, blood coming from the mouth as it coughed and spluttered, obviously dying. Another was busy outside the cave entrance, its back to him, obviously intent on using magic to dig him out. Only two? Where was the third, there were always at least three or at least that's what he'd read in the forbidden texts. As the Dremrel near the cave started to turn around, a rush of wind alerted Darjoon and he dropped quickly and rolled to the side. A Dremrel crashed into the ground in front of him, spinning around with elbows bent and wings extended, the things clawed hands held close together and pointing at him. The hands were glowing and he ducked and rolled again as a bolt of fire flashed into the space he'd just occupied. The other Dremrel was hissing and moving across to cut him off from the path.

Darjoon's heart was racing and his mind was crowded with little thoughts falling over each other in panic. The Dremrel on the ground gave a last, coughing gasp, spewed up thick, black blood and fell back dead. The other two, temporarily distracted, looked over at it and shrieked as if in agony, howling out their anguish and deafening him, the air filled with crackling lightning, fire-bolts and sound. Without thinking, Darjoon flung his hands up and two shield spells locked into place around the Dremrel. He continued applying magical power as they slowly, agonisingly began to contract around each monster. He could tell they were confused, as they couldn't see outside the spell, and were cut off from each other, scrabbling against the shield but not breaking free. Not even their telepathy was able to penetrate the shields he'd locked around them but he could see their muscles straining as they tried desperately to fight against the inexorable force of the shields. At the end, he heard bones cracking and snapping, heard the agonised shrieks as first one, then the other were crushed into two round wet balls of bone, gristle and blood. The shields snapped out and dropped the balls onto the trail with twin wet thuds as he slumped to the ground in exhaustion. Every part of his body was aching and there was an army of sledge-hammers behind his eyes pounding at his brain. His muscles felt like jelly and he was dizzy. He looked up as the mountain peaks spun around him and slowly he fell back to lie still and unmoving in the dirt.

Before the darkness took hold, he remembered that his Grandpa had once told him, "Defensive spells are often stronger than offensive ones. You might think that a ball of fire will just blast your enemy into bits, but most often their shields can counter your offensive spells. Think creatively, Darjoon. Real success is not always achieved through the obvious option. Be prepared to defend yourself, and if necessary, to escape. Honour and valour are fine things but they are of no use to you when you find yourself on the back of the Great Raven, flying to the Stream of Life. Make sure you live to fight again in this life."

After coming round. it seemed like ages before he could drag himself out of the dirt, grab his pack and crawl back into the cave while his body protested at even this feeble effort. As he slumped into oblivion again, he barely heard the voice in his head, "... three Dremrel, and two simultaneously with defensive magic. By Zukar, that's never been done before!"

Darjoon woke up and stared at the dust motes floating in the faint light that came in from the cave's entrance. Using his magic he could sense that his body was close to its last reserves. The walking and climbing were nothing to him physically, he could do that for days, but the magic he'd been using was starting to eat into his body's reserves. His clothes were just hanging off him now. Grabbing a mouthful of chranth and berries, neither of which were particularly fresh, he used a swig of water to help him swallow them down. He'd been dreaming, and in the dream his mother and grandfather had been arguing. In fact, he was pretty sure it was more a memory from his childhood than a dream. Closing his eyes, he replayed the dream.

"No father, I'll not hear any more about it", he'd heard his mother saying, "Darjoon will go to the college and that's that. I don't care what you think of the instructors or the headmaster or the Council. He needs an education and the company of boys his own age, and he needs to learn what it means to be raven-born."

Darjoon had been lying awake in bed at night, his mother and grandfather's voices floating up from downstairs. With no conscious effort, his magic had augmented his hearing so that it seemed as if they were in the room with him.

"But daughter, just listen to me for a moment. That college has been nothing but a sham for decades. What they teach the poor children is just drivel. Not one raven-born will come out of there with a sense of their true heritage or an awareness of their true power. They will never survive outside our lands and you know this. None of the true mages among you learnt what you know from the college. You were hand-picked after you graduated and then retrained, but what about those that aren't, those that you judge unworthy but are still raven-born? Do you think your precious Council is that good, that perfect? What makes you any different from the Circle of the True Ones?"

It wasn't often that he heard his grandfather so upset. He was almost shouting now, and his mother started shouting back.

"You don't know what you're talking about, father! There is a reason that we don't let them unleash their true potential. Uncontrolled magic is inherently dangerous, as you should know all too well. It is exactly because of the Circle that we cannot let young raven-born develop their powers unchecked. We must monitor and control those with potential, and that's why only those selected are chosen for the Kasram. If they survive that test then they can become senior mages and may eventually sit on the Council. This is what I had to do and I almost died doing it, don't you remember? What would I have done if I'd had access to my real power without guidance? Burnt myself out and ended up like you?"

"Oh, so that's it! Your father, the embarrassment that you must endure, the shame you must carry! The farmer who can barely enchant a candle-flame. To think that my own daughter has so little skill she cannot detect true magic when it is wielded. What about this then?", Darjoon felt a familiar tingle across his skin, and knew his grandfather was using his magic. It had a different quality to his mother's magic, being raw and unrefined but also very powerful. He hadn't realised it before, but it was only with Darjoon that grandfather had ever revealed his real magic, and never with anyone else around, not even his own daughter.

There was a deep silence, and then suddenly the tingle again followed by the sound of his mother sobbing. He heard a door slam and knew his grandmother had gone into the room.

"What did you do, Dasmorn? What did you do to your own daughter, to your very flesh and blood? Have you gone mad? Both of you? You'll wake Darjoon at this rate. Do you want him seeing the two of you duelling like those crazy magic-users from Sorcerer Isle? What's wrong with you both?"

His grandmother was in full flow as usual. He could just see grandpa and mother cowering.

"I'm sorry Trameta, you're right, I shouldn't have done that. I've never shown her the extent of my magic before. Misroan, don't look so alarmed. There was never any need and as an outsider I didn't want to ruffle the feathers of the raven-born. You know how paranoid they can be", his grandfather's voice was softer now.

"But father, you're one of us. You are a raven-born, even if you grew up in Lower Srinth on the farm. It's not your fault that your parents abandoned you there."

"They never abandoned me, little daughter, they were doing what they thought was right. They had a war to fight, and the farm was a safe place for me. They didn't want to leave me here. My uncle was on that farm. He never made the grade in your precious college so they kicked him out of these lands, as you well know."

"But father, where did you learn to use magic like this? I've never been in a shield spell that was so powerful before! How could you develop your powers without a mentor, without the Kasram?"

"That's what I'm trying to tell you. The college and the Council are not the sole owners of magic. My parents and even my uncle taught me the basics, but the rest I learnt by myself, out in the fields among the beasts, insects and plants. Nature showed me what I needed, that the magic was always inside me, deep inside. And it showed me how I needed to reach and free that instinctive part of me, that deep subconscious life that is in all of us. That's what I've been teaching Darjoon. To surrender to what is in him and around him and let it out into the world."

"You, what? How dare you show him magic! Do you know what harm you could do to him? He could burn out. He could die from it. You know who his father was and how dangerous his magic could be. Do you want him to go mad as well? Do you?", his mother was really upset now.

"Misroan, stop! What they've taught you to believe is nonsense. This isn't magic that's at fault here but the training. The raven-born's power is dwindling fast, with every generation weaker than the one before. We're controlling our children so much that our people are losing their natural abilities. The Dremrel numbers are growing again and they are getting bolder. The Circle is an ever-present threat to us as well. And do you think the Empire will stand by idly while we cut off even some of our best from their true power? What a dark road and a dark place we're flying to. We are travelling ever further from our nest with our wings clipped and soon we'll not get back, although it might already be too late. A bird on the ground is no bird at all, Misroan, you know that. I'll not have Darjoon become another slave to this place, especially as none of us know the full extent of his power, let alone the boy himself. Do you think that stupid college is going to be of any use to him when his power wakes of its own accord? This place hates outsiders, you know that from experience, from their response to his father, their response to me. Have you seen what he's growing into? Every day he looks less and less like a raven-born and more and more like his father."

"Shush, Dasmorn, what's wrong with you! He'll hear both of you", he could hear his grandmothers voice again, "Now stop this nonsense and go to bed the pair of you. I'll not have you fighting in front of him. That poor child has no father and you've hardly been here, Misroan, and quite likely he has no future. So just give it a rest, both of you. Misroan, you know your father is one of the gentlest men you'll ever meet. He's doing that boy a world of good, magic or no. And Dasmorn, well, you cannot change an entire civilisation overnight. Darjoon will have to adapt to our raven-born ways or... or... Well, he has to find a way to fit in. Yes, he's different, but he's also strong and good, just like his grandfather and his mother. We all have to raise him to be strong, to shun the madness that might be in him. Don't look at me like that, Dasmorn, you of all people must remember who his father was. You know this is no place for crazy people. No-one knows what the union of a raven and a bat will bring, but I have a feeling that the raven-born will need Darjoon one day and so we must protect him, even if it is from himself. Now off to bed with both of you."

In the silence he'd thought about what his grandmother

had said. She'd almost seemed fond of him, even though she usually never so much as blinked in his direction. She ruled their home with an iron fist and beware any fool who crossed her. He had heard his grandpa and mother meekly heading off to their rooms. Not for the first time, small tears had escaped his closed eyelids and trickled down his cheeks. Why did he have to be so different? And who was his father, that enigmatic mage that no-one would tell him anything about.

Darjoon opened his eyes and blinked into the twilight of the small cave, the memories bitter-sweet. The dream about his childhood had been strong and Darjoon had to shake himself into the present world. He was older now and had been through that college his family talked about. It seems his grandfather had been right, they weren't teaching them anything about their true power. But what power did he now possess? What power had he inherited from his father and his mother? And what had his grandmother meant by "bat"? He did not know of any people in the Old Lands that were known as bats. His mother was the raven, that was obvious as they were the raven-born. That his father had not been born in the nest of the ravens was also obvious in his own large physique, round face and strange magic. Only his hooked nose was remotely similar. But who was he then? He climbed out of the cave, shouldered his pack and continued walking along the trail up through the mountains, deep in thought. Every day he had worried at the puzzle like a wolf gnawing on a bone, but he could not unravel it. He knew he did not have enough information. After another long day of trudging up and down the mountain, he rounded a corner lost in thought when a sharp, shrill scream jolted him out of his reverie.

Darjoon flattened himself against the rock wall at his back. He could see down the path and there were two recognisable forms silhouetted in the setting sun. Looking like old, stooped men wearing long, flowing coats, he could see the Dremrel were intent on prey lower down the trail. It had taken another day of uneventful walking and a dreamless night of deep sleep before he started to feel like he'd recovered from his previous ordeal with the Dremrel coven. Finally getting through the rest of the freezing mountain pass without mishap he was now heading down towards the immense forest of Spidral that was laid out before him. The densely packed trees stretched from the foot of the mountains all the way to the horizon, and there was a faint mist that blurred the morning air above them. The breezes that blew were slowly starting to warm up now that he was descending out of the mountain, and he could almost smell the deep, rich earth of the forest far below.

So he was surprised to see Dremrel that were so far down from the Darken Hills. Normally they would stay higher up and keep to themselves, living in caves and feeding on the deer, as well as the odd traveller. Although they were known to occasionally venture further down, they tended to go into Lower Srinth, not here towards the dangerous forest of Spidral. There was another shriek from below followed by the dry hissing noise that he'd heard the other Dremrel make. He saw the two creatures below him tense, looking as if they were readying themselves to jump on their prey. Suddenly they relaxed, arching their backs and extending their clawed hands in front of them. Again a scream, this time the unmistakable cry of a woman in distress. If she was using words, he didn't recognise them immediately as they were clearly in a foreign tongue.

Darjoon quickly and quietly crept over to a small spur of rock overlooking the Dremrel and their victim. He saw the young woman sprawled on the trail with her belongings scattered around her. Standing before her was a Dremrel, the arms flung wide and wings outstretched, hands curled forwards with menacing claws extended. The creatures head was flung back, as if lost in some great pleasure. He'd read that Dremrel sometimes toyed with their prey, their malicious evil expressing itself through fantasies implanted in the mind of the creature they were to eat. They would do this for hours and if their prey was a person then their mind could be destroyed by the sheer horror they experienced. It was said a Dremrel coven could enjoy their victims fear vicariously, being able to link to the attacker and the victim. This was obviously what they were doing now. He could see her face as it contorted into a wordless, open-mouthed scream.

Darjoon sat back on his heels and thought about the best way to deal with them. It was a mark of his character that even though at college he'd always pretended to be a coward, in reality he would never run and leave someone in trouble. He closed his eyes, feeling the magic rise up in his blood. He couldn't hope to get lucky again and defeat three Dremrel, so he needed another angle. Throwing an opaque shield spell tightly around the woman lying on the ground, he created an illusion of her standing up and running back up the trail.

"Please Zukar, don't let them see through the illusion", he muttered to himself.

If the Dremrel were to become aware of another magic-user then they would immediately abandon her and come after him. He'd read they could feed on magic and would always prioritise their attack on those who had magic in their blood. Which might buy her time to escape but would probably mean death for him, not that he was a coward but he did have a healthy sense of self-preservation. The Dremrel below hissed and let out a thin shriek as the shield blocked access to the victim's mind. At the same time, the two on the rocks took off after the figure of the fleeing girl, closely followed by the one below. He sent the illusion dashing off up the trail just fast enough to stay ahead of them. They weren't very quick across the ground so he had to be careful not to outdistance them. Learning from his previous experience over the last few days, he used short bursts of magic to make her appear and disappear among the rocks without draining himself.

Walking quickly down the trail, he could see the girl fighting the shield spell and quickly dropped it. She went mad, screaming and throwing herself at him in an effort to claw out his eyes and he had to throw her back. Dropping the illusion spell he had used on the Dremrel, he conjured one for her where she found herself standing on a thin ledge high up on the outside of a tall tower. She froze into immobility, afraid of losing her balance and falling and put out her arms as she teetered on the edge. Into this illusion he projected himself reaching out a window and offering her a hand which she gratefully accepted. Pulling her slowly up and through the window into the tower, she sank gratefully onto a chair. In reality, she'd sat down on a rock next to the trail, hugging herself. He dropped the illusion and watched her closely to see the reaction. She looked up at him, blinking slowly. "Where am I now?", her voice was light and husky, probably sore from screaming.

"You're safe now. You're above Spidral, in the foothills of the Darken Hills. You've just been attacked by Dremrel and I'm afraid they were messing with your mind. How are you feeling?", Darjoon groaned inwardly. What a stupid thing to ask. He'd basically just told her what had happened, so how did he think she was feeling.

"Umm, I mean are you okay?", he cringed inside, that wasn't any better.

"How do I know I'm not still in an illusion?", she asked, looking at him intently and then getting to her feet quickly as Darjoon stepped over to her.

"Owww! What did you do that for? That really hurt you know. You've got great big fingers", she exclaimed as Darjoon pinched her.

"I... I'm sorry, I... I mean you... Well I was just helping you realise that this is all real now. Would you feel real pain like that in the illusion?", to his ears he sounded like a little boy and nothing like the brave mage he wanted to be.

"No, I suppose I wouldn't. I mean, I don't know, I did feel pain before though. Anyway, it doesn't feel like an illusion, and if it was, who would be silly enough to magic you into it", she glared at him from under her bangs.

She had long blonde hair, cascading down to her waist, with a short, straight fringe just above her eyes. They were a piercing blue-green, bright and sparkling in the late sunshine. Her small stub of a nose floated delicately above soft, full lips. Her jaw was small and determined, with a long neck underneath. As for the rest of her, Darjoon could just stare. She was petite and very, very attractive. Her blouse had been pulled down and to the side during the confrontation with the Dremrel and clung tightly to her. He started to speak, and then began to blush, as she looked up at him mischievously.

"Are you quite finished, or should I stand up and turn around? I'm not a bront for sale at market you know. Eyes up here, young man. Actually, better yet, why don't you turn around while I make myself decent."

He turned around, still blushing bright red down his face and onto his neck. She pulled and tied her wayward blouse closed and then, grabbing a jacket from the mess around her, pulled it on and tied up her hair. Then she grabbed the rest of her belongings and stuffed them back into her pack.

"Ok young man, you can turn around again. Hopefully this will help you to be less distracted. You do know that those creepy bats will probably come back, right?"

When he turned around, she was standing with her hands on her hips looking back up the trail.

"The Dremrel! Oh Zukar, I'd forgotten about them. Oh, uh, we'd better get moving", he started heading down the trail.

"Oh, so I was right. You weren't watching for the Dremrel, were you? You know you're staring again? Have you never seen a woman before?", she was almost laughing now, her eye's sparkling.

A faint hiss overhead was all the warning he had, along with a flicker of shadow just before the Dremrel landed on the path in front of them. He knew the creature's companions wouldn't be far behind. Throwing the girl away from him, he rolled to the side of the trail and threw out a shield spell. This time, the creature resisted and he felt the spell fizzle out before it could take hold. He threw out another one, but instead of going for the creature, he put it around a rock balancing precariously on a ledge just behind it. Bringing the spell towards him with as much force as he could, he released the shield just before the rock hit the Dremrel's head. He heard the wet smack and the crunch of the thing's skull as it sprawled full-length on the trail. There were a few twitches and then it lay still. She was lying on the ground where she'd fallen, staring in shock at the dead creature. He grabbed her by the hand and pulled her to her feet.

"Run! The others won't be far behind", he yelled at her and took off.

They ran down the trail and then stopped as they heard shrieking and wailing behind them. Lightning flew into the air and slammed into the cliffs around them. Great shadows jumped and danced up the trail. She ducked down behind a rock while he grabbed her arm, trying to pull her out and drag her with him.

"They're shooting spells at us, they're going to kill us", she yelled at him above the din.

"No, that's just a reaction. They're upset because the other one is dead and so their magic is out of control for now. Let's get out of here before they recover."

He finally managed to drag her out from behind the rock and they took off running down the trail. Darjoon stopped to catch his breath, his chest heaving with the effort of running.

"She doesn't even look like she's been running, how fit

is she?", he thought, glancing over at her.

"I think we've lost them", he said to her, "they seemed pretty upset at the other one being dead. They usually hunt in packs, so I think we're safe for now."

They both slowed to a walk, their chests heaving after the run and Darjoon could see that although he struggled to catch his breath, she was already breathing normally. Who was she?

"So what were you doing in the Darken Hills?", Darjoon asked. He flinched at how it came out. It sounded as if he was interrogating her.

"Well, someone's nosey. I could ask you the same question you know", she stared back at him. He snorted at her and then together they both doubled up in laughter. He was laughing with deep belly laughs, while she was snorting and laughing at the same time. Looking at her he couldn't help but admire the way her eyes crinkled up at the corners and how straight and even her beautiful white teeth were between her perfect ruby lips.

As he looked at her, he could hear his grandpa speaking to him like it was yesterday, "Be careful my son. Woman can be the worst illusion a mage can face. They can get into your head quicker and slicker than the fastest spell. Before you know it you'll be as tongue-tied and foolish as a new-born bront trying to walk. And they'll tie you up in knots so you can't sleep at night and with all the power of your magic you still won't stand a chance."

"So, are you going to introduce yourself properly this time?", she'd stopped laughing and was standing looking him up and down with an appraising smile.

"Uh, um, yes. Of course. Sorry! I should have... I mean, I could have... I mean yes, my name's Darjoon, I'm meet to please you", he mumbled back.

"Oh sweet Zukar, what an idiot I am", he thought, cringing and beginning to blush again.

"Well, Darjoon, my name's Sirroya, and I have to say that despite looking and sounding like a complete twit, you actually saved my life. So I'm very meet to pleased you. It's not often a young lady like me happens across a real gentleman", she smiled as Darjoon blushed even deeper.

"And may I ask, young sir, what are you are doing up in the Hills? I can't imagine you were just waiting to save damsels in distress, or are you a bandit in training?", her voice and her stare got a little harder and her eyes narrowed.

"Yes, no, that's right. I mean no, I wasn't waiting for you. Or anyone. I mean I wasn't in training. I'm not a bandit, actually. I meant yes, I'll tell you", he stammered again as the blush started to slowly creep down his neck. He thought about how he could explain his situation to her. She was definitely not raven-born, so she wouldn't care or understand that he was exiled. Or would she? Actually, most people were nervous around raven-born, and yet she didn't seem anxious at all. Then again, he wasn't really raven-born, was he.

"I'm on a training mission of sorts", he began.

"I knew it", she said, "you are a bandit."

"No, no, I promise you I'm not. I'm a raven-born apprentice and they've sent me into the Hills for training."

That at least was partly true. Young raven-born were sent into the Hills, although not many came back.

"Oh, I see. Finished at college have you? You poor thing, and now you're supposed to learn how to be a man", her voice was sad, "You don't look raven-born though. Well, the nose is sort of right, but your hair's not black enough, the nose isn't sharp enough, and you're a little on the large side."

"I am a man", he exclaimed indignantly, "and I'm not fat, I'm just big-boned. You're not much older than I am anyway."

"Okay, okay. It's not like I'm saying 'Fat Man Walking', is it? The kids in my village used to say that every time they saw the innkeeper. It was a game of theirs, and he really was a big, fat man. Until one day, one of them fell in the pond and couldn't swim. The innkeeper was passing by, dived in and saved her. After that they never teased him again, in fact they used to visit him and sit outside drinking cold berry juice while he told them his stories. He'd been an adventurer you see. Such amazing stories too, and every time he told one that girl was spellbound.", she had a faraway look on her face, then abruptly smiled at him, "Stories just like you must have?"

"Well, I don't know about that. I'm only just starting my adventures. What about you then? Why are you out here? What stories do you have to tell?"

She looked at him for a long time, her eyes slowly blinking as if she was remembering something from long ago.

"I used to live in a small village in the Empire. My parents were poor and so I used to help out at the local store, getting paid in goods we could use at home. One day, I saw someone steal something and they blamed it on me. The thief had parents that were well known around town, so no-one believed me, not even my parents. They locked me up in the cellar as punishment but I escaped and ran away. I've been running ever since, and so I thought I'd go to Spidral where I could start a new life among the free-folk in the forest. They don't care about how much money you have, or don't have, and they accept you regardless of your past", she stared wistfully past him into the distance.

"I don't mean to be rude", Darjoon said, "but you don't look that young. I mean, I can't see how anyone would be able to lock you away easily or without a fight."

"Well, aren't you full of compliments. Not young indeed. Care to try some more flattery on me? You obviously know a lot about me so what else can I say. I've been running for a long time you know", the last she said over her shoulder as she brushed past him haughtily and tramped down the trail.

"I'm sorry, I, I didn't mean anything. It was a silly thing

for me to say. Of course you have, and you are still young", Darjoon hurried to keep up, trying to appease her.

As they walked down the trail, Sirroya glanced over at the young man walking beside her. He was of average height, a little taller than she was. He had a fine head of dark brown hair, piercing dark brown eyes with a hooked nose and small, full lips. He walked with a straight back, broad in the chest and although certainly not fat, would obviously become a large, well-built man. She could see in his shoulders and arms that he was already strong and he had an air of power around him. He'd casually and calmly distracted two Dremrel while dispatching a third, as if he'd been doing it all his life. She'd heard stories of powerful mage's living in the mountains, of a cabal that kept to themselves and who individually might even be a match for a Dremrel pack. But surely he was too young and naive to be involved with them? She knew the raven-born occasionally sent out boys they didn't consider up to their standards to survive in the Hills. Maybe they, like her, didn't see him as raven-born and had rejected him, although it was strange they'd so easily get rid of such a powerful mage.

Still, he could be of use to her. It wouldn't be hard to enlist his help in her plans. With her experience of men, she could see that he was already infatuated with her. Now that really was a weapon. She smiled to herself. Oh yes, this was going to be a good day after all. Once they were in Spidral, she knew a few ways they could make some money, especially with the powers he had. Enough coin to buy information about the free-folk village and finance an expedition there.

"Well Darjoon", she thought to herself, "it looks like this could be the start of something special after all."

She started whistling as they walked, but stopped when she saw him frowning at her. Hmm, she was going to have to teach him to relax and learn how to have fun. Raven-born men could be so uptight..

4 TWO'S COMPANY

They'd spent a day slogging down the trail out of the Darken Hills and finally camped just outside the forest in an alcove formed by two great rocks that had rolled down from the mountains above. The thought of entering that great, brooding forest in the twilight and trying to find a place to camp didn't appeal to either of them. Darjoon, and particularly Sirroya, were quiet and contemplative. Occasionally he'd give her a sidelong glance but she was too wrapped up in her own thoughts to notice. She looked so young and so vulnerable, it made him want to reach out and comfort her and tell her that everything was going to be okay. But he could see that underneath the cheeky, bubbly exterior was a determined woman who would not take kindly to such gratuitous displays of affection. He'd seen it in the way she coped after the Dremrel attack, composing herself quickly despite the mental anguish she must have suffered. To think in the college they'd been taught that Empire women were useless and only fit to wear fancy clothes, yet the first one he meets is strong and courageous.

"I guess running away from home when you're young must do that to you. Something I'm finding out all too well", he thought to himself.

After they spent the night in the secluded alcove and had a sparse breakfast of some berries and a few crumbs of chranth washed down by water, they headed into the Great Forest of Spidral, following a well-beaten path that led through a small grassy field and into the cool of the forest. There were two enormous tree's on either side of the path, their massive trunks towering high overhead and it looked as if they'd been planted as a gateway to the forest ahead. As Darjoon walked in between them, he heard a faint sigh and what sounded like an old, wheezing voice that spoke to him, "Welcome back, friend". Glancing quickly at Sirroya to see if she'd said anything, he shook his head, wondering if the Dremrel attack was still affecting him. The magic of the evil bat-like creatures had been very powerful and maybe he was experiencing some after-effects. Hearing nothing further, he shook his head again and followed Sirroya into the forest.

After walking for some time in the leafy gloom the path split in two directions and they paused for a moment to consider which way to go. She looked at him inquiringly as if to say, "What now?". He tried to remember what he'd learnt about the Great Forest at the college. He only remembered being told it was very dangerous and it was not wise to stray from the path or get lost. There was meant to be a large town not far from the forest entrance, one that most travellers visited as it was the gateway to the rest of Spidral. He seemed to remember it was to the north-east, which meant they should follow the right-hand fork, although he couldn't be entirely sure. Just as he started to walk that way, Sirroya interrupted him.

"I think we should take this left-hand fork. We want to go to Roikba, don't we?"

She'd been silent all this time and he'd forgotten the charming, lilting tone of her young voice and so smiled at her indulgently, "Yes, that's right, it is Roikba we're looking for. And as that town lies to the north-east, we must take the right-hand fork."

He felt smug and sure of himself and the knowledge he had.

"Okay, big man, if you think so", she replied, "But I'm pretty sure it was the other way."

She had her hands on her hips again in that cocky stance of hers, complete with raised eyebrow and a little curve to her lips like a secret smile. He wanted to be angry with her for doubting him, but when she looked like that he just couldn't be.

"Well, I know for a fact that this is the right way. You're welcome to trip daintily through the forest, but getting lost here is pretty dangerous, as everyone knows", he was showing off now.

"Oh, everyone, is it? I thought it was just you that knew what you were doing. Well, don't let me stop you, big man. I'll follow behind and if something dangerous comes along, I guess the great mage will protect me", she was definitely smirking at him now.

Darjoon blushed and stalked off down the trail along the right-hand fork. How could she get under his skin so easily? He'd never had brothers or sisters and back home had pretty much been a recluse, so his experience of girls was limited. The colleges were divided according to gender and the boys and girls were not encouraged to fraternise. In fact, there were often harsh physical and magical competitions between them and a raven-born girl was more likely to take your head off than play romantic games, as many a young man distracted by shapely curves had discovered. After waking up with a splitting headache a few times, a boy learnt to be careful around girls. Yet, were all girls so downright annoying and enticing at the same time? He'd have to watch himself and make sure he didn't get distracted. He needed to remember his mission and why he was here. His grandfather had tried to warn him about the dangers of pretty women.

Sirroya had found her voice again and was prattling on

about the town of Roikba and all the traders that stopped there and the amazing goods they had to sell, as well as how you could make a lot of money there, lawfully of course. She described the amazing houses in the trees, how some of the Spidralites liked to build up high in the branches of the massive, fragrant Brisla trees, using a form of magic to shape branches and trunks into beautiful shapes. Darjoon recalled reading that Brisla trees were old and massive and grew for hundreds of years, providing shade and shelter to the many animals and people that lived in their branches. The trees could often be seen towering above the canopy, like the two they'd walked through in the morning at the entrance to the forest. It was said the trees were sentient and for certain people they would speak to them, but then only a few could understand what they actually said.

Darjoon stopped suddenly, "Wait, what? What did you say? Trees that can talk?", he remembered the voice he'd heard on entering the forest. Then a thought struck him.

"How do you know so much about this place if you've never been here before?", he stared at her intently.

This time it was Sirroya's turn to blush prettily, but she covered it up with a huff and a sigh, rolling her eyes.

"Oh excuse me. The great mage is the only one to be all-powerful and all-knowing, is he? No-one else could possibly know anything, is that it? Would you prefer if I simpered a little and smiled vacantly at you while I shook my head so hair flew round my face? There, how about that, did you like it? Is that all you think Empire women are good for? Oh, don't look so surprised, I know what you raven-born are like. You train your women to fight like hellcats and then believe that all the other women are just silly fools and only good for decoration. Well? Has a bat got your tongue, young raven?"

Darjoon stared at her. He couldn't make out if she was red in the face because she'd blushed, or if it was anger, but she looked really pretty all the same. He was tongue-tied and just turned and carried on walking while she followed him, her eyes laughing.

"Well, I can see that the great mage isn't completely defenceless. It's true you know, the best defence against an angry woman is to just turn around and walk away. Although that's probably not a good idea with a raven-born woman, is it?"

She laughed out loud this time, a rippling, musical melody that echoed through the trees. He grinned to himself, knowing she couldn't see his face as he walked in front of her.

His grin quickly faded as they entered a clearing that seemed to have no exit on any side. An old, broken-down well had been built right in the middle and after walking around the clearing, he stomped over to the well and sat on the edge, fuming. Sirroya also walked around the clearing, then examined the broken pulley and bucket and flopped down on the grass with her back against the old stone wall of the well.

"So, great mage of all-knowing power, I don't see where the trail continues, do you? I wonder, do you think maybe the left-hand fork was the way to go? Oh, I'm so hot and thirsty and they've obviously been neglecting this well lately. Please tell me you have some water?"

Darjoon hauled his waterskin from his pack and handed it to her, saying, "I still think you know more than you're letting on, Sirroya. It definitely seems like you've been here before. How is that possible?"

"Me? I thought I told you already. I ran away through the Empire and into the Darken Hills. When in my sad, short little life would I have come to Spidral? I just assumed that someone would look after this well, wouldn't you? I mean. surely it's obvious that others would end up here."

She watched him, his dark eyes glittering in the sunshine and boring into her soul. She shivered slightly, feeling as if he was seeing her from the inside. He had that penetrating look that she'd finally recognised, the same look as his father. It was in the way he cocked his head and scrutinised her. It was also in the way he dealt with the Dremrel, and, come to think of it, he seemed to have similar magic as well. But did he have the same flaws? She shook her head slightly to clear the memories that seemed to be from so long ago and yet felt like they were only yesterday.

"Well, this is obviously not the right way. We better head back to the fork and go the way you said", Darjoon sighed, heaved himself off the well and started walking back along the trail.

Trudging all the way back to the fork, they headed down the left trail which after some time turned and headed north-east. They were tired and foot-sore and the gloomy light that was filtering through the trees deepened as the sun went down. A little later, just as they were thinking of camping for the night, they saw lights glimmering in the distance through the trees. The path they were on broke out of the forest and now entered a wide clearing, with an impenetrable line of trees on the the other side. In the middle of the trees there was an opening in which someone had built a large gate. It had twin massive doors, easily twice the height of Darjoon and they were blackened, as if they had been treated and hardened somehow. Intricate carvings with looping whorls surrounded stylised shapes of the great Brisla trees. As they approached the gates, a smaller door in one of the gates swung inward and a dark, helmeted face appeared. The eyes above the nose guard narrowed as they saw them and the thin-lipped mouth barked a command, "Halt! Who are you and what do you want in Roikba?"

The face stared at them and then turned and glared at Sirroya. The crease in the forehead deepened as it took in her obvious Empire features and appearance.

"Listen, we don't like the Empire here, girl. Perhaps you should come back when you lot have got tired of butchering our men and raping our women and children!"

The guard started to close the door when he was interrupted from within. They could hear a muffled exchange and then one of the voices a little louder than the other said, "Or maybe we should get a little revenge of our own?"

The door opened again as another helmeted head appeared beside the first, staring out of the gate at Sirroya.

"Gentlemen, she is with me!", Darjoon's voice almost broke on the last syllable.

He'd tried his best to sound manly but wasn't sure he'd pulled it off. The helmets turned to look at him a little closer, one of them producing a burning torch that he shoved towards him.

"Oh-ho, a raven-born, is it? So is she your prisoner, lad? I can't see why else a nice young man like you would bother with her sort. Or is she one of them free-folk, eh? Should know better than to still dress in her Empire clothes. Well, that's fine, young apprentice, we trust your kind, if not hers!"

The guard turned to Sirroya, shoving the torch almost in her face, "Now listen here you Empire scum, as long as you stay with your raven-born friend then you can both come in. But no trouble mind you. We'll be watching both of you, and you, young raven-born, just remember that there is no magic while you're here. You should know the rules, and if you don't, well then we'll have fun teaching them to you, eh, Bloorin?"

The two guards laughed together and withdrew, allowing Sirroya and Darjoon to enter. The guards were armed with long pikes which they rested on their shoulders while they lounged against a small hut just inside the gates. As Sirroya walked by, she tripped over an outstretched foot and would have fallen but for Darjoon catching her.

"Careful girl, this is a dangerous town, especially for an attractive Empire lady like you. I wouldn't stray far from the young raven-born if I were you. Unless you get bored and want better company? Then you know where to find us, eh!", the guards burst into laughter again.

Sirroya's face was turning that bright red colour again and he could see she was getting ready to give the guards a piece of her mind. Darjoon hastily grabbed her arm and hustled her along, whispering to her as he did.

"Look, they hate the Empire so just ignore them. You're going to get a lot more of that before we leave. We can change your clothes, but we can't do anything about your blue eyes and blonde hair. Just try to control your pretty temper would you? You'll get us both into trouble and I can't afford to use my magic here. They take an extremely dim view of that!"

Sirroya gave him that lazy, dangerous smile, "Oh yes of course, kind sir. Did sir know that I can in fact change my hair colour, or is sir just pretending to be as dumb as a bront?"

He blushed. Of course he had forgotten that women from other nations coloured their hair. No self-respecting raven-born woman would dream of doing that. Even if they went grey early which was very rare.

"Oh but poor little me, I must be so glad to have the big mage for protection. What would I do without the all-knowing wise one?", she dropped a curtsy and fluttered her eyelashes at him.

Darjoon sighed, exasperated. Again, he wondered how someone so pretty could be so downright annoying. What was wrong with her anyway? He stalked after her as she marched off down the street. As he followed her, he looked around at the town. It was one thing to read about Roikba in the college library and see some crude illustrations, quite another to actually see the cobbled streets with their ornate lanterns on tall poles shining down warm puddles of light. Looking up he saw well-lit houses up in the trees with ornate walkways that connected them in a web of comfort. Some had winding wooden stairs that curled around the great trees, thereby allowing easy access to the house itself which was usually embedded inside the trunk. There were additional rooms built around the trunk as well. Most of the houses had a rope-and-pulley system for bringing up goods in large wooden boxes. He guessed they could also be used to bring up people or animals that couldn't navigate the stairs. There were brightly-coloured flags fluttering from short flag-poles outside most entrances. Spidralites had a rigid class system and people inherited their titles, although being canny traders the titles sometimes changed hands for the right price, for example when an old, noble family fell on hard times and sold their inheritance to survive. The poorer folk and commercial buildings were built on ground level, some even on muddy tracks that led off the main, cobbled street. This time of the evening there were not too many people around as the shops had already closed for the night. What people there were moved briskly and with purpose, offering the couple only a cursory glance. Spidral had for many years resisted the Empire's domination and still employed a slave system, something the Empire had abolished. The slaves wore a large, silver sleeper in their left ear to denote their status. Senior slaves wore gold, and those lucky few that earned their freedom were given another gold ear-ring in their right ear. Many of these freed slaves simply continued in their master's employ but were allowed to move around independently. He saw a few, and they moved slower than the others, some of them talking together as they headed to the taverns.

Sirroya led them past the first tavern they found. It had an overpowering smell of unwashed men, stale drink and rotten food and the men sitting outside had large gold sleepers in either a single or both ears, so it was an obvious hangout for the freer slaves. Outside the second ramshackle establishment, there were two groups of people egging on their respective champions as they wrestled each other in the mud. They gave that a wide berth as some of the less salubrious characters started eyeing Sirroya in an unfriendly way. By their long hair and various weapons that hung around their person they were either off-duty guards or sell-swords for hire. Finally, towards the middle of the town, they found a quiet inn with well-tended gardens out front. It was flanked by a neat, white, small temple on one side and a shop with an ornate door and a large gold chalice on the other. A smartly-dressed couple stepped out of the inn and headed down the street. Sirroya gave the shop next door a speculative, experienced stare as she pulled him inside the inn.

On pushing open the old, battered door they found a well-kept front room with tables and chairs neatly arranged around a large central fireplace. At the bar, a few locals stood chatting and at one end a man in a dark hood leant on the bar and slowly sipped from a silver goblet. He looked up when they entered and stared at Darjoon for quite a while. They sat down at a table near the entrance and when Darjoon looked up and saw him watching, the man turned his head away and continued to drink. Sirroya strode over to the bar and came back with a jug and two pewter mugs.

"Okay, we're here now. So what are your plans?", Darjoon asked her in his typically blunt way.

"My, my, are you so keen to get rid of me, mighty mage? Well, I need to find out if there's any work going. I'm handy with, well, my hands, so I'm sure there'll be something I can do. I just need to earn some coin for a while and then I can get some supplies and information and go looking for the free-folk in the forest. What about you?"

"I'm also looking for information. My, uh, uncle, well he came through here a while back and my family want to know what's happened to him. So I'm looking for him. It's also part of my assignment."

"Right. Your uncle and an assignment. I see. So what

does he look like? Maybe I can help, you know. If I see him or hear anything about him, I can let you know."

"Uh, thanks, I'd appreciate that. He's, um, well, he's tall, dark, lean, with brown hair and brown eyes. He's a mage, so is most likely wearing a dark cloak and uh, well, that's about it."

She stared at him incredulously, "You're kidding, Darjoon! That's the best you can do? You just described almost every raven-born male in the Old Lands. Well, fine, maybe their hair runs to black and hardly ever brown. Still, in that case, it's every Spidralite male who might have some magic and fancy themselves to be a mage. Come on, Darjoon, there must be more you can give me than that, surely?"

"Well. He is very powerful, magically speaking. And he wore a wide-brimmed hat with a pendant in front. And maybe he wasn't so much lean as broad in the chest."

"Right, that's better. So why didn't you just say that in the first place? Do you remember what the pendant looked like?"

"Yes, it was a bat with wings spread out and holding a broken staff in its claws."

Sirroya jumped as if she'd been bitten, "What? Shush!", she looked around anxiously, "Are you mad? You just can't blurt that out and you should definitely not tell anyone about it. Do you have any idea what...? Are you...?", she trailed off and stared at Darjoon helplessly.

"Any idea of what?", Darjoon asked innocently, "I only want to find my fa... I mean my uncle. And as you said, there's not much to mark him out from either Spidralite or raven-born. Why, what's wrong with a bat? Oh, the Dremrel, I see. So what, you mean you think they could be related somehow? I hadn't thought of that before. But what would my... uh, my uncle, have to do with a Dremrel?"

Sirroya stared at him, and then just as she was about to reply, Darjoon felt someone bump into him from behind.

The man in the dark hood that had been at the bar stumbled against him and Darjoon could smell the strong drink on his breath.

"Shorry, shir. Little unshteady on my feet sho to shpeak", the man knelt next to Darjoon's chair while Sirroya glared at him.

Leaning over, he whispered clearly in Darjoon's ear, "You're not safe here, you should leave right now. This is no place for you, young raven-born. They know you've come and are looking for you even now."

Darjoon looked up and saw the man was also raven-born.

"Shorry shir, muss gerron now", he said and was up and gone before Darjoon could stop him.

"Do you know him?", Sirroya asked.

"No, why would I know him? Of course not, don't be silly."

"Well, I only ask because he's obviously raven-born. I've heard you all live together in the same nest", she smirked at him.

"I'm hungry, what do you want to eat?", Darjoon ignored the insult and focused on a more important matter.

"Hmm. Well, the roast is absolutely delicious here which is why I came", she said, and then quickly, "or at least that's what I was told back home. To come here, I mean. Because the food is so good."

Darjoon watched her closely as she went up to the bar to order. She seemed so assured and well-travelled and he definitely had a feeling that she'd been here before. But given how young she was, how could that be possible? And what did that raven-born mean by telling him to get out? What danger was he talking about? He should have rushed out the inn and asked him but the man would be long gone by now.

A few more Spidralite locals had wandered in and he watched a couple of women as they waited at the bar to order. They were unlike the raven-born ladies, being brown-haired and big-boned with plump cheeks and small round noses. Their skin was lighter than the raven-born too, although not so light as Sirroya's, who was obviously different from anyone there. As he watched he saw the two women huddle together and whisper to each other, casting glances at Sirroya and then at him. It looked as if one of them said something to Sirroya, who with a casual flick of her hair answered back. In an instant, the woman had a knife out and was jumping towards Sirroya, aiming it at her belly.

Darjoon didn't even twitch nor did he bother chanting. The shield-spell snapped into place around the woman before she was halfway towards Sirroya. The other woman jumped forward to help her but was repelled back by the shield, striking her head on the bar and crumpling to the floor. Sirroya turned and yelled at him, "Drop the spell, Darjoon, drop it now! She can't breath in there you fool!"

Letting go of the spell, he cursed as he saw the woman's face had turned blue. She gasped for breath and then slumped to the floor as well. He rushed over and quickly knelt down next to first one and then the other of the women, making sure they were breathing easily and sensing for anything broken. Relieved to find no major problems, he revived them with a little magic push inside their heads and they began to stir.

Two men with swords walked into the inn while he was standing over the second woman trying to help her up and Sirroya was wiping blood off the first one's head.

"Get them, they tried to kill the Rintar sisters. The raven-born was using magic to kill her", the man behind the bar shouted at the two guards.

They quickly grabbed Darjoon and as his face took on a familiar, tense look and his lips started to move, Sirroya jabbed him in the belly with her elbow, causing him to gasp and lose focus.

"Don't be a fool", she hissed in a whisper, "do you

want us both to die?".

He relaxed as the guards hustled the two of them over to the town's watch house and threw them inside a cell, glaring at them.

"We'll let the magistrate decide what to do about this. I expect it of Empire scum like you, golden-hair, but not from you, raven-born. You should know better than to use magic here, even if you are just out of the college. You won't be the first mage they've blinded, or worse, for illegal use of magic. Can't throw spells at people you can't see, can you?", the soldier shook his head and walked away, leaving them in silence.

Darjoon slumped in a corner of the cell, feeling the chill of the cold night air. Thrusting his hands in his pockets in an attempt to warm them, he felt something odd in one pocket and drew out a crumpled note. Sirroya looked on with interest, seemingly unconcerned about being in prison. He assumed from what she said of her past that she'd been jailed before.

"What's that then?", she asked.

"How should I know? Never seen it before and it wasn't there in the morning, was it. Let me have a look and I'll let you know. Is that okay, miss nosey?"

Darjoon was biting off each word, feeling cold, tired and hungry and wanting to blame her. She looked at him, then quietly sat down in the opposite corner of the cell and pulled her cloak around her, closing her eyes. He stared at her, feeling confused. How could she make him feel guilty when she was the one who was nosey and bossy. Not to mention they were here because of her. She looked so small and frail in the large cell they were in and it reeked of past inhabitants. Was she shivering now? Sighing, he put the note back in his pocket, stood up and walked over, slumping down next to her.

"Listen, I'm sorry, I didn't mean to snap at you. It's just that I was looking forward to that roast and a healthy draught to wash it down with. This really isn't my idea of a picnic, but I shouldn't have had a go at you.", he looked at her keenly, "What did you say to that woman anyway?"

"She called me an Empire whore and I told her that at least I knew how to pleasure a man, whereas she probably couldn't pleasure a goat."

Darjoon shook his head and then laughed heartily.

She looked up and smiled. Well, this one was different from the others. Maybe he wasn't like his father at all. Very promising. She liked how Darjoon kept surprising her. He was naive and innocent, yet powerful and composed. It was obvious he knew nothing about women and yet here he was, apologising and doing it rather well. Very intriguing. His stomach rumbled loudly in the quiet cell and she started giggling. Darjoon snorted and then they both dissolved into laughter. As they quietened down again she took hold of his arm and then snuggled up to him for warmth, putting her head on his shoulder.

Darjoon looked down at the small blonde head pillowed on his arm. He desperately wanted to put his arm around her, but had a feeling that might get him a few broken teeth. He'd seen the way she moved and knew that despite her youth she could definitely handle herself. Deciding the risk wasn't worth it, he closed his eyes, then jerked them open as he remembered the note. Taking it out slowly so as not to disturb her, he began reading.

We've been expecting you ever since you left the raven-born lands. As you must have realised by now, all is not well in our beloved homeland. Not only are our youth like you cast out, but you are given no real instruction or direction on how to deal with the world at large. The training you received was rudimentary at best, and destructive at worst. There is much important knowledge that has been withheld from you, knowledge that could save your life and the lives of your fellow countrymen. You are more powerful than you know. If you want to learn more, then come and meet me on the night of the full Tregora moon, beyond the wishing well in the forest that lies on the path least travelled, beyond the talking towers. See with more than your eyes to join us or never see us at all. The Circle of the True Ones awaits you. Do not dare the journey lightly for only a true raven-born will succeed.

There was a symbol of a wolf on the bottom right of the page. What on earth was this about? He had vague memories of something his mother had once said to his grandfather. Something about a secret, magical society of raven-born that had been expelled from their lands. They had created a base in the Darken Hills somewhere and wanted to overthrow the raven-born leaders. So was this the same secret society of the wolf? The note wasn't addressed to him in particular, so it must be a standard message they gave to young raven-born who left or were forced to leave the country of their birth. This was probably how they conscripted their members. Wait, could the well it spoke of be the one he'd blundered into recently? But there'd been no other path than the one that entered the clearing. Both Sirroya and himself had looked, there was no way out of the clearing. What did they mean to "see with more than your eyes"?

"What's it say?", Sirroya looked up and blinked wearily at him.

"Oh nothing, just an old potion recipe or something. I forgot I left it in there, wasn't important really. Why don't you get some shut-eye and I'll keep watch."

He didn't want to share it with her just yet. And besides, she wasn't raven-born, she wouldn't understand. But the note was right in that something was wrong back home. People weren't getting all the knowledge they needed and the raven-born leadership were too secretive and controlling. He yawned, feeling sleepy after all the day's excitement. They'd taken their packs away but he found a few old seeds and dried berries in his pocket and munched on them. Somehow, he didn't think Sirroya would appreciate what amounted to pocket fluff and when he saw the look of disgust on her face, he just shrugged his shoulders.

"You know", he said speculatively, "I could get us out of here pretty easily. There's no other magic in use that I can sense, so there's nothing to really stop us leaving."

"Yes", she said sleepily, "but how far would we get? Do you want to fight every guard and Spidralite assassin here? And they'd catch us in the forest, make no mistake. No, we need to see where this will go and state our case. It was only self-defence on our part and they did attack me first. The Spidralite magistrates are known to be firm but fair. If that fails, then we'll have to consider our options. Now go to sleep, I'm tired."

"Okay, okay. Goodnight", he muttered.

Despite his best attempts to stay awake, he drifted off, feeling her warmth where she lay against him. In his dreams, wolves ran across an open plain, howling, and he knew they were searching for him. Behind them was a darkness, darker than the night and spreading out as it came, reaching for him and trying to drown him in blackness.

The rattling of the cell gate woke him up. He blinked into the light that was streaming in through the open door of the watch house. Sirroya woke up and sleepily stretched her arms above her head, to the admiring glances of the guards as her cloak slipped down. She blinked and smirked at Darjoon, who was obviously irritated at the guards clear interest. Grimacing, he stood up as they opened the cell gate and jabbed their pikes at them.

"Out, you lot. Someone wants to have a word with you. Seems like it might just be your lucky day. And you there, no magic or anything funny right? See my friend's crossbow, what he's aimed at your head? Any magic and it'll go off, so don't wave your arms or start chanting because it's on a hair-trigger. And you love? Do you think I've got all day? You might be pretty, but you're no princess, so move yourself", saying which the guards dragged them out the cell and into the front of the watch-house.

Through the open front door stepped a lean, scarred, dark-skinned assassin. He had a black robe that was tightly wound round his body but left his legs free. A black felt skullcap sat tightly on his head. From the nose down, his face was covered with a black scarf. A long, white scar ran from just above his right eyebrow, down towards his nose and under the scarf. The eyes smiled coldly as he looked at Sirroya, then scowled when he glanced at Darjoon. He crossed his arms and his hands came to rest just above twin daggers nestled in a broad leather sash that went around his chest. His fingers twitched and rested lightly on the handles.

"No troubless little ssorcerer. I'm quicker than the crossssbow, sso don't you even think about it. There'ss never been a ssorcerer could beat me yet. You could assk them but I'm afraid they're all dead, sso you'll have to take my word for it", he had a husky, sibilant voice with a strange forked tongue that slithered in and out his mouth as he spoke, and then again as he laughed at them.

The laugh never reached his dark, almost black eyes which glittered malevolently and flickered here and there as he kept watch. Following the assassin was a tall, spare man wearing a maroon velvet cape over a red and gold tunic. He was wearing black stockings and ornate, gold-buckled black shoes. Various rings of different colours glittered on his fingers and he had a large, dangling gold and ruby earring in his right ear. His hair was black, long and trailed back down onto the cape. He smiled knowingly as he looked at Sirroya and turning to look at Darjoon, inquiringly lifted an eyebrow.

"He looks a bit young to cause such trouble, sergeant? Are you sure it was him? It looks like he's barely out of the egg, as their people say", the laughter was soft and melodious, the words clear and clipped. His dark eyes glittered dangerously in the sunlight streaming in through the door. He had a handsome face with a large, aristocratic nose under which were a pair of full lips and a small, pointed, oiled beard.

"Yes, it was definitely him. Old Krigar said he'd never seen the likes of it. He used his magic without speaking and reacted like lightning. The poor hunter ladies never stood a chance, he stopped 'em cold."

Darjoon had tensed at the raven-born phrase. He didn't like the way this was going, and he particularly didn't like being called a child, but he wasn't sure he could deal with the guards and the assassin. It was rumoured that any top Spidralite assassin could use magic and often carried magic amulets and weapons. The daggers the assasin wore might be magically charged and could fly at someone on his command. A charm could mean that any spells used against him would rebound on the caster.

"Oh relax, young man, I meant no disrespect to you. I was simply surprised at your age given your more than capable exploits. My apologies, I should introduce myself. I am Lord Gromtag, the lord of Nefarglos. That may not mean much to you, raven-born, but I see your friend knows something of it."

Darjoon could see Sirroya's mouth had fallen open when the Lord introduced himself.

"I'll say I do", she said, clearly impressed, "You might not have much land but what you have is the richest in Spidral. The rubber and medicines from Nefarglos are well known throughout the Empire."

"Well we may not be the richest but we do well enough. Lucky for us our territory is the only one where the rubber wasp nests, and as the rubber tree won't pollinate without that particular insect, we have become the sole proprietors. And it's true, the same plant that miraculously produces our rubber has some medicinal benefits. In the right doses of course, otherwise it simply kills, doesn't it, my silent one?"

The assassin smiled coldly. They were well-versed in all manner of poisons as part of their trade.

"Now guards, please may I have a word with our two young offenders in private? Thank you so much for the good care you've taken of them, I'm sure they'll not make a nuisance of themselves and will be on their best behaviour. Of course, if they are not then my, uh, assistant here will ensure they comply."

After a brief look at each other and a nervous glance at the assassin, the guards stepped outside and closed the watch house door.

"My dears, I have need of both of you. And it seems I am in a position to, ah, well, let's say I can assist with the evidence, in our dear magistrates case. I'm afraid you will have to appear in court before him as I simply cannot spirit you away, now can I. But I'm certain he'll be amenable, provided you're willing to take me up on my little offer?"

"What's the offer, Lord Gromtag?", Darjoon wasn't smiling and he was in no mood to be messed around by some Spidral aristocrat.

"Hmm. Straight to business, young mage? Not much experience in commerce I suppose. Normally, people will banter for a while and then certain offers are made and rejected, until finally an equitable deal is reached that suits both parties. But I suppose you're not really in a position to barter, are you? You do have what I want, but what value your eyes over performing a small service for me, eh?"

"My eyes, but Sirroya said that the Spidralite magistrates are reasonable, they're not likely to uphold that ancient punishment?", Darjoon was incredulous. He was sure that a civilised nation like Spidral wouldn't do anything so barbaric, cruel and out-dated.

"Well, of course, normally she'd be right you see. But unfortunately for you, those two hunters you almost killed are a particular favourite of the magistrate. They keep him well supplied with a particular, ah, let's call it a berry, shall we. A berry that has some, ah, interesting and distracting properties when harvested at the right time. That's also not the only, ah, service they provide him with, so you can imagine how protective he is. But not to worry, it's amazing what a few words in the right ear can accomplish. Oh, and the small matter of a few gold coins between friends. Naturally, I'd be reluctant to let two such promising young people come to harm. It wouldn't be right at all, such a waste."

He turned to Sirroya with an appraising look as he said the last.

"Sirroya, was it? An unusual name, although it does sound rather familiar to me. Where could I have heard it before, I wonder? Even your looks are not entirely unknown to me, I'm sure. Have you or your family ever visited Spidral previously?"

"What offer were you talking about?", Sirroya asked quickly.

"Ah, yes. Well it seems that I am to host rather important people at a little party in a few nights time. Now naturally, most magicians are unwilling to simply perform for entertainment, and those that are, well they're not really worth it, are they? However, if the young man could see his way to, ah, demonstrate a few choice spells, especially those that showcase the remarkable talent he undoubtedly has, well that would be a fine repayment for services rendered. And as for you my dear lady, with your beauty I think you'd be an excellent companion for the mage. If you could, ah, be included in some of the spell-casting, well I think that would be splendid. That, and keeping your eyes and ears open for a few particular details that I'd be interested in knowing about. People do so love chatting to beautiful young women, don't you think, silent one? Quite interesting what they end up saying when they're suitably distracted."

The assassin's eyes roved up and down Sirroya's body appreciatively and his head nodded slowly.

"We can work out the finer details of our little contract

before the event itself. That's only if you're interested, of course. Otherwise, well, just the magistrate and yourself and trusting to, ah, the dubious chance of good fortune and the roll of fate's loaded dice", Lord Gromtag smiled coldly at them.

Sirroya looked across at Darjoon. She knew that most mage's, particularly raven-born, wouldn't dream of public displays of power just for entertainment and she could see how tense he was.

"If you don't mind, kind Lord, perhaps you could give us a few minutes to discuss your attractive offer in private? I'm sure we can come to some sort of arrangement."

"Of course my dear. I can see you will certainly be an asset to me. But please don't take too long as I know the magistrate is keen to meet the magic-user himself. We don't want to keep him waiting, do we?", he bowed politely as the nobleman and his assassin bodyguard left the guard house.

After a cursory glance and muffled conversation with the nobleman, the guards remained outside to wait and closed the door.

The minute the door closed, Darjoon turned on her, "Are you crazy, Sirroya? We can't accept his offer. Who knows what he's up to? I don't like him one bit. Nor that creepy friend of his, and the way he looks at you makes me mad. Don't you know that I can't use my power for entertainment? It's... it's... well it's unheard of, it's against the code."

"Hang on a minute, Darjoon! Do you mean you can't or you won't? I mean, how does the magic work, are you in control of it or aren't you? Does it only work when you're in danger? Don't you see what he was saying? The gold he gives the magistrate can be used for either of two outcomes. If we don't take his offer, he'll make sure we won't live to talk about it. We either go with him, or you'll be blinded and probably tortured and I'll become the city guards new plaything until they tire of me. We don't have much choice now, but that doesn't mean we can't change our minds later. Let's do what he says and see what opportunities we might have later on. At least we'll be alive to take them."

Darjoon lowered his head and then nodded reluctantly. He could see the sense in what she was saying, but he didn't have to like it. The first chance he got, he'd use his magic and they'd be out of this place.

"Okay, Sirroya, that makes sense. Of course I have control of my power, don't be ridiculous, I'm not some entertainer, I'm a trained apprentice. Let's just play along for now like you said and see where it goes. But if this doesn't work out, we're gone."

5 THREE'S A CROWD

The magistrate seemed quite happy to believe that Darjoon and Sirroya had been attacked and then reacted in self-defence. Despite some boo's and mutters from the assembled crowd in the courthouse, he simply gave a verdict of self-defence and set them free with a warning that if either of them caused any more trouble they would be dealt with severely. The silent assassin was waiting outside the court when they left and he quickly and quietly escorted them down various alleys and lanes until they came to an imposing residence. It was surrounded by four large Brisla trees and a high stone wall. The assassin did something to a flowerpot on a pedestal by the gate, although so quickly they couldn't see, and out of nowhere a doorway seemed to magically appear in the wall. Walking into blackness, they found themselves going down a gently sloping, cold, musty passage and then up a flight of stairs and finally through an old, wooden door into what looked like a cellar. The wooden door closed behind them and all they could see were the regular bricks of the cellar wall as the passage opening disappeared from view. To the casual observer there was no door. The assassin escorted them up a few flights of stairs and then across a corridor that was actually suspended between two of the Brisla trees and finally through a secure door that opened into a small hallway. Off the hall were a few rooms and he pointed out two of them.

"You will sssleep in there, young one's. The door to thisss hall will be locked. Don't even think of leaving without ssssaying goodbye, or I will, permanently", he whispered at them, smiled, then slipped back out the hallway door and they could hear it locking behind them. Darjoon walked into one of the rooms and threw his pack on the large four-poster bed. The sofa, curtains and carpeting were rich and sumptuous, decorated in gold and maroon with what he believed was the royal crest of the nobleman who was their host. It looked like four trees on a yellow field, with a single-stemmed plant in the middle that had a bristly, purple head. He guessed it must be the rubber plant that gave them their fortune. Sirroya had disappeared into the room next to his, and he could hear the floorboards creaking as she prowled around, no doubt exploring every nook and cranny.

Before he could go and see what she was up to, the hall door opened again and slaves appeared with basins, soap and clean clothes. The young woman went into Sirroya's room and the young man came to his room. It was obvious he wanted to shave Darjoon, who wasn't that keen on having someone wield a sharp blade anywhere near his face. The man was also reluctant to speak to him and Darjoon was just about to shout at him to get him to start talking when he opened his mouth and looked at Darjoon mutely. Where there should have been a tongue, there was simply a stub of muscle. Darjoon sat down suddenly, appalled. The man rolled up his sleeves and picked up the blade again. This time Darjoon let him get on with it and found he was very, very good leaving smooth skin and not a single scratch. When Darjoon thanked him, he simply smiled back although Darjoon noticed the smile didn't reach the slave's eyes.

After he was finished and the young man had helped him dress and then left his room, he walked out into the hall to see Sirroya come out of her room, look at him and slowly twirl round. She was dressed in a midnight blue, long velvet gown speckled with silver glitter and just above the hem on one side was a large, shiny, silver crescent moon. On the back of her dress, it was open to the waist and just under the deliciously sweeping curve above her small bottom was a silver shield containing the crest he'd seen in his room. Her hair had been coiled and piled up, her eyes lined and some colour applied to her cheeks to accentuate her blue eyes. She was wearing silver slippers with glass heels that peeked out from under the dress. Darjoon was spell-bound and stared at her in fascination.

"Oh good, I see it's working on him. I never doubted for a second that you would be radiant, my dear. Really, I think it's even better than we expected. Not all the men will be as naive as our young friend here, but even for the most cynical, I daresay the reaction will be the same. Come Darjoon, don't stand and stare like that, you'll embarrass yourself. Let's all head down to dinner shall we, I think we're going to enjoy this."

Lord Gromtag had appeared almost out of thin air. The servants opened the hall door for them and they went out onto the landing, crossing to the first Brisla tree and passing through another door to the head of a large staircase. Sirroya, flanked by Darjoon and Lord Gromtag on either side, slowly descended the marble stairs while holding up her long dress. At the end of the steps they entered a large foyer with a beautiful crystal chandelier suspended above their heads. Lord Gromtag led them across the foyer and into an ornate panelled room with a large, dark brown table in the middle surrounded by blue velvet upholstered chairs. A sumptuous feast had been laid out in front of them.

"Expecting many guests, Lord Gromtag?", Sirroya enquired.

"Not tonight dear, but I want you both to experience what it will be like in a few nights time. This is where you'll be, ah, performing, shall we say. Darjoon, won't you be a darling and go stand on that podium in the corner. Oh, stop sulking now, I want you to enjoy this, and why not? Now there are a few particular spells that I want you to perform, if you can, that is? Firstly, I want you to levitate this dining table. Now, now, don't look so amazed! I have every confidence that you can do it. Then at the same time I want you to raise Sirroya and her chair above the height of the floating table and bring her over to where you are so she ends up sitting next to you. Can you do that, do you think?"

Darjoon just stared open-mouthed at him. What the man was talking about involved the use of very powerful magic, not simple parlour tricks. It was one thing flying, which as he had discovered was a subconscious act that required a great deal of power. However levitating other objects was very difficult indeed, and for whatever reason, levitating people was even harder, certainly given the forbidden texts he'd read. It would require a great deal of magic and experience to achieve it. What was this crazy Lord thinking?

"What, Lord Gromtag, you want me to do it now? I need to eat first and recover all my magical strength. I haven't eaten properly in a few days and certainly not yesterday when we were in prison", he shrugged apologetically.

Lord Gromtag frowned and tugged at his small beard. Wiping his hands ostentatiously on his napkin, he gestured at the table magnanimously.

"Oh very well, if you must, please help yourself. Perhaps we can wait until tomorrow night for you to try this simple thing, but please don't test my patience or underestimate my resolve, young mage. You'll find it's not without limits, even when it comes to wonderful young people such as you two. Now, if you'll excuse me, I must attend to my other business. Please, eat, drink and be merry. My servants will take you back to your rooms when you are finished. Sirroya, I will discuss your part in this, ah, small affair, tomorrow morning over breakfast. Perhaps you should sleep in, Darjoon, to conserve your, ah, magical strength. No, no, not to worry, we won't wake you and what I have to discuss involves just Sirroya."

After they both ate in silence, the servants took them back to their bedrooms. They could hear the hall door being locked as the servants left and as soon as it was quiet, Sirroya went to Darjoon's room.

"Well, can you do it?", she asked directly.

"I don't know", Darjoon shrugged his shoulders, "that is asking a lot. I mean we did some small levitation exercises at college but they were with pebbles and small objects, nothing on the scale he's talking about. That dining table is massive, after all it is made of solid wood. As for lifting you, well, everything I've ever read says that lifting people is really difficult and needs a lot of practice. I've certainly never done it before. The truth is I'm just an apprentice."

"Well, you had better start to practice then. Why don't you start now? See if you can lift me", Sirroya sat down on the bed.

Darjoon looked at her. She'd thrown off the beautiful dress she'd been wearing and was just wearing her slip, which wasn't exactly opaque. He could see a faint outline of her fit young body revealed by the candlelight on the table next to the bed. She looked at him quizzically and smiled in that mysterious, knowing way.

"Oh, I'm sorry, does this help you?", she laughed as she grabbed a blanket off the bed and wrapped herself in it, "I don't want to distract the great mage from his amazing spells."

He grimaced at her but she was right. He'd need to concentrate to do this properly. He slowed his breathing, allowing his subconscious to enter his conscious as his grandfather had shown him. Sitting on the sofa, he imagined her sitting beside him and reached out with his magic.

"Owwww, stop it Darjoon, you're hurting me. Ouch!", she squirmed on the bed in obvious pain.

Withdrawing his magic immediately, he rushed over to her, "I'm sorry, Sirroya, this is a lot harder than I thought. Let me see that", he took her arm and looked in horror at the red welts that were starting to appear.

"I could feel your magic pressing on my skin and it hurt. Are you sure you can actually do this? Maybe you should practise with inanimate objects first. How about that fine bowl on the night-stand, see if you can levitate that without breaking it. I'm just going to run some cool water on these welts."

Back in her room, Sirroya peeled off her shift and looked at the welts that had now appeared all over her body. She shook her head in wonder. His magic was so powerful, it was like nothing she'd ever experienced before. Even his father's magic hadn't had that power to it. It was strange, a combination of magics that she couldn't recognise. Every magic-user had their own personal signature, and underlying that was their heritage, passing through the generations although appearing with different strengths in different children. So for example, raven-born mages were identifiable versus Empire magicians or Spidralite assassins. But Darjoon was very different from any of those. Could he really be the one that was foretold? She'd not even heard or read of anything like this magic, she thought to herself while she sponged down the welts. Fortunately, they already seemed to be fading away as was often the case with indirect magical pain. She heard a faint tinkling noise from Darjoon's room and guessed it was the bowl falling and probably breaking. He was going to need a great deal of practise before he could move an entire table, let alone that, her and a chair all at the same time. She really did have her doubts he would be able to do it, despite the strength of his magic. She'd have to see what Lord Gromtag had planned. Maybe she could find out more tomorrow and stall him so that Darjoon would have time to practice. She heard a thud from next door and heard Darjoon muttering to himself. Yes, they were going to need a lot of time. She pulled back the covers and climbed into bed. As she drifted off, she hoped that she could sweet-talk the Lord into waiting for a while, without revealing that Darjoon had never done this before. Despite worrying over the problem, she sunk into a deep sleep.

Sirroya yawned, stretched and swung her feet over the edge of the low bed. She sat there, waking up slowly while her feet dangled below her, then slowly realised something was wrong. The ceiling seemed to have slid down the walls during the night and the small chandelier above her bed was perilously close to her head. And the bed was actually quite low, so her feet definitely shouldn't be dangling in space. She looked down and gasped, seeing the chair next to her bed some way below her. Then she heard a chuckle from just outside her open door.

"Darjoon! Are you doing this? Stop it at once and put me down right now!"

The bed floated gently down to the ground and her feet gratefully sank into the plush carpet as the ceiling and chandelier once again resumed their normal place high above her head.

"How? How are you... When did you...", Sirroya stared at him, speechless for a change.

Such power, such incredible power. How could he have learnt to do that in such a short space of time? This massive four-poster bed was so heavy, how could he lift it? Gasping, she quickly checked her arms and then pulled the top of her shift away from her body, looking down at her chest. Nothing. There were no marks of any kind.

"Well, it wasn't that hard really. I was up most of the night practising. My first attempt on the fine bowl broke it, so I thought I might as well try something bigger and kept trying my bed. Mostly it just went up then thumped down but eventually I got it to lift up. I just wasn't sure if I could lift a person as well. Then I sensed this mouse in the wall and coaxed it out to me. I figured if I could lift it and the other unbroken bowl, then that was a start. Did I hurt you just now?", there was a genuine concern in his voice.

"No, not a mark. Nothing at all. Well, Darjoon, it looks like you're going to pull it off after all. I'm... I'm just surprised. I mean, I wasn't sure the great mage could do it this time."

She was only half-teasing him, as she had really doubted he could. Then she shrieked as she lifted up in the air, hovering over the bed.

"Put me down at once. How dare you, Darjoon. You have no right to control people without their say-so, you know that."

She bounced back down on the bed as he sheepishly relinquished his control of her.

"Yes, I know, but... but you didn't feel anything, did you? I got it right, didn't I?"

She smiled up at him. It was hard to be angry for long with Darjoon, he had such a puppy-dog look to him when he'd done something wrong.

"Yes, Darjoon, I think you definitely got it right. Just please don't use your magic on me unless I give you permission. It is very rude for a gentleman mage to act against a lady's wishes. I don't want you turning out to be that kind of man as well. Now I've got to get ready to go and hear what our host has to say. At least I'll get a good breakfast out of it. I'll see you later, perhaps you should catch up on your sleep and get some rest."

Darjoon returned to his room and lay on the bed. He was very tired and the magic he'd used had taken a lot out of him. Had she really doubted him? Had he revealed too much power this time? He wasn't being as careful as at the college, where he'd kept his ability so well hidden. He wondered what the high and mighty Lord Gromtag wanted with her? Why did it make him jealous, that she'd be meeting with him? He felt all these conflicting emotions when it came to Sirroya. She was young and quite beautiful, there was no denying that. But sometimes she acted a lot like his mother. There was a raven-born saying that a man often returned to the nest for his woman, meaning they would likely choose a woman that was similar to their mother. Is that what he was doing? She seemed so strange sometimes, like she knew more than she was letting on, as if she'd been to more places than seemed likely given her apparent age. His grandmother used to say that birds who flew high saw a lot more of life but they also risked getting their wings burnt. Who was this strange girl-lady that he was with? Darjoon drifted off to sleep, dreaming sweet dreams of Sirroya and himself running through the forest and falling into the soft grass of a gentle meadow washed with the subtle scent of flowers and a light, fragrant breeze blowing over their faces.

He started awake, the breeze on his face not dying away. A face was near his, blowing softly on his cheeks. Sirroya drew back with a half-smile on her face, her perfume lingering in the air above his face.

"Wakey, wakey, sleepy-head. Your breakfast got cold but they've exchanged it for a nice, warm lunch. Best you eat that while it's hot. I can't stand cold, congealed meat, can you? We've got to have a private conversation, can you shield us without anyone knowing? I don't want what I'm going to tell you being heard by anyone else."

Darjoon nodded at her and sat up, throwing out a shield spell that wouldn't repel sound so much as absorb it. To anyone who didn't have very strong magic it would seem like there was no-one there, but they shouldn't be able to detect anything. And if they tried to breach it, he'd know immediately. He sat down at the little table and started tucking in, surprised at how hungry he was, while Sirroya sat on the edge of the bed and started telling him about her meeting with the Lord.

"Do you know that creep actually thinks he's charming? Brrr, he gives me the chills. He's so proper and polite, but in a slimy way. The thing is, Darjoon, I think he can help us. I was looking for free-folk, and he knows someone who can help me find them. A hunter called Y'sarryn often travels to Roikba to trade. He lives with the free-folk and with Lord Gromtag's introduction I could go with him. Oh, and Darjoon, he knows something about your uncle too. He says he could help you get more information about him. He'll also reward us handsomely for our help, so you'll be well-equipped to continue your search. We just need to do a few of these meetings where we can impress people with your power, while I extract the, uh, information from the gentlemen that attend."

"You mean I distract them while you steal from them? Is that the idea, Sirroya? Do you think I'm so innocent and stupid I can't see what's going on? He's paying me to do a magic show and show them that he's got a powerful mage working for him, and paying you to work the room. So much for nobility, huh."

"Fine, Darjoon, so you think you're smart. But we don't have too many options do we? Do you really think we can fight our way out of here? I guess they may have taught you a thing or two about combat at your precious raven-born college, but these are Spidralite assassins and warriors we're talking about. Lord Gromtag has said that his assassin will teach me to fight, can you believe that? Here, he showed me something already this morning. Come and attack me", she stood in the centre of the room.

"What? Are you joking? I'm not going to attack you, don't be silly. And why would you want to learn from an assassin? Planning to add murder to your thieving skills? Hey, stop doing that right now. What are you doing? Leave me alone."

Sirroya was pulling on his arm, and then, as he resisted, she shoved his chair back. Darjoon rolled out of the chair and across the floor, springing to his feet and ending in a half-crouch next to the bed. She grabbed a knife from the table and while jumping at him brought it around in a smooth, twisting overhead motion. He crossed his wrists and lifting up his arms caught her wrist in his, then grabbed and twisted her arm to the side, forcing her to drop the knife. At the same time he rolled back and to the side, taking her with him and then throwing her down he rolled on top and pinned her there, holding her wrists above her head so she couldn't move. She tried biting him but he just laughed at her as she couldn't reach. She tried to kick him but he moved his legs so he had her completely pinned. She was breathing hard and glaring at him.

"Ok, wise guy, lesson over. So maybe the college did teach you something after all. Now get off me you lump and let me up. I can't breathe with you on top of me."

Darjoon stood up, offering her his hand which she glanced at scornfully and jumped to her feet. He shook his head and sat down to his meal again.

"Why do you want to learn to fight, Sirroya? I'd have thought a nice lady like you would have no interest in that sort of thing."

"Oh very funny. A girl on her own has to be able to defend herself. And the free-folk often have to defend their territory from Spidralites and worse. I don't want to be a complete novice when I meet them. Hey, seeing how you're so good, why can't you teach me instead?"

"Teach you? What? Okay, listen up then. Seeing how you're so good at making deals, here's one for you. I'll teach you what I know about combat, and you'll find it's a lot more than some dirty assassin, and you stick with me until we get to the free-folk. You must also promise me we'll get away from this horrible Lord Gromtag as soon as we can. I don't like him, I don't like his house and I don't like what we have to do. We're as good as prisoners here and I was born to fly free."

"Okay, Darjoon, you have a deal. I'll stick with you and

help you get away from here, and in return I'll learn from you."

She spat on her palm and after he did the same, they shook hands. They stood looking at each other and Darjoon suddenly and self-consciously dropped her hand which had been so warm and soft in his. Putting his finger to his lips to caution her, he dropped the shield spell just before a discreet knock on the door announced the arrival of the servants to prepare them for the evening's meeting with Lord Gromtag. They got dressed and made their way downstairs. Darjoon demonstrated how he could lift not just the dining table but also Sirroya in her chair. Lord Gromtag was overjoyed and kept applauding them. He promised that they'd be well-rewarded, and that he would do all in his power to get more information on Darjoon's uncle and introduce Sirroya to Y'sarryn, the free-folk hunter.

The following day Darjoon spent time recovering and rehearsing the tricks he was going to use while Sirroya alternated between practising her own sleight of hand and babbling at him. Later that evening Darjoon and Sirroya could hear the guests arriving downstairs. They got dressed and joined Lord Gromtag in the dining hall. Once Darjoon had demonstrated his magical power with the table, Sirroya, and the chair, she mingled with the guests while Darjoon performed some other minor spells that had been requested by the Lord. Darjoon couldn't help but be distracted by Sirroya's obvious charm and beauty. She chatted gaily to several men in a group nearer the back of the hall, surreptitiously touching first one and then the other as she made each feel like he was the centre of her world. Later that evening, she met with Lord Gromtag, and after providing him with a few crumpled notes and other items as well as information that she'd gathered, she came upstairs and into Darjoon's bedroom. He was sound asleep, having made his excuses and retired earlier, exhausted due to the magic he'd expended. She leaned over and breathed softly on his cheek again.

"Ugh. What? Sirroya? What, is it morning already? Wait, what's wrong, what happened?"

She had a flushed, worried look to her face he hadn't seen before and she was breathing hard. He could sense something wasn't right and immediately came fully awake.

"Darjoon, we have to leave here right away", she shook her head as Darjoon started to speak, "Yes, I know you've been saying that all along, but just listen now. Lord Gromtag is not what he seems, he's actually a spy for the Empire. In fact, I think he's a double agent, playing both Spidral and the Empire for his own advantage. I think he intends for me to marry one of the men that was here tonight."

She put her hand on Darjoon's chest and pushed him back onto the bed as he tried to stand up, outraged.

"Just hear me out first. Did you see that group of men I was speaking to? They're all minor nobility from the Empire who are colluding with him. If I marry one of them, then I'll go back to the Empire and I can use my position to get more information for Gromtag and Spidral. You'll have to come with me, as my brother, and will do the same sort of thing you did tonight. You'll also have to use your magic to get information", she was breathing hard.

"He's had to convince the Empire nobles that he was serious, that he had someone who could counteract the Empire court wizards and further their own political aims. They think you'll be strong enough to do that. He wants to make this happen sooner rather than later."

Sirroya had been speaking in a rush and now took a few deep breaths. Darjoon shook his head, forcing himself to focus on what she was saying.

"Slow down, Sirroya. Really? I mean, I have to say, this sounds a bit far-fetched even for our crazy Lord Gromtag. How did he think we'd react to this? There's no way I'll let him marry you off."

"Well, that's touching Darjoon, thanks. But actually I lifted this document off his desk while I was giving him my report. It's a letter he was sending to someone in the Empire, warning them to expect a woman and her brother who will be sent to them, drugged and bound. They are to pressure us on the basis that if we don't cooperate, then we'll be revealed as spies and executed. Don't you see? He was going to drug us and then once we were in the Empire, blackmail us into doing what he wanted. He's not planning on helping us at all."

"Well, I have to say I told you so, didn't I? I told you from the start that this was a bad idea. Now what are we going to do?"

"We get out. Now! Tonight! We can't stay here any longer. As soon as he finds the letter is missing I don't doubt he'll suspect me. We probably have until dawn and then..."

A servant knocked politely on the door. Sirroya started and went pale. Darjoon opened the door and the young manservant put out hot wine for him, indicating with gestures that Sirroya's was already in her room. Darjoon thanked him and lifted the goblet, flinching at the heat and putting it down again. He stared at the cup as the servant left.

"What do you think he heard?", she whispered.

"Nothing", Darjoon replied, "I had a shield up from when you said we have to leave here. I wouldn't touch that wine if I were you, I can sense it's drugged. Looks like he's moving fast, just as you said. Right, get your things and follow me."

Sirroya went to her room, stuffed her things into her pack and rushed back to find Darjoon gone. She searched under the bed, behind the screen, then went out and up and down the hall and into the other rooms but he was nowhere. She returned to his room to find him sitting on the bed, waiting for her.

"Where have you been?", she hissed at him in a

whisper.

"I've been right here all the time", he grinned at her.

Motioning to her to move quietly, he walked across to a panel on the far side of the room next to the fireplace. Pressing on a moulding to the side of the mantelpiece, the panel slid quietly back and a narrow hallway appeared. Darjoon told her to be quiet and led her down the stairs, conjuring a small globe of light above his head. At the bottom, he touched the side of the wall and the panel slid back into place, blocking out any light. She crept closer to him in the darkness.

"I was down here checking earlier while you were taking time powdering your face, and I know which way we should go. Now don't make a sound, this passage runs between rooms for a while and we won't know who's on the other side", he whispered at her.

She shook her head. Once again, he surprised her. The large, clumsy-looking boy could fight well, had serious magical power and could think ahead. What were the raven-born doing, letting someone of his ability go? They really were sliding back into darkness. One day all they'd be able to do was peck food, squawk and fight among themselves like their namesakes.

After following a number of narrow passages between rooms, they went down some winding stairs that seemed to be inside a tree, then through some dark tunnels and emerged into the sewer system under the town. Holding her cloak over her nose she followed Darjoon who finally led them up some stairs and through a narrow cleft in a rock, where they stumbled out into the Great Forest outside town. There'd been a few locked doors and gates along the way which Darjoon had easily opened with his magic, making sure he locked them again once they'd gone through.

Sirroya reached inside her pack, taking out and unrolling a map that she showed to Darjoon.

"I was able to get this map out of Lord Gromtag's

cabinet. It shows the most recent location of the free-folk. We should find this hunter, this Y'sarryn, and see if he really knows something about your uncle. Do you think you can get us there?"

He smiled grimly at her, studied the map, then turned and began a quiet incantation. Soon, a soft green line of light appeared in front of them, leading off into the forest. He started following the light and after a moment where she just stared at his retreating back, Sirroya stepped out and quickly caught up. Here we go again, she thought to herself. Please let this time be different. She couldn't go through it all again, not like last time, that would just be too much. The darkness deepened as they headed further into the Great Forest, a soft breeze causing the branches to rustle and leaves to fall around them while the great old trees slowly swayed and creaked, muttering to themselves in a language no-one could understand.

6 UP IN THE TREES

Darjoon stretched as he climbed out of the tent. The gloom of the forest around him obscured the morning sun which was shining down long beams of light as it tried to penetrate the green canopy above his head. He sniffed the rich, earthy smell of mould and decay that only the really old forests had. It was said there were areas of the Great Forest that had never looked on man. Which was an interesting way to put it, given the belief that parts of the Forest itself were sentient. Like the Brisla trees themselves, the entire forest was known to communicate with people who took the time and trouble to listen and who had the right magical ability. As he stood there remembering what he'd learnt in college about the forest and trying to listen, he thought back to the two trees that stood as gateways to the Darken Hills. Could it be that they had been talking to him? But then why would they welcome him back, as if he'd been here before? Maybe they had him confused with his father.

"Yes", Darjoon muttered to himself, "that's exactly what it was, my father must have come this way". He jumped as Sirroya suddenly appeared at his elbow.

"So, oh great and wise mage, are you going to stand

there all morning staring at nothing and muttering to yourself, or are you going to help me pack? Oh wait, is packing beneath you now? I could fight you for the privilege if that'll make you feel more at home. I know you raven-born men like your women a bit feisty. Or hang on, is it the women like their men feisty? It's hard to tell you lot apart sometimes, given you all came from the same egg."

She dissolved into laughter and he grinned in spite of himself. He was getting used to her odd sense of humour, especially now he knew she wasn't really insulting him or his people.

"Well, we're not all as stuck-up as you think we are. Let's get packed and get going. I've no idea how far away the free-folk are nor if we're actually heading in the right direction. This forest magic might be throwing me off a bit, although I don't think so."

"Oh great, now you tell me. This dark forest hates us Empire folk, you know, and it's no wonder. Before the Spidralites and the forest itself pushed our armies back we'd burnt a good chunk of it. I'm sure some of those thorns and prickles were avoiding you and lunging after me, and I swear the midges are doing the same as well. I've got a hundred little bites and I can't see one on you. Have you been using magic on them? Anyway from what I'd heard back at that fool Lord Gromtag's house, and from looking at his map, it seems we're heading in the right direction. Let's give your magic a chance, it's saved us before."

He grinned at her, She babbled away merrily, then stopped and smiled at him shyly, turning to finish her packing.

They had a quick and sparse breakfast, packed up camp and headed off into the trees, continuing to follow the soft green line of light that was Darjoon's direction spell. It glimmered ahead of him in the gloomy depths of the forest and when he chanced to look up he could see only tiny snatches of sky far overhead.

They'd been walking for some time and the forest appeared to be getting even gloomier. Just as he was thinking of throwing up a light-globe above their heads, he heard a voice calling him.

"Psst. Over here, raven-born. No, silly man, not there, over here, here in the darkness by the pretty red flower."

As Darjoon wandered over to the red flower by the side of the trail, Sirroya gratefully took off her pack and sank to the ground.

"Oh, thank the Gods. You go do a bit of botanical rooting around with herbs and things and I'm just going to rest my eyes for a bit. Those stupid midges kept me up all last night with their biting and whining. I really didn't sleep well at all. Oh and hey, Darjoon, could you snore a little louder next time? I don't think Lord Gromtag heard you back in Roikba although I'm deaf as a post now."

Darjoon ignored her prattling, concentrating on the well-beaten trail he'd discovered just to the side of the flower.

"Yes, yes, that's right, young raven-born. Just follow the trail and you'll find me waiting", the strange voice whispered to him.

Sirroya opened her eyes suddenly and looked around the trail. Had she really nodded off? That wasn't like her, she normally struggled to sleep in the daytime. She yawned and then sat bolt upright as her skin prickled and the hair stood up on the back of her neck. Looking around quickly, she couldn't see Darjoon anywhere.

"Darjoon? Hey Darjoon, where are you?", she called to him but there was just a deep silence. Remembering that he'd been looking at a stupid red flower, she looked around but couldn't see it anywhere. Maybe he'd picked it and then walked up or down the trail. Calling out to him again just resulted in that deep, eerie silence that settled on her like a shroud. Shaking herself, she tried to dislodge the heavy weight that threatened to pull her back into dreamland. Something was definitely wrong and after calling out for the third time, she grunted in annoyance as there was still no response. There wasn't even bird noise, nor any of the usual scurrying of insects and fluttering of birds, not even the infernal whining of the annoying midges broke the silence.

She looked around cautiously, then quietly muttered a brief incantation under her breath. A red flower appeared at the side of a large tree with a well-beaten path to the side of it. So, she'd been right. This was magic at work. Hurrying quickly down the path she frantically scanned for signs of Darjoon's passing. What had that big fool gone and got into now. Making her way around the thick trunk of an old tree, she stopped and stared at the scene in front of her. Darjoon was waist-deep in a large pond, qiute oblivious to what was around him and slowly wading further in. His head was tilted slightly to the side and he smiled and nodded, as if he was listening and talking to someone. Without a thought for her own safety, she ran and jumped from the bank of the pond, landing behind him. He turned in one fluid motion and thrust out his arm and she suddenly found herself airborne and flying back through the air. Moments before she smashed into a tree-trunk she stopped dead, unable to move, and then just as suddenly dropped to the forest floor. Darjoon was standing and staring at her with a surprised look on his face and she could see the concern in his eyes. Then his eyes glazed and his head tilted again as he turned around, wading forward into the pond which was soon up to his chest. Sirroya picked up a thick, solid branch lying next to her and moved forward stealthily. She was going to have to do this very carefully as Darjoon had shown he wasn't completely lost yet. She crept up behind him, raising the branch in the air. With what she hoped was a blow intended to stun, she hammered down at his unprotected head, watching in horror as the ash of the now blackened branch fell down around his cloak. Staring at the charred end of the branch that she was still holding she looked up and saw he was continuing to walk forward and the water was now lapping at his chin. Throwing the smoking branch into the pond, she suddenly started to sing, loudly and lustily. It was an old tavern song from her village in the Empire.

A chicken and a cat, you know they can't do that!
The raven or a lizard? I'd sooner face a blizzard!
But once you walk in through my door,
I'll lay you down upon the floor.
And we'll be loving all the way,
'Cos Empire girls know how to play.

Darjoon stopped, turned around and focussed on her. He laughed once, a short bark, then stopped, looking around at the forest as if he didn't know where he was. He began to walk out of the pond towards her.

"What's going on, Sirroya? I was following my mother towards our house. Where did this pond come from? Wait, it's... It's all fading again, I... Mother? Mother, is that you? You want me to... To follow you? What trouble? Where are you going, wait for me. I...", he was turning around again.

Sirroya ignored him and just carried on singing.

Step to the left and step to the right,
Avoid their blade and lift your knife,
Watch their face and guard your life,
Step to the front and you're in the fight!

"Sirroya, I'm struggling to see properly. There's powerful magic at work here and I can't fight it. If you can keep singing, I'll follow your voice. Just don't stop singing, whatever you do."

She sang almost every fighting song and lusty tavern ballad she knew and pulled him back through the forest.

Once they got back to the main trail and she'd picked up their packs, singing the whole time, she grabbed hold of his arm and marched him deeper into the murky depths of the forest. Eventually they came to a small clearing of fine grass lit by dappled sunlight that filtered softly through the foliage that connected above them. Darjoon stopped and hung his head and she pulled on his arm.

"It's okay. I'm fine now, Sirroya. You can let go of my arm, don't worry, I'm not going to be wandering off in a hurry. This crazy forest was trying to drown me, can you believe that? And after it gave me such a nice welcome too. I thought we could be friends!"

She looked quizzically at him, then shook her head slightly in understanding and smiled.

"Oh, you think it was you... Oh", she stopped, then carried on, "Well next time you want to go for a swim you should strip first. No point getting all your clothes wet, is there. Here, you'd better change into something dry before you catch cold."

"Good point, I'll do that right away. Well? Are you going to turn around so I can change? I'm feeling a bit self-conscious after all those, uh, interesting songs you were singing. By the way, where did an innocent young thing like you pick up songs like that?", Darjoon was already taking off his cloak and beginning to to pick off his tunic.

She grinned as she turned around.

"My brothers were often at the local Empire games. They liked to test themselves, although they weren't particularly good. They used to sing those fighting songs around the house and I guess I picked them up. Oh, and I also used to sneak into the tavern when they weren't looking. I've got a good memory for that sort of thing and well, once those men have had a few ales, there's no stopping them."

"Brothers? I thought you were an only child? I guess you're not, I must have misheard. Still, I'm not sure I've ever heard, ah, such graphical descriptions before."

"Really? Hmm, I suppose you raven-born don't get out much, what with all the training and being stuck up your own bum. I hope these free-folk have a decent tavern so I can teach you how to have a good time for a change. Are you finished already? Coming, ready or not."

She turned around, but Darjoon wasn't listening to her. He was staring intently across the clearing at a beautiful, bright green bird perched on the branches. It was watching them, its head cocked to one side when suddenly it let out a piercing whistle, turned and flew onto another branch, stopping to look back at them. Sirroya grabbed Darjoon's arm and dug her fingers in hard.

"Ouch! What? What are you doing that for? Oh, I get it. No, no, relax, this isn't the forest again. Magical but something else, a different kind of magic. We should probably follow it. I have a strong sense the bird was sent to guide us."

"Oh, yes of course you do. This after almost drowning yourself. Do you really think I should trust you now? As if you're a good judge of what's right or...", she stopped in mid-flow as Darjoon chanted briefly, "Oh, I see! Okay, maybe you're right."

Darjoon's direction spell glimmered straight towards the bird and beyond. It looked down and chirped quietly. The glimmering line faded and disappeared. He picked up his pack, and after a raised eyebrow at Sirroya, started following the small bird which spread beautiful iridescent green wings and flew on into the dark forest. They walked along in silence as the bird flew on, occasionally waiting for them to catch up.

"Okay Darjoon, we've been following your little birdie for a while now. I wasn't so happy when we veered off the trail to begin with, and now we don't seem to be getting anywhere. What makes you think it has been sent by someone? For all we know this is just a friendly little bird that happened to be going the right way. Well, to begin with anyhow. Are you sure it's not a magic bird?"

"Well, I did try to nudge it with my magic but discovered there was a magical barrier in the way. I couldn't even sense it and I think it's pretty strong magic. As you saw, it was even able to cancel out my direction spell. For all I know the bird is magical but I don't think so. I remember reading about the brightly coloured birds in the Great Forest, and this must be one of them. Another thing I noticed is that one of the claws is damaged, and a magical bird isn't likely to have any flaws, is it? I mean, they're pretty much perfect copies of what the original should be like."

Sirroya looked at Darjoon closely. He was still big, but over the last few days had got even broader in the shoulders and slimmer in the legs. He was a strong, formidable fighter, as she'd discovered during their training exercises in the evenings. She knew that magically he was very powerful, with a blend of magics that augmented each other, rather than disrupting each other as so often happened. And he'd been showing her that he could really think too, able to reason out possibilities and opportunities. He'd make a formidable enemy someday. His excited voice jarred her out of her reverie and she ran forward.

"Oh look, a rope ladder. See how the bird is flying up? I guess this is our way up. I've always wanted to see the tree towns of the free-folk."

Darjoon was excited, his face red and beaming. Still just a young boy inside that large body, she thought as she laughed and grabbed the rope ladder, swinging herself up and beginning to climb.

"Race you to the top, great mage. And no flying, that would be cheating."

After a little while, panting and puffing, Darjoon pulled himself up onto the platform next to Sirroya who was sitting patiently with her legs dangling over the edge of a wooden platform.

"Okay, okay, you win. Great Zukar, how high are we? I felt like I was climbing forever. I'm not sure I like tree-living after all. Doing that every day would kill me."

"Don't be silly, Darjoon. Do you think the free-folk climb up and down all the time? What's the point of living in the trees if you ever go down? They've got everything they need up here: food, water and sturdy accommodation. Come on, look, they've even made an easy way to travel."

Darjoon looked dubiously at the rope-and-pulley system someone had erected. It ran between the tree they were on and another large tree in the distance. Resting on the small wooden platform was a large wicker basket that was attached to the rope overhead.

"Did you say easy? Do we really have to get in there? I'll fall through that thing, it won't hold my weight. And where's the safety harness? Do they really expect a person to trust their lives to a small basket like that?"

Sirroya had already pushed the basket over the edge where it dangled free, and was throwing in the packs and clambering in as it swayed from side to side.

"Oh come on, great mage. Have you forgotten already? You don't need a safety harness. You can fly, silly man. Just don't forget to fly me with you if we start to fall. Now let's go. Woohoo! Hold on tight!", as Darjoon climbed in Sirroya waggled the basket from side to side and laughed at Darjoon's obvious discomfort.

They pulled on the rope and in turn were dragged along over a large ravine below. Another basket passed them halfway along and Darjoon swore as it did so.

"No wonder this is such hard work, we're pulling two baskets and not just one."

They could make out a platform on the large tree at the other end of the ravine as they drew closer. On a branch sitting patiently above the platform the green bird waited for them. Once on the other side, they simply climbed out and gave the ropes a final pull to haul the basket up onto the platform. Then they set off along a rope bridge to another large tree. In this way, using a combination of rope bridges and baskets they travelled through the forest canopy for some time, surrounded by bright, sparkling birds, flittering butterflies and other insects and howled at by monkeys who travelled in parallel with them for a while. The air was fresh and crisp up here, the cool breeze blowing away the warm, rank odour of the dark forest below. The sky stretched out overhead, big and blue and the sun was a welcome sight, softened by a slight haze in the air. It seemed they had been travelling for ages when up ahead Darjoon saw an obvious walkway, wooden planks laid out as a floor along the usual ropes, leading to the side of a truly massive tree that towered over those around it. Great birds of prey circled lazily overhead, intently watching the forest below. Halfway across the walkway, Darjoon nudged Sirroya, who was staring up at the birds. She looked across to see a broad-shouldered man dressed in simple green cloth standing on the other side waiting for them. He had a large bow slung over his shoulder and a broad blade at his hip and stood easily with feet apart and hands on hips. The green bird they'd been following landed on his shoulder and looked back at them with its head to the side. It shrieked and then disappeared.

"Obvious flaw, huh? So much for your non-magical bird. Oh yes, you flew out early from the nest, I can see that", Sirroya laughed at Darjoon.

"Nice. She obviously thinks highly of you, doesn't she. Welcome to the village of the free-folk."

Darjoon stumbled and stopped, looking up at the man and realising his lips hadn't moved and the voice was definitely inside his head. Sirroya stopped and looked quizzically at Darjoon, then turned to the man standing in front of them, put her hands on her hips and glared at him. He smiled faintly and shrugged his shoulders.

"I apologise, young lady. I'm so used to communing with nature and those who understand me in their minds, I forget not everyone does. Please, let me welcome you both. I am Y'sarryn, the hunter, and you are obviously Darjoon, the apprentice mage, and Sirroya, the, uh, runaway. Come, let me show you our humble village", his voice was deep and soft.

Darjoon and Sirroya followed Y'sarryn as he led them through the walkways, pointing out the meeting hall and other rooms and dwellings of interest in the village. These rooms were all built into the massive trunks of different trees, connected with rope bridges and walkways, some of which had covered roofs that were painted in different colours and most of the buildings had flags suspended from the eaves that whipped in the wind. There were also beautiful carvings of thin, delicate faces on the tall posts that were used to anchor the ropes and Darjoon could swear the faces turned to watch him as he walked past. People were walking and climbing among the walk-ways, dressed in bright silk clothing that fluttered in the breeze. Y'sarryn had told them that a lot of the people were away during the day, foraging and creating what they needed to survive. The people that were there walked with obvious freedom, laughing and talking with each other, with only the occasional curious, friendly glances at the three passing by.

"We use everything from the forest in our village, the vines and grasses for ropes, certain birds and tree sap for the glue, a form of cotton for the clothing I wear, all of it is available here in the canopy. Even our pet birds are much like your large, fat ground-birds back home in the Empire, Sirroya. Here they run along the broad branches and feed off insects and they are used to lay eggs for food in the same way."

"But what about meat? Surely you don't just eat birds, or dear Zukar, tell me you don't eat the monkeys?", Darjoon looked at him in alarm.

"No, Darjoon", Y'sarryn chuckled, "we don't eat any meat at all. The birds are only for eggs, and that is used with some ground up bark from a particular tree to make a delicious bread. And the monkeys are our friends, they warn us if anyone is approaching and show us where the best fruit is. Some of the children have made pets of them and trained them to fetch and carry. But those are typically the injured one's they are taking care of, not the healthy monkeys who are too independent anyway. We even have milk up here."

Y'sarryn laughed at the look on Darjoon's face and responded before he could ask his question.

"Don't worry, we don't milk the monkeys. Our milk comes from the sap of that tall red tree over there. It's actually quite sweet and delicious and otherwise very similar to the milk you'd know from your domestic animals."

While he was talking they'd arrived at a nursery, a large open area of planking strung between five trees and currently occupied by children of various ages engaged in different activities. It was fenced off with netting and had an ornate wooden roof painted in stripes of different colours. There were three symbols carved into the gables: a raven, a snow cat and a large bat.

"That bat symbol looks familiar? I'm trying to remember... oh wait, the one my fa... I mean my uncle wore around his neck. Do you know what it means? What, Sirroya? Oh, well, I've said it now", Darjoon blushed red as Sirroya glared at him in warning.

In reply, Y'sarryn called over one of the women who was looking after the children.

"Sirroya, this is Timras. I'm afraid we are always needing help with the children. Please would you go with her and look after the children for a while? I need to have a private chat with Darjoon. I really hope you don't mind, Sirroya."

"Mind! I'd be glad to have a break from this mad mage. Darjoon, what have I told you about blurting things out to just anyone? Well, it's on your head who you trust. He seems to be okay but looks can be deceiving, no offence mind you", this last she addressed to Y'sarryn then turned back to Darjoon, "Come say goodbye to me when you're done. I've finally found where I want to be! Let's go, Timras, I'm keen to see the children ag..., uh, and see how they feel about living as free-folk. I've always dreamt about...", her voice faded as Sirroya and Timras headed over to the children, chatting away as if they'd known each other all their lives. Something niggled at Darjoon's memory again, the way she spoke and how she always seemed to be at home wherever she was. He dismissed it, thinking that she was just extrovert, gregarious and always eager to please. It was natural that she'd fit in anywhere. He turned back to Y'sarryn who was watching the ladies walk off with particular interest. Darjoon felt a burst of jealousy as he realised the look was directed at Sirroya. Silly boy, why did he care? It was obvious she thought him a great, big, fat lump of idiot. He had no chance with Sirroya so why care who looks at her.

"Ahem! So, are we going far?", he tried to distract Y'sarryn.

The older man looked up at Darjoon and smiled. He had an honest, open face, although careworn and sunburnt with wrinkles and touches of grey about the temples. He stood relaxed, but in the same way that a coiled spring appeared relaxed, as if it were waiting for the right moment to react and jump forward. Beckoning Darjoon to follow him, Y'sarryn ran around the tree trunk and grabbed hold of a rope ladder, quickly climbing up into the higher reaches of the canopy. Darjoon sighed and hurried to keep up as the older man was fit and nimble and soon they were running along walkways and climbing ladders, racing each other to the top. Darjoon was panting and his muscles aching as he finally joined Y'sarryn on a platform at the top of a particularly tall, massive tree. Below them, stretching into the distance was the Great Forest, a distant green floor of waving trees with patches of grey mist and a few open, cleared areas that sent up puffs of dark smoke, the obvious locations of the Spidralite villages. Beyond the forest stood the blue outlines of the Darken Hills. There was a stiff breeze so high up and Darjoon huddled into his cloak as Y'sarryn and himself settled onto the platform.

"I like to come up here to get away and just think", Y'sarryn said, "This is so beautiful and peaceful and I can still feel that I am part of that world out there, even though I hardly ever venture into it any more. You mustn't worry about trusting me Darjoon, I knew your father well. As for your mother, I, um, I knew her very well too. Let's just say I would have liked to be the better man in her life, but I wasn't. I was the best man at their wedding though. They said their vows up here, just the three of us and one other to witness."

He turned and looked at Darjoon, appraising him.

"I can see both of them in you. The large, powerful physique of your father and the nimble agility of your mother. You move surprisingly well for a big man, and for that you have your mother to thank. She loved it up here and we'd often meet and chat about many things late into the night. Oh don't look like that! You don't have to worry, nothing happened. Your mother was madly in love with your father. There was nothing he could do that would condemn him in her eyes, nothing at all", Y'sarryn sighed and looked up into the blue sky.

"He wasn't from here, your father. I suppose you guessed as much. I can sense his raw magic about you, but tinged with the raven-born subtleties and something else that I cannot place, something strange. I have a feeling you have no real idea of your true power, do you? And what are the chances that anyone has informed you of the amazing prophecy and so the real reason you are here? Oh yes, I know you want this information. I can see you are so very keen on finding out more, but are you sure you really, really want to know, Darjoon? Information always has a price of some kind. You see, the more we learn about this life of ours, the more responsibility we have to the world around us."

Darjoon, who'd leaned forward and listened intently, sat back and stared at the hunter. A man who knew both his parents and who had loved his mother, and who it seems could give him the information he wanted. Or so he fervently hoped. What would he do when he found out, when he finally knew the truth about his father? The hunter didn't make it sound like it was all good news. On the other hand, he couldn't go back to Upper Srinth until he had found the knowledge he was supposed to have, and to find that out, he definitely needed more information. So yes, he wanted to know. He simply nodded once at Y'sarryn who nodded back slowly with sympathetic eyes.

"Very well, but don't say I didn't warn you! And remember, when we hatch from the egg, we don't always find a loving wing to guard us. We have to become harder than that fragile shell that gave us life", as Y'sarryn was speaking, his features were slowly changing until Darjoon gasped in recognition. In front of him was no longer a tanned, brown-haired, green-eyed Spidral hunter, but a black-haired, brown-eyed raven-born with the tell-tale hooked nose.

"Yes, I am not always what I seem. It serves me to deny my origins and there are very, very few who know my true identity and none who find out that shouldn't live to tell of it. You are now one of them. The one's who live, that is", he smiled dangerously.

"And to keep living, I know you won't tell anyone else. Why put them in unnecessary danger, eh? But enough about me, let's talk about your parents."

Y'sarryn composed himself, slowed his breathing and looked inward to revive old memories.

"I remember like it was yesterday. When your mother and father arrived here I hadn't been long among the free-folk myself. Your father wasn't in good shape, he'd been burnt down one side of his body and was totally blind. Your mother and I worked for hours every day healing and repairing the obvious wounds that he'd sustained. Unfortunately his vision never came back. I don't believe that was just a physical hurt, we all believed it was a mental wound that had seared him from inside as much as the fire had burnt him outside. You see, Darjoon, your father was a great mage from Sorcerer's Isle and back then it wasn't the glass mess it is today, it was lush and verdant, with a forest as beautiful as this, if a lot smaller", Y'sarryn shook his head, then looked out at the forest.

"That beautiful forest was like this one, in that it was sentient, and they used to communicate through their seeds that would float in the ocean or stick on the birds that flew between them. Just like the little raven friends we used back home to fly little messages from one person to another. The people on the island were largely self-sufficient and hardly ever left it, not even to trade. Trade-ships would stop in their port, but all the business was conducted on-board the ship and no sailor ever put foot on shore, or lived to tell of it.", Y'sarryn took a deep breath, let it out and looked at Darjoon.

"There was a college of magic there, much like the one you attended but also very unlike it. The people on the island had a powerful, old form of magic that was buried deep in the blood and bone of them, not superficial and empty like our raven-born magic has become. It is said they also acquired an even older beast-magic from some unknown race of people, and this had allowed them to do terrible things that I have only heard hinted at, and that I heard in the ravings of your father during his bouts of fever."

Ysarryn shivered, drew his cloak tightly around him and continued with the story.

"Your father was slowly going mad and nothing we could do was able to slow it down or stop it. I had developed a close friendship with both of them, and your mother and I continued to work on various potions, poultices and spells to heal your father's eyes as well as his mind. We had little success, and even though he was fine physically, other than his blindness, a part of his mind was leaving us every day.

"One morning he called us both into their dwelling and put a shield-spell around it. He was good at those, they just came naturally to him. No-one could see or hear what was going on inside, and it was then he revealed to us the beast-magic he had learnt.", Ysarryn's mouth pulled down in disgust.

"A friend and himself had managed to transport themselves magically to the mist-lands of Fr'bazim, the home of the Y'shtim. They are an ancient race of furry creatures and in a way, they resemble truktari with whiskers and sharp, pointed ears but they have feet and hands like humans and stand upright. They live in a cold, strange land to the south of us and at the time they had an uneasy, fragile alliance with some giant snow wolves. These wolves can think and speak like us but still run on all fours and have large, sharp teeth. The two races hunt together, the cat people catching fish and seals and the wolves protecting all of them from the fierce, giant snow-bears. It is a violent, rugged land and the inhabitants are no different.", Ysarryn's eyes took on a distant look as he dug deep into his memories, replaying what he had learnt from Darjoon's father.

"The cat people have great magical powers including the beast magic and a special form of frost magic which is unlike anything we have in the Old Lands, be it here in Spidral, with the raven-born or anywhere in the Empire. It is believed that the Y'shtim created or altered the great wolves in some way and it was this terrible magic that your father and his friend had been taught. Naturally, the Y'shtim were reluctant to teach them what they knew, but your father gave them something precious in return, something that would change their world forever. He taught them how to command the beasts that their beast-magic had created, how to take control of them and make them do anything that was asked.", Ysarryn shivered again and looked around him, as if he could see the creatures he was speaking of.

"This is something we raven-born learn to do, although what we learn is insubstantial and incomplete. We can 'nudge' creatures, but your father's people had a very real control over animals. For the first time, the Y'shtim could have their independence from the wolves they had made, avoiding being forced into an alliance with them. They could control both the wolves and the great snow-bears, bending them both to their fierce will. Of course, that meant the end of any freedom that the great wolves had ever had, and so they hated your father for it as it was he who had ended their freedom. They had never loved the Y'shtim anyway and I believe they are simply waiting for their chance to rain down death and destruction on them and somehow take vengeance on those who helped them."

Darjoon shivered and huddled further into his cloak. The sun was starting to drift towards the horizon, casting long beams of light across the forest and creating furtive shadows twisting in the mists. What kind of blood did he have running in his veins? It is said that when a mage learns new magic, that magic is transmitted to his offspring in their blood. Did he have these abilities too? Y'sarryn moved over and put his back against Darjoon's, sharing his body warmth and looking down at his feet as he spoke, almost as if he didn't want to look Darjoon in the eye.

"Your father learnt one other secret magic from the Y'shtim, and that was the ability to age slowly. He was old when he came here to our village in the trees, very old indeed, although I still have no idea just how old. Your mother knew that apparently, but it didn't seem to matter to her. Nothing about your father bothered her because she was so blinded by her love for him. Even the fact that he'd been to see the foul Circle of True One's did not stop her. I asked her why he'd been there, what possible purpose could he have for seeing those renegades, but she didn't know. Who in their right mind would associate with such crazy fanatics? They are a menace to themselves, and to everyone in the Old Lands, not just the raven-born", Ysarryn now looked over at Darjoon, "Make sure you stay well clear of them, Darjoon. Nothing they could offer you would be worth that involvement, or the terrible price you'd have to pay."

Darjoon closed his eyes and shook his head slowly. His mind was whirling with everything Y'sarryn was telling him. What sort of man had his father really been? Y'sarryn glanced at him again, then continued his tale.

"Your parents met when your father was visiting the raven-born on official business, something unheard of then and now. Your mother was only recently appointed to the Council so the Council put them together, wanting her to learn as much as she could from him. She was one of the youngest mage's ever appointed to the Council, in part because she displayed some unusual magical traits. The most notable was the ability to fly long distances and with great accuracy. This intrigued your father, who was in fact really there to learn everything he could about raven-born magic in order to help his faction in their civil war back on the island. So they spent some time together and I can only imagine he must have felt something for her, although in his long life and extensive travels who's to say he hadn't had many, many lovers, most of whom would have died long before. Not that your mother cared at all", he shook his head.

"They had a brief affair, but then he had an urgent summons to return home and left immediately. Years later, he reappeared at her door, broken and burnt, babbling on about the end of it all, about the fools who had unleashed living hell. The civil war on the island had erupted into open violence and swiftly spiralled out of control, and they had destroyed themselves. Can you imagine, an entire nation wiped out in a matter of days", Y'sarryn's voice grew husky and soft and Darjoon had to lean in to hear what he was saying as the raven-born stared out into the twilight.

"I can still remember when it happened. For nights we'd seen flashes of light and heard sounds like thunder and then from this observation post one night we could see smoke rising from the ruined slag that is now the Glass Isle. It rose for many days and the smoke blocked the sun and spread a deep gloom over every land. According to your father, they had completely destroyed each other as well as the whole island in some final, mad, beast battle. The forest here had literally wept, the trees shedding bark and dripping sap for many days as if in mourning over the loss of a sibling or friend or whatever relationship the two forests had shared. It was terrible for us living here among the trees, many of us had violent nightmares filled with horror, full of burning and death", Y'sarryn himself had a tear running down his cheek now.

"As for your father, the raven-born wanted nothing to do with this crazy, burnt wreck of a man from a nation of such terrible violence. All they could think was that their beloved balance was at risk and so they demanded that he leave immediately. Your mother flew him here, to the place where everyone gets accepted regardless of their past. She was a wonderful woman, your mother. She was kind and considerate, always willing to help out among the free-folk, to lend a hand and share her magic. We all became very fond of her and I must confess I grew to love her deeply, but it was no use, there was nothing to be done about it. She was blinded by her mad infatuation with the strange mage that was your father!"

Y'sarryn stood up and wiped his cheek, strong emotions playing across his face. Darjoon could see that he had really cared for his mother, that in fact she had meant everything to him. The raven-born features slowly faded, as did the expressions on his face until once again the smooth-featured, smiling Spidralite hunter stood before him. He wondered if the mask wasn't more for

Y'sarryn himself, to hide away from who he was or from what could have been, rather than an attempt to conceal his true identity from anyone else.

"I cannot tell you more than that, Darjoon, because I honestly don't know any more. Your father passed away in the end. Unfortunately by then he had gone quite mad and your mother and I buried him in the forest. She grieved for a few days and then left, never to be seen here again. She had already known that she was pregnant with you and she said she wanted her baby to be among those of her own kind, back among the raven-born. I... I asked her to stay, told her that I didn't care about the baby, but she wouldn't listen, she...", his voice broke.

"It was no use, you see. Once your mother had decided a thing, it was done and so I never saw her again after that day, that final farewell, and then I got word years later that they'd found her in the Darken Hills, alone and dead. She never did let anyone else close to her, never let anyone in. As if she knew, as if...", Y'sarryn turned and looked at Darjoon, then shrugged his shoulders and offered him a hand to lift him to his feet.

"I realise this is a lot to take in now. Come, there are some items that she left behind for you and a note that may shed some more light on all this. She seemed to know that one day you would travel here and I would be the one to give them to you. I know she wanted you to hear the full story from me because when she left, she hugged me goodbye and whispered to me, 'Tell him everything he needs to know'. I've been waiting for you for a long while now. When I heard about your mother's passing and you still being so young, I wondered if you would come. Obviously she didn't tell you much but you must realise that it's not because she didn't want to, Darjoon, it was for your own protection. Some things are, well, are just better left unsaid, some knowledge, some facts can be too heavy a burden, especially for the young. Come, let's get back now, your friend will wonder where you are."

In the bright moonlight, they made their way back down to the meeting hall, collecting Sirroya on the way. The last few children were just leaving with their parents who had come in from wherever in the trees they had been working for the community. The chatter of little voices and tired, parental responses slowly faded away. Sirroya looked quizzically at Darjoon and Y'sarryn and joined them as they walked away from the nursery and past the great hall, an ornate building embedded in the heart of a truly magnificent tree. A few trees away from the great hall was Y'sarryn's dwelling and they sat outside together on a small balcony facing towards the great hall, eating and talking and even, occasionally, laughing. Sirroya, as usual, was sharing from her seemingly inexhaustible supply of Empire jokes and tales. She claimed that as a child her mother had taught them all to her. According to her, her mother had worked for a while cleaning a great man's library, and so had been allowed to borrow some books to read. It was as much as Darjoon had ever heard Sirroya talk about her family. He sat and looked out across the forest, at the twinkling lights of the Spidral villages scattered in the darkness. He wondered what his mother had thought, probably sitting in this very spot so many years ago as his father lay dying and going insane.

Y'sarryn broke off his conversation with Sirroya and tapped him on the knee, "Okay, Darjoon, I need to go and get those items I mentioned. I'll be back soon enough, it's just that they're not here but safely hidden away."

He was up and gone before either of them could reply, moving with subtle swiftness for an old man. Sirroya shuffled her chair closer to his until their knees were touching.

"So? What did he tell you? What have you learnt about your, uh, uncle? Anything juicy you want to share?", Sirroya leaned forward eagerly, placing a hand on his arm.

He looked down at the beautiful hand resting there, feeling its warmth through his cloak, and then he shivered slightly. What should he tell her? He took a deep breath, "Well, I, um, I mean, uh, I now know that he was a great mage, and, uh, and he died here long ago and, well, that's why my mother left here and returned to the nest."

"Really? And that's it? Oh, come on Darjoon! Do you really expect me to believe that's all he told you?", Sirroya withdrew her hand and sat back.

"Okay, okay, I understand. You don't want to trust me with your history. I think that's wise, I really do. I told you, you can't be too careful. Did you at least learn the significance of the amulet your uncle was supposed to have worn? The one with the wolf's head that I see you look at every now and again when you think I'm sleeping or not paying attention."

Darjoon blushed. He'd forgotten all about that. Trust her to think of something he'd missed. Now she would get that smarty-pants look on her face and start chiding him for not remembering. She was so insufferable sometimes.

"Actually I did! I learnt all I could but I can't share it with you! It's too dangerous for you to know more about it", he lied.

"Dangerous? Really? Oh, wow, that's so kind of you! Impressive, really. It warms me inside knowing you care so much about me that you want to protect me from such deadly information. Thank you, Darjoon, that's so very sweet of you", her voice dripped acid as she pushed her chair back from him and he winced.

"Well! And how would you know if it wasn't? You don't know everything!", he responded without thinking.

At that moment, Y'sarryn returned, carrying a large leather bag and an oilskin wrapped and tied around something tall and thin. He dumped it on the table between them.

"Sorry! Am I interrupting a lovers quarrel? You could cut the atmosphere with a knife you know. You kids are too young to argue, you should cherish the time you have together and not waste it squabbling", he looked from one to the other as they sat glaring at each other then turned to Darjoon.

"I have no idea what is in that bag or that oilskin as I have never opened either of them. Your mother made me swear to never touch any of it", Y'sarryn looked amusingly from one to the other again, "So I'll leave you to the night and your, uh, angry mistress, and see you both in the morning."

Y'sarryn disappeared inside his dwelling while Sirroya and Darjoon were still spluttering out their denials.

"Mistress?", Sirroya exclaimed, "That'll be the day! As if", she stood up and stalked inside.

He could hear her banging around inside her room for a while and then the noise died down. Darjoon shook his head, and then sat staring at the items on the table. Would he ever understand a woman or her reactions? What was wrong with her? He sighed, then reached out and grabbed the leather bag first, sliding it over in front of him and trying to untie the knot that held it closed. After a few minutes picking, pulling and tugging at it, he found that the harder he tried, the tighter the knot became. When he stopped trying, he could see it visibly loosen again. Frustrated, he took the small knife that he wore around his side and tried to cut the rope around the knot. No matter how hard he sawed at it, nothing happened. Then he tried to cut into the leather itself, but he could quickly see that the blade wouldn't penetrate. Drawing his finger across the blade and feeling how blunt it had become, he sat scowling at the knot as if his frown would cause it to unravel. Then, slowly, with dawning comprehension, the frown melted away. Smiling now, he closed his eyes, put his hands on the bag and muttered a small incantation. The rope around the bag magically untied itself, the bag fell open and he shook out the contents on the table.

"Well, mother, your magic lives on even if you don't", he whispered to the night air, "I remember how you used to pack my school lunch, and my gym clothes, and tie it like this so no-one could touch it. Some things never change"

He chuckled to himself as he remembered how he struggled with her knots in the beginning, starving every day until finally he begged her to show him the spell. She'd smiled and gently guided his magic until the knot had fallen apart. He reached forward to examine his prize. One of the items was an ornately carved ivory dagger, the long, sharp blade curving up slightly with a notch at the end, making two small prongs. The handle had a sea-green velvet binding that was tied off at the end, leaving two trailing ribbons dangling free. In the top centre of the steel pommel of the dagger was a dark blue chiselled stone. The stone had a faint glow inside, even after he placed it in the shadow to check if it was just the torchlight. He turned it over and over in his hands, feeling a slight buzzing as he did so. Touching the blade to a corner of the discarded leather of the package, he stared in awe as it flared white, crystallised, then shattered as he flicked it with his finger. Picking up a piece of the white leather, he quickly shook it from his hand, sucking on his fingers. It was ice cold, the sort of freezing frost that makes objects stick to the skin. Turning to the other object from the package, he saw it was a neatly folded, finely woven grey robe. He stood up, unfolded it and realised it would be a perfect fit. Putting it on, he smiled, wondering how his mother had known what size he'd be when he received it as the robe fit like it had been tailor-made for him. He thumped his chest with his left fist in the age-old gesture of raven-born gratitude, acknowledging the gifts from his dead mother. Wincing in pain, he sucked his stinging knuckles. It had felt like he'd just hit solid steel. He felt the robe again, but it was fine and soft, evidently of good quality.

"Darjoon, are you imagining things again?", he muttered to himself.

He slapped his chest hard, and again, it was like slapping steel. Picking up the knife he'd been trying to cut the cord with, he held the blade between his forefinger and thumb, and tapped the handle lightly to his chest. He could feel the handle touch his chest through the soft robe. Trying again, he put some effort into the blow. Clang! The ringing of steel on steel reverberated through the night. He grinned in delight. A robe that became armour would be very useful, especially as it had the element of surprise. He looked forward to trying it out at his next training session with Sirroya, that would surprise her. The smile dropped from his face. That would obviously not be tonight based on the mood she was in. Oh well, he sighed, she'd be fine by morning.

Picking up the long, thin, oilskin-wrapped package leaning against the table, he used the same magic on the knot and it unwrapped easily. He slid out a long, wooden staff that was as tall as himself. There were intricate drawings all along the length of the staff, and at the top, the wood formed a natural cradle for a large, green ornately chiselled gem that also glowed faintly in the shadows. Looking around surreptitiously, he thrust the jewelled end of the staff out away from him into the night and muttered some magical words. Nothing. He tried a few more times, but still nothing happened. Oh well, he'd have to find a way to unlock the magic that he knew was inside the gem. He was about to discard the leather and oilskins, when he saw something white in the bottom of the first package. Taking out a neatly folded letter, he rested the staff against the table and sat down to read.

My dearest Darjoon

If you are reading this, then I am probably no longer in this world and am flying on the back of the Great Raven to the Stream of Life. I would rather die than see you thrown out of our lands, so that's the only way you could be here in the Great Forest unless I brought you myself. In which case I would have got this letter first and destroyed it.

My son, there are many things that you need to know about your father. Y'sarryn himself only knows the little he's probably already told you. I'm afraid you will need to travel a long road to learn all that you need to and it's very important that you do learn slowly, my boy, even if that's the harder way. I don't want to do this to you, dear one, but you might be the only hope of our once proud nation. Please remember your training, and remember that magic learnt quickly is never magic learnt well and is never good magic. There are no shortcuts.

I cannot tell you everything now and even the little you already know is dangerous for you. I wish there was another way, Darjoon, but there is other knowledge you must first acquire before you are ready for the whole truth. As hard as it must have been for you to leave our lands, you must never return, no matter what the Council or anyone else has told you. Especially if they talked about the Garduin moon. I realise that means you might never see your grandfather and grandmother again, but it's for the best, you must believe me.

You must travel immediately to the Desert of Thoth and there find a warrior called Turmoos. He will know what you must do next. Be warned, my son, it will be a dangerous road for you, but there is no other option. Turmoos will also help you to unlock the true power that is inside you. You will know what that means when you find him and you can trust him completely.

I've been fighting the Dremrel for some time now and they are getting stronger. Their magic is on the rise, while we as a nation grow ever weaker. It is not only the raven-born that are at risk, but all the Old Lands are in great danger. The Empire is too dull to understand what a threat these creatures are to them. They think they can treat them like their stupid bront's, penning them up in the Darken Hills. Yet the evil creatures now begin to travel further afield than ever before and are gathering together. I've seen gatherings of almost one hundred Dremrel in a single location, something that was once believed to be impossible. They no longer only hunt in small parties of three like they used to but instead are organising in great numbers, like an army.

Darjoon my son, I have read a prophecy that tells of a young man who will save the Old Lands. A young mage with great power and a greater heart. A young man who is alone and independent. I know it may be hard to hear, but I believe that this is you. The combination of magical abilities that you have received from your grandfather, your father and myself will be very powerful once you learn how to harness them together. I know that you will save us, I just wish I was there to see it and be part of it.

Darjoon, you must not trust the Circle of True One's. They will seek to use your power for their own gain. I don't know how, but they have become aware of you and will try to hunt you down. Stay away from them, no matter what they offer you. They are mad and dangerous and will stop at nothing to further their aims. What they believe is only half the truth, and even that is twisted and bent. If they try to contact you, ignore them. Please, you must avoid them at all costs.

You will know more about the prophecy when the wolves make contact, which should happen soon. The wolves have helped me in the past and they will help you too. Darjoon, you must know that you cannot join them, no matter what they say or what they promise, for yours is a different destiny. They are naturally secretive and stealthy, but know that you can trust them with your life, as I have in the past.

I will always be with you, Darjoon, whether we meet in Khamoos or whether I travel down the Stream of Life again. You must know that I am very proud of you and I have loved you dearly, even if I cannot or know not how to show it. You and my raven-born people are the reason I hunted and fought against the Dremrel so hard. I know that you will be the saviour we have all been waiting for throughout the Old Lands.

You will make us all so proud of you and I will see you again, never fear.

Love
Your Mother

Darjoon read and re-read the letter, tears running down his cheeks. He wiped his face with the back of his hand, knowing that this ability to show emotion was another aspect that set him apart from the raven-born. Displays of emotion were discouraged as a sign of weakness and a true raven-born was expected to fly away from the nest, not keep loving those in it. He wasn't sure how long he sat, looking out over the tree-top town and watching through tearful eyes as the lights in the village winked out slowly one by one. After a long while, a shiver ran through him and he pulled the grey cloak he was still wearing tighter around him. As he did so, it snuggled against him and he felt a blissful warmth envelope him. "Well, you would've been useful in the Darken Hills", he whispered quietly.

Sighing deeply he wished this was all just a dream, a bad dream from which he would soon wake. If he listened, carefully, then it was as if he could hear his mother calling him down for breakfast. She would have set out a steaming bowl of hot oat porridge with honey and goats milk for him. He pinched himself just to see if he would wake up from this other, wretched dream, but no, it was still all there in front of him: the staff, the packages, a letter and beyond that the dark village in the trees.

In a daze, Darjoon put the letter into his new cloak with its handy inside pockets. Carefully folding and storing the oilskin and leather, he blew out the lamp, went inside the little cottage and climbed into bed. Lying there staring up at the ceiling for what seemed like hours, he wrestled with what he had read. He knew his mother had to be wrong. There was no chance that he was a hero and pretty much everything he'd encountered in his life so far showed him that he was definitely no saviour. It seemed that there was so much conflicting information, everyone else told him something different. What was it with the wolves that everyone kept talking about? Who could they be? What were they? He knew he had to find this warrior in the desert and get more information. Hopefully he'd be able to solve some of these conflicts as he had to know more, why else would his mother send him that way. Darjoon slowly drifted into a fitful sleep with wild dreams, in which a hundred Dremrel chased him down a mountain path forcing him to dive into a little cave. They started digging around the entrance to get in and just before they broke through and a myriad clawed hands reached out to grab him and pull him toward rotting fangs, he woke up.

7 THROUGH THE FOREST

"Are you sure that's what you want to do, Sirroya?", Darjoon asked again, "It seemed you were pretty keen on staying with the free-folk and settling down here. That was your dream, wasn't it? I have to tell you that I honestly don't know what lies ahead of me. It seems I must travel out of this Forest, across the Plains of Breath and probably through the Desert of Thoth to find some warrior called Turmoos. Given that neither of us have ever been that way before, it's not going to be easy."

Sirroya looked at him and crinkled up her forehead in the way she did when she was about to argue with him. He smiled and before she could draw breath carried on talking.

"Please, don't get me wrong, I'm not saying that it hasn't been great having you along, well, actually, it's not been all that great... Ouch! What are you doing?", he ducked back and to the side.

She threw another punch at him but this time he was out of reach. Darjoon was laughing out loud now.

"Okay, okay, I was only joking. What a fun time it's been with you, getting chased by Dremrels, thrown in prison and working for a spy. But I really don't know what it's going to be like in future. I can't promise you that you'll be safe, you know that", Darjoon looked at her with real concern.

"And, well, um, you see, well, actually, well, the truth of it is, I kind of like you. So I don't really want anything bad to happen to you", Darjoon was blushing now and the last words came out in a rush.

"Oh really?", Sirroya looked at him with a grin, "You like me now, do you?"

"Yes, I.. I mean like, like, like a sister. Of course. That's what I meant. Just that I... I mean you... I don't want... You might get hurt, that's all I'm saying."

Darjoon folded his arms and glared at her, the blush having enveloped his face and travelled down his neck.

"Well, oh great and glorious and wise mage, you just listen to your little, what did you call me? Your sister! Don't think that being with you is a picnic for me either you know. And while we're talking about brothers and sisters, well, if you only knew. I mean, the fact is you are like a brother to me, Darjoon, so of course I want to protect you too. Now can we stop all this mushy nonsense and finish packing?", she had her hands on her hips, daring him to disagree. He shook his head, knowing he didn't have a choice. She grinned at him and went back to her packing, including grabbing food off the table.

"Darjoon, don't you think it is rather kind of Y'sarryn to provision us like this? I mean this chranth he's given us will last a long time, although I must say it isn't exactly a favourite of mine. Too dry and sweet for my taste.", she looked up from her packing and saw the young mage standing with a perplexed look on his face.

"No, Darjoon, no more arguing. I'm going with you to keep an eye on you, and that's all there is to it. I'll not hear another word."

Sirroya picked up her pack and stalked outside while Darjoon rolled his eyes. She was so stubborn sometimes. In fact his mother would have said to her what she used to say to him, 'stubborn as a bront'. He laughed suddenly, thinking of that silly bront his grandfather had kept. It was such a dumb, lazy, brute of an animal and once it decided not to move, there was no shifting its massive bulk. He used to be naughty and set the tip of its tail on fire to make it move, although only when his mother wasn't looking of course. His grandfather used to roll in the dust laughing as the stupid beast suddenly ran the length of the paddock to get away from its own burning tail. That certainly got it moving, but then one day his mom had set his shoe on fire, which burnt his foot, making him dance around until he'd hopped across to the water trough and plunged it in to quench it. His grandfather had been rolling around that day too, laughing like mad. His mother had innocently asked him what it felt like and whether he had liked it.

"Magic, Darjoon", he remembered her saying, "is not to be used against animals or people unless it is for your or their defence or to help them. When helping people you must ask and they must agree. Now that you know what it feels like, maybe you won't be so quick to hurt that poor bront. Did you ever think that maybe there was a gentler way?"

It was the first time he'd seen her magically "nudge" an animal into doing what she wanted. He'd never forgotten that lesson and it was why in the Darken Hills he'd not attacked nor hurt the mountain lion, even though there'd been some danger to him.

He looked up as he heard Y'sarryn's voice through the open door and realised why Y'sarryn had fallen for his mother, they were kindred spirits in so many ways. The hunter had a deep respect for all the forms of life that were around him, including the so-called dumb animals.

Darjoon finished his packing, swung the pack onto his shoulder and walked outside. Y'sarryn and Sirroya were deep in conversation and he caught the word "brother", assuming that she was telling the hunter about their little conversation. He blushed again, thinking what a young idiot he must look. He worried that he was really beginning to like her, maybe even falling in love with her. Shaking his head, he walked over to Y'sarryn who turned to smile at him.

"Well, Darjoon, it seems that you won't be alone after all. I wish I could come, but I'm afraid my exploring days are well and truly over. There are too many grey hairs on this head, too many old bones in this body and far too much responsibility here in the village for me to wander around the countryside. A pity, as I'd love to travel into the Desert again.", he had a wistful look on his face. Then he turned to Darjoon, looked at him piercingly and clapped a hand on his shoulder.

"Be careful what you find out there, young raven-born. Not all is as it seems. The desert might look bleak and empty, but it hides many secrets including much danger. If you hurry now, you should be able to get through the Plains before the Dragon Breath stirs, otherwise you will have to dig fast and deep to survive that scorching wind. Legend says it can melt the flesh off a man's body. Remember, both of you, to watch the animals closely. If you see them running, then run with them because they will know where to go and what to do."

Y'sarryn looked over at Sirroya and turned to Darjoon again, "Take care of this young lady, Darjoon, I have a feeling you'll both need each other before this is all over. I'll be here waiting for you, so make sure you pass this way when you're headed back. Don't look at me like that, Darjoon, you will be coming back.", the hunter smiled at Darjoon's perplexed frown. Darjoon shook himself and smiled back.

"My thanks for everything, Y'sarryn. May the falling feather of fortune bring you the Great Raven's many blessings."

As he said this, he traced a feather on his brow.

"We will stop by on our way back, if we actually make it out alive. I've been lucky so far, but, well, I'm just not sure how far my luck will stretch."

The hunter laughed, "Just remember that you make your own luck, Darjoon, and from what you two have told me, you're not doing a bad job of it. Now off you go, don't waste any more of this wonderful morning. It'll be clear skies today and good weather for travelling. Just remember that as long as you have each other, you're never far from the nest."

The hunter turned and led them back along the walkway and out past the great Brisla tree. People were already heading out to their day's chores and as they walked past the school Timras came out and gave Sirroya a hug goodbye. Darjoon could see the emotion in Sirroya's face and how hard it was for her to leave. She kept turning back to look at the school as they walked away. Finally, they came to the same entrance to the village where Y'sarryn had been waiting for them.

Darjoon turned and gave Y'sarryn a traditional ravenborn salute as they headed out on the rope bridge they had found on their arrival. As they looked back, Y'sarryn was standing in the same place and he lifted his hand again in a final farewell. Darjoon imagined he could see the ravenborn face, Y'sarryn's true identity and not the mask he habitually wore. Darjoon and Sirroya travelled in silence through the forest canopy until they were eventually back on the ground again, heading down the forest trail back towards Roikba. Late in the afternoon, they pitched camp and then as they had been doing every day so far, Darjoon continued his physical training of Sirroya. She was nimble, quick and sometimes pre-empted his commands, as if she already knew a particular move. At other times though, he could see she was genuinely surprised, usually when he showed her the combat drills he'd picked up on his own through the unofficial and sometimes illegal books he'd lifted from the college library. While they were sweating their way through one of the drills, Darjoon threw Sirroya back with a fairly strong blow. He was always careful to temper his natural strength when sparring with her, but was a little distracted this evening. She lay back on the ground panting and getting her breath back. Just as he leaned forward to apologise and help her up, she looked past him over his shoulder and suddenly jumped up, moving her hands in the air and muttering something. He was just about to respond in kind, thinking she was really trying to do him damage in retaliation, when he felt something heavy drop on his neck. Falling sideways he ducked and rolled, coming up and turning around in time to see Sirroya grab the long, sinuous length of a large, deadly tree snake from the ground. The reptiles head was a charred mess. These were lethal as their poison first paralysed and then killed in minutes and they were known to ambush prey by falling on them from the tree branches above. Darjoon stared at the burnt, dead snake, then glared at Sirroya.

"You! You used magic! How? You have magic? Since when? Who taught you that? How did you...", he wanted to be angry, but somehow he wasn't that surprised and Sirroya was shaking, seemingly in reaction to what had happened.

"I thank you, Sirroya. Now I truly owe you a life-debt. What did you do to that snake?"

"I... I'm not sure", she stammered ,"I, I just... I wanted the head to explode, and it caught fire. It was just about to drop on you from the branch above. I guess I've always been able to call fire. A travelling bard in our village, he, I mean she, taught me a simple spell. I've never really thought anything of it. Just, well, it's not something we normally do in the Empire."

"What?", Darjoon exclaimed in surprise, "No magic in the Empire? But you have mage's there, in fact I remember reading that there's a college of magic somewhere up in the mountains. I also read that your bards are known to perform small acts of magic, although they're so good at illusion, sometimes it's hard to tell if it's real or not. But what do you mean you don't do it there?"

"Yes, no, I mean there are mages and yes, the bards are taught a little magic. But none of it is encouraged among the ordinary folk. It is really just a privilege reserved for those who have either money or true power. Only the nobles and a few others with real influence are admitted to the college. In fact, anyone found practising magic on their own without being sanctioned is arrested immediately, and they are seldom heard from again", she could see the amazed look on Darjoon's face.

"This is all because of the Glass Isle. There was a really nasty war where they used magic and basically destroyed themselves and now the Empire is scared there will be more mad mages if they don't, well, keep control of how the magic is used. They don't want a repeat of that."

"But... that's not... I mean... Wait, what? We never heard about this back home. In fact, we were taught that the Empire was dangerous precisely because there were lots of magic-users. That's why we are predominantly taught defensive spells and not offensive ones. But, from what you're saying, this is not true and most Empire folk are not magical? Wait, is that really what you ran away from? Because you used magic and they found out?", Darjoon stared at her.

Sirroya hung her head. He couldn't see her face in the deepening gloom of the forest, but he could've sworn her eyes were glistening. That must be why she ran away, it must be part of the abuse she'd spoken of! Darjoon stared down at the burnt snake as he tried to digest this new information. The raven-born were never told anything about the Glass Isle. In fact, it was actually forbidden to even speculate on it and there was nothing about it in the libraries, not even in the restricted section that he had raided so often. The only rumour he had ever heard was something his mother and grandfather had spoken of, that there was a link between the Dremrel in the Darken Hills and the Glass Isle. He remembered them saying that the creatures were a weapon that got out of control. He walked over to Sirroya and took the snake, looking it over and then throwing it into the bushes.

"Well, I think we need to extend our training sessions now. You need to learn to use your magic properly and we need to see how powerful it is. I must be honest with you, even though you are still relatively young, when magic is found late in life and hasn't been developed in a child it is never very powerful. That is why the raven-born are sent to college while still so young, it means their magic is developed from an early age and has the chance to fulfil its true potential. If the power of magic is not harnessed effectively while young, then it tends to dissipate as the years go by. This is why those raven-born that do not show promise are banished to the farms. It is thought that through time and disuse the magic will simply fade away. Don't worry, we'll see how you get on. It won't be the first time they've been wrong."

They hunted briefly then drifted back to the camp-site, sitting together companionably and eating a small rabbit-like creature that Sirroya had snared and roasted. He'd found over the weeks that she was an able hunter and cook over and above her other surprising skills. She'd explained it away by saying that her father had often taken her out on hunting trips. At least she'd had a good upbringing, what with her mother's tutelage and her father's interests.

In the firelight, Darjoon showed Sirroya the gifts that his mother had left him, including the staff with the green gem on top.

"I tried to use it, but can't seem to access the underlying magic. It feels quite strange, being remote and distant yet palpable and powerful", he held it in his hands, the gem glinting in the firelight.

"Well, try it again. I'm sure you can learn to unlock it, Darjoon. Such magic will come in handy given what we'll be facing. Any help we can get will make our chances of survival that much better."

He pointed the staff away from them into the darkness and tried again to invoke it's power, but as before nothing happened and he groaned in frustration.

"Patience, Darjoon. I don't think that you can force that kind of magic. Try again", she encouraged him.

"Oh wait. I think you've given me an idea. You're right, I think patience is required here, not sheer magical power. I think I've been overdoing it. Here goes", he lifted the staff again and tried again, but this time, just as his grandfather had taught him so long ago, he let his subconscious enter his conscious in the same way that he did for flying. As he stood with the staff pointed out away from them, he felt a strange, alien magic coil around his own, the two combining and feeding each other, growing and shifting. It seemed strange, unformed and felt like the direct opposite of his own magic, as if it had twisted itself inside out. The gem pulsed once, briefly and then darkened again. He staggered and immediately felt a slight headache and nausea, but figured it was the strange magic he'd just experienced.

"Oh Darjoon, did you see that? I can't believe you got a result from it so soon, did you see it glow? That's amazing", Sirroya exclaimed excitedly. Darjoon rubbed his head and frowned at her.

"Well, so much for that! I don't know why you're so happy. A small glow isn't much use to us, is it? It was really strange. The magic it created felt familiar to me but at the same time quite odd. It was like looking into a mirror, where everything looks the same but isn't really because the image is reversed, a sort of distorted reflection. Well, something like that. It's, well, it's a bit hard to explain", he put down the staff, sat and then glared into the fire with his face in his hands.

"Don't worry, Darjoon, it's still progress. Relax, at least you got some sort of response. You should keep trying and don't give up. Your mother gave it to you for a reason", Sirroya yawned and stretched, "Well, I'm tired now so I think I'm off to dreamland. Good night, Darjoon, sweet dreams."

He nodded to Sirroya as she bedded down for the night, while he continued to sit and stare into the flames, mulling over the strange magic he'd experienced. After a while he got up and rolled out the sleeping mat Y'sarryn had provided. Lying back and wrapping his cloak around him as he felt the stirrings of a faint, cool breeze, he slowly fell asleep listening to the crackling of the fire.

Out in the night, just beyond the glowing flames, twin amber, glowing eyes watched him, their black pupils dilated in the darkness. Darjoon watched as the wolf approached him through the cool mist, the grey pelt thick and shaggy but also well-kept, the moisture beading and trickling down it's rough length. It rose up from all fours as it came and walked easily and nimbly on rear paws with an almost feline grace, the body swaying delicately from side to side. The thick, furry tail was balanced behind, sweeping just above the forest floor and the wolf's ears were pricked forward, the muzzle withdrawn from the teeth, not snarling but in a smile of greeting. The nostrils wrinkled and the muzzle quivered as it drank in his scent. Stopping in front of him, it stood and looked at him, and then he heard it speak, even though the massive jaws didn't move.

"Greetings old friend. It has been many moons since you were among us. We have waited, great wise one, waited with baited breath for your return and for the restoration of our people. But come, let us first hunt together as we once did. Surely you remember, wise one? To truly know the wolf, you must hunt with the wolf, you must be the wolf. We are the hunters and all the rest are prey. Aaaooooooooo!", the wolf howl split the night air.

It turned smoothly and began to run at incredible speed on all four paws. Darjoon accelerated and drew alongside without missing a beat, running next to the wolf in an easy motion. The snowy trees flashed past in a blur and they bounded and leapt over and through the deep snow drifts. As he jumped over a melted pool of water he looked down, seeing in the rippled surface a tall, distinguished, handsome man in an ornate, deep purple robe with glittering yellow threads. Overlaid on this was a transparent image of a large, black shaggy wolf. It was as if he was dreaming, but actually dreaming someone else's dream. He felt like a thief, as if he was stealing a memory.

Darjoon woke stiff and sore in the morning despite the soft sleeping mat Y'sarryn had provided. He actually felt as if he had been running all night, and yawned and stretched, opening his mouth wide and hearing his bones and joints crack and pop.

"My, what big teeth you have, great mage. Could you at least put your hand up in front of your mouth? I was wondering if you were ever going to wake up. You didn't spend all night practising with that staff, did you? Don't make a habit of doing that, silly apprentice. Young men need all the sleep they can get. Here, I've made us some porridge for breakfast, and I've brewed coffee. That should help get your morning started."

He smiled at Sirroya as she continued chatting away while finishing her preparations. Trust her to wake up every morning in a good mood. He was actually very glad she'd come along, otherwise it would have been a horribly lonely road, not to mention she'd saved his life already. After breakfast, Darjoon tested Sirroya's magic skills, asking her to show him what she could do. She drew out a pack of cards and performed some minor tricks, including some very good sleight of hand tricks that couldn't be done without real magic. Disgusted, Darjoon lectured her on the uses of magic, especially on the point that cheap card tricks were a waste of talent and ability. She frowned at him and her forehead crinkled.

"But, Darjoon, I've seen many bards perform these. In fact that same bard I told you about showed me these. I thought I could at least earn a living from it?", she protested.

Darjoon shook his head vehemently, "No, Sirroya. Magic is not meant for cheap illusions, it is used for defence first and offence only when there is no other option. Yes, of course, when you're young and learning, you might do silly things with it, but magic is not silly, it's serious. As you get older and use it more, you begin to realise that this is not some trivial pursuit, that there is a cost to using magic that affects your body and your mind. You should ration it, not abuse it."

She looked at him, seeing his serious expression and smiled inside. "If you only knew", she thought to herself. They continued this routine of walking, hunting, and training as they made their way through the forest in the days that followed, making sure they skirted around Roikba so as to avoid any accidental meeting with the traitorous Lord Gromtag or his cronies. During their training sessions, Darjoon threw in a few tips on augmenting some of the moves with magic, and once all the chores of the day were done they would sit around the fire. As was his habit lately, he sat still as stone, staring into the fire and trying to make sense of everything he had learnt. One evening, as he looked into the fire, he blinked, and then suddenly found himself back in the college. He was in the common room, looking at the fire in the hearth. The familiar smells of old books, young children and pipe tobacco from the duty teacher mingled in his nose, causing him to sneeze, as he used to do so often. He felt the rough fabric of his simple college robe, and putting his hand in his pocket, felt the half-eaten apple he'd left there for later. He looked down at the book on his lap and saw it was his second year work on shield spells. His fingers still had the ink from the morning's class work. He lifted his head and his eyes caught the eyes of the large, good-looking boy at the end of the hall. The boy smirked at him, pulling his finger across his throat under his chin in that time-worn gesture meaning he was going to get his weekly beating before bed tonight. He quickly looked back at the fire, hoping they'd get bored and go away. He blinked again and suddenly he was back in the forest, feeling disoriented at the change and looking around. Sirroya was laughing and saying something to him.

"What? What did you say?", he exclaimed.

"You see Darjoon, illusion can be used for anything, not just cheap tricks. So where's your staff gone now?", she teased him.

He grabbed at the rock next to him where he'd leant the staff only minutes ago. It was gone, there was nothing there. Sirroya took it out from behind her where she'd been hiding it.

"I could have killed you just as easily and you wouldn't have known anything about it. I might even have led you through the forest without your knowing it", she said, handing him the staff.

He stared at her in recognition. She'd given him that memory, had created that dream, that illusion. That was impressive! She had definite talent in that area.

He grinned up at her, "Okay, okay, you got me. Illusion is definitely a strength of yours and you've proven that, but what I said still stands. You can't just use it for trivial purposes and you should definitely not use it to make money. There is a price we pay for magic, and that's what I'm trying to teach you. To balance that price against the power of your magic, otherwise you may even burn yourself out. In fact, you could end up killing yourself if you're not careful", Darjoon looked at Sirroya who swayed, yawned and sat down.

"Look at you now! See how tired you are just from creating that illusion spell? Come, I think it's time we went to sleep. We can continue the lessons another night."

In this fashion they travelled through the forest with the weather clear and the sky cloud-free. Not that it mattered to them as they were trudging under great trees anyway. The ever-present gloom of the forest was interspersed with occasional bright blinding rays of sunshine from above. One day, they crested a slight rise and broke out into an open clearing, one of a few that they'd come across. As they burst into the sunshine, Sirroya turned her head facing back along the trail, averting her eyes from the brightness before they were blinded. As she did so, she saw the glint of something in the distance along the straight trail behind them, lit by one of the shafts of sunlight that rayed down into the forest gloom. It was there just for a moment and then disappeared, but she knew intuitively that someone was following them.

"Uh, Darjoon? Don't make it obvious by looking back, but I think we're being followed. I can't say for sure, but I saw something way back on the trail, through that straight section we just came through. There was a spark of sunshine glinting off something metal. I'm not sure what exactly but it definitely didn't look natural. Do you think our dear Lord Gromtag or your precious raven-born have set someone on our trail? If that's a Spidralite assassin then we're going to be in big, big trouble!", she frowned and looked back again.

"Are you sure, Sirroya? How would anyone know that we're headed this way? I did wonder if someone would turn up at the free-folk village looking for us, but no-one other than Y'sarryn knows where we're going. Okay, okay, don't glare at me, I believe you. Let's pick up the pace and then we'll hide out on the side of the trail. We'll see if we can catch them out that way."

"Right, we can do that. But listen, I'm telling you if that's an assassin then they'll know we're there anyway. You can't hide from them, not even using magic, which just so you know, they can sense anyway. We'll need to be on our toes."

Darjoon smiled. He knew that his shield spell was very powerful and unless the assassin was equally as powerful magically, they wouldn't have a clue they were there.

Spidral assassins often used magic as part of their arsenal, but they weren't true mages.

"Well, let's take that chance. I think it'll work, but we won't know unless we try. We can't just keep walking and hope they don't catch us. They'll never lose our trail, especially not here in the forest.

The two of them strode briskly across the clearing and plunged back into the cool dark of the forest beyond. Some while later Darjoon spotted a bush off to the side between two massive trees. Grabbing Sirroya, he pushed his way into the natural shelter and cast a shield spell around them. They waited close together in the gloominess of the forest, listening to the nearby rustle of insects, and slightly further afield the noises of small creatures moving around on the forest floor. In the trees they heard birds fluttering, chirping, whistling and squawking. Further away, a tribe of monkeys called out to each other as they busied themselves with their daily foraging. Suddenly the birds were silent apart from a few angry squawks back up the trail. Darjoon and Sirroya tensed, waiting for any tell-tale jingle or thudding footfall but there was nothing, not a single sound now. The silence of the forest began to press in on them and now not even the monkeys in the distance were making a noise any more. Frowning, Darjoon dropped the shield and crept forward out of the bush with Sirroya tugging on the back of his cloak.

As he angrily turned around and swung his head to hiss at her to let him go, a blade whistled through the space his neck had just vacated. Without thinking, Darjoon tucked forward and rolled to the side, coming up with his back against one of the large trees. He twitched rapidly to the left as a slender, short blade embedded itself in the tree where his heart should have been. Wrenching the blade free and with a momentary recognition of perfect balance and weight, he flung it with speed back the way it came. At the same time he flung out a finding spell for the dagger to follow. Gasping with surprise, he twitched to the right just in time to avoid the same blade as it simply reversed course and flew back at him, again embedding itself in the tree. Before he could move, he felt the bite of cold steel on his throat and cursed. He'd let the attacker slip behind him without even seeing him. At college they'd been told that if a Spidralite assassin came for you, you should make sure that you'd paid all your debts, and that you were ready to enter Khamoos and take the long journey on the back of the Great Raven to the River of Life. Few people, if any, survived a contract the assassin's had accepted. He prayed that Zukar would make his death swift and sweet and that she would grant Sirroya extra life in place of his death. As he felt the blade begin to bite deeper, he tried to see if he could see her anywhere, hoping she had stayed safely hidden.

Sirroya had watched in horror as the blade first missed Darjoon and then again as it reversed back at him. Before she could react to either event, she saw a flicker of movement behind the tree and watched the arm and blade reach around from behind. She knew she didn't have long before Darjoon would be spraying out his life-blood on the forest floor. She couldn't know if they wanted him dead or alive. Chanting quietly, she threw out an illusion spell, hoping to trap the assassin in the belief that he was back in Roikba. She prayed he came from that town or at least knew it well. In the illusion she created, she imagined him standing in the pub, reaching down with his left hand to pick up his pint of ale. She stared in wonder as she watched the assassin's hand holding the dagger to Darjoon's throat slowly lower and reach down. Darjoon didn't hesitate, he simply stepped away from the tree, spun around smoothly and kicked straight up off the ground, launching the assassin up in the air to crash down and lie inert on the forest floor. Sirroya scrambled out from under the bush and ran over to him.

"Quickly, Darjoon, kill him and let's get moving", she

said, looking around in obvious fear.

"We cannot kill him. Leave him and let's go!", Darjoon grabbed her arm, but she resisted, pulling her arm away violently.

"What! What do you mean you can't kill him? You're raven-born aren't you? You lot kill just for pleasure!", she was angry now, standing with her hands on her hips.

"We do, Sirroya, but only in honourable combat", he calmly replied, "This man is now incapacitated and no longer in any condition to fight us, so we will not kill him in cold blood, even though that is what he wanted to do to us. It is our way!"

Darjoon reached down and quickly frisked the assassin, removing what weapons he could find, of which there were many. He avoided those he felt were booby-trapped, knowing this was not an uncommon trick of the Spidralites. Sirroya stared at him in consternation then rolled her eyes.

"I give up, I really do! Alright let's move quickly now. There'll be others not far behind", she kept looking around them nervously.

As they collected their packs and ran down the trail, Darjoon thought on what she'd said, "What makes you think there will be others? And why did you give in so easily, I expected you to argue like you always do?"

"Because!", Sirroya puffed alongside him, "Don't you know that there are always two Spidralite assassins. One to kill, and the other just in case."

"In case of what, Sirroya? I thought the assassins from Spidral never missed their targets?", Darjoon looked perplexed.

"Oh yes? Like the one back there that just did? No, Darjoon, they do occasionally miss their targets, after all, they're only human. Just that when they do, they don't come back to talk about it. There's always a second assassin that follows the first to make sure of that, and to finish the job. There are very few people who can survive the attentions of two Spidralite assassins, and most will assume that if they killed one then it's over, just like you did. Which makes the second assassin's job that much easier because the target isn't prepared. Then of course, if neither of the two report back in due time, another two will be sent out just like the first. So an individual assassin might miss, but a Spidralite contract is always honoured and completed. That's how they keep the legend alive."

Throughout that day and into the night they hurried along the forest trail, entering the mouth of a deep, dark valley. Darjoon conjured two globe lights that hovered above each of their heads to light the way, despite Sirroya's protests. He assured her that falling down the side of the path, or stumbling over a root and breaking a leg, or blundering into one of the deadly night-time creatures that patrolled the forest was a surer fate than the assassin catching them. They pushed on relentlessly into the dark valley. Towards the bottom end, the trail brought them into some dark, dank caves, the walls dripping with water and the cavern roofs teeming with bats. Way into the next morning they wearily stumbled through the cave system, stopping only for brief rests and the occasional sip of water. The trail through the caves was used regularly and so was marked in some places, probably by occasional travelling assassins and those traders that were brave enough to enter Spidral and the Great Forest. Exhausted beyond belief, Darjoon drove them on relentlessly, knowing the assassin couldn't be too far behind.

8 THE HEAT OF THE DAY

By midday of the next day they broke out of the cave system into the full glare of the sun. As they stood blinking in the strong light and feeling the warmth on their faces, they found themselves standing on a crumbling ledge looking out over the vast Plains of Breath. These were flat, green-blue grasslands that extended into the hazy horizon, which was itself obscured by a slight mist. The trail off the ledge made its way down the side of a steep incline and below that were some old, frayed rope ladders supposedly to help on the treacherous bits. Darjoon and Sirroya slid, scrambled and clambered down the dusty path, grimacing at the creaking noises the ropes made on the steep descents until they finally arrived on the plain feeling sore, tired and hungry. After the cool of the forest the blazing sun beat down on them like a hammer on an anvil in a heated forge. They rapidly shed their coats and stripped down to their tunics. The air was still and breathless and at first the only life they could see were some large birds that circled in the distance, lazily riding the hot air in loose spirals. Darjoon looked at the angle of the sun and the shadows and taking his bearings began walking to the north with Sirroya striding jauntily next to him in her thin tunic. He marvelled at how lithe and fit she was and how quickly she recovered from any ordeal she went through, almost as if she'd seen it all before. After a while, Sirroya looked over their shoulder and said to him in a loud stage whisper, "I don't think we're being followed, you can probably slow down a bit", then laughed out loud.

He shook his head then walked onto a rise where there was a patch of soft, green grass and dropped his pack, slumping to the ground. Exhausted after the hectic pace, Darjoon nibbled some chranth and took a swig of water, already starting to feel better.

Seeing a few strange looking deer further down the hill from where they reclined, he pointed them out to Sirroya, "I think we'd probably best avoid those. Who knows what might be hunting them nearby?"

Sirroya however, seemed pleased to see the creatures. Jumping up, she quietly beckoned him to follow her while she moved slowly and confidently towards the deer. Darjoon carefully slid out his dagger, thinking that perhaps she was going to do some hunting. Once she spotted what he was doing she hissed at him, gesturing for him to return the knife to his sheath and to keep quiet. Frowning at her, he did so reluctantly but stayed quiet as she requested and tried to crouch lower in the short grass. They inched closer to the animals and Darjoon could see they were in fact roykili, large barrel-chested, six-legged creatures with four short rounded horns on their wide heads. He'd read in the illegal books that he'd smuggled from the college library that they could be harnessed and ridden, although as the Plains were so hostile it wasn't thought that anyone living had done it for generations.

Sirroya stopped and began to chant quietly under her breath, using the "nudge" magic that he'd taught her. After a little while, two of the roykili left the herd and moved towards them. Darjoon watched in fascination as the creatures slowly drew near, then placidly lay down at her feet. He shook his head in wonder. Once again she'd shown how quickly she absorbed what he taught her. Sirroya vaulted nimbly onto one of the creatures which then stood up and under her guidance dashed off across the plain. After a few canters back and forth, she came riding over to Darjoon and slid easily off the roykili's back and onto the ground, smiling and breathless, her cheeks flushed with delight.

"Well, they'll do, but we definitely need to have harnesses. I might be just about able to control them, but there's no way that you will, definitely not without reins. That is unless the raven-born have suddenly acquired a love of riding animals that I hadn't heard of?", she bared her teeth at him in a mock smile. He shook his head and took a step back as the animal tried to nuzzle his shoulder.

"Uh, no, we definitely have not, thank you very much. Have you seen that thing's teeth? Think of the bite it could give you. And how massive are these hooves? How can you be sure the silly thing won't stand on my feet? I'm really not sure about this, Sirroya, maybe I should fly while you ride? Raven-born were never meant to be in the saddle, we were born to be up in the sky. Hey, let go of that", Darjoon grumbled as he tried to pull his cloak out from between the roykili's teeth.

"Oh right, and who was giving me the lecture about not wasting magical energy? No, if you fly then the assassin that I'm sure is still hot on our trail will be able to see you up in the sky and follow you easily. Then, when they finally catch up to us, you won't have enough energy to resist them. Be sensible, Darjoon! Lets travel with the herd across the Plains so they can mask our tracks. Once we're across then we can leave them and head into the desert. Come on Darjoon, we better hurry if we want to beat the Dragon's Breath. I don't want to be caught out here in the open.", she grabbed him and led him back to the hill, still protesting. The two roykili meekly followed after them.

"Oh, shush Darjoon. You'll be fine. Can you make us

some harnesses for these big boys? You did say you repaired your tent using magic, didn't you? Don't look so worried, Darjoon, I'll give you a mental picture of what's needed through my illusion magic. Think of it as a crash course in how to ride a roykili. Well, don't just stand there staring at me, let's go make some harnesses", she tossed her hair and put her hands on her hips, looking across the roykili at him. He snorted. She was a bit much sometimes. It was easy to forget how young she was when she acted so bossy.

"If I must but don't think I'm going to make saddles, not unless you want to kill one of these things for all the leather we'd need. Hey, that's actually not a bad idea. Okay, okay, relax, Sirroya, I'm just teasing you", Darjoon grinned as she looked at him wide-eyed, then he sighed, "You win, again. I suppose we'll just have to ride bareback, not that it'll make much difference to me as I don't know how to ride anyway".

While Sirroya got to know their new friends, Darjoon went looking for ore-bearing rocks and the right grass for ropes. At worst, he had a few spare ropes left in his pack from when he had repaired the tent.

A few hours later and Darjoon sat nervously on top of a roykili, his thighs tightly clenched as he watched the big head nervously. Currently it was lazily flicking its ears back and forth to drive off a few annoying flies. Darjoon swatted at them himself, accidentally catching the ear of the beast, who promptly turned its head and rolled an eye at him. He snapped the reins tight, well aware from Sirroya's illusion training that animals like this could bite your kneecaps if they got really annoyed and managed to turn their heads all the way round. He got a huff in return from the beast and an irritable shake of the head. He was definitely not making a good first impression as a rider. Through his legs he felt an excited quiver that ran through the massive torso and simultaneously he sneezed as a cloud of dust enveloped him.

"Woohoo, let's go big boy!", Sirroya was loving the freedom and had already raced out in front of him, heading towards the herd. Watching and waiting to see the herd scatter, Darjoon was amazed to see it docilely turn and follow Sirroya, who had slowed down once she'd caught them.

"Come on Darjoon!", she yelled back at him, "Hurry and catch up, don't keep us all waiting for you."

The next minute Sirroya was practically falling off her roykili from laughing so hard. Darjoon bounced up and down on his poor beast who looked none too happy at this ungainly lump of weight it had to carry. She recovered herself and took in deep breaths, yelling at him again, "Try and feel it under you, Darjoon. Don't fight it, just let it take you where you want to go. Be one with the animal. You'll feel yourself connect and then it becomes an easy motion for both of you."

Easy motion indeed! It reminded Darjoon of how his grandfather used to toss around the bags of potatoes when he was mad. Having grown up on a farm in Lower Srinth as a youngster, his grandfather had been determined to have his own version in the raven-born lands the Empire called Upper Srinth. This was despite the other raven-born who were openly derogatory of his weak attempts at farming. The wet, miserable highlands they lived on were not good for most crops although potatoes seemed to do well. Not that anyone really liked the earthy taste, but it made his grandfather happy to grow something. Occasionally when grandpa was mad, he would pretend to be stacking the bags of potatoes, when in reality he was flinging them around all over the place. Darjoon believed he now understood what it was like to be one of those bags. His legs were already quivering from the strain of gripping the massive body under him and he could feel new bruises beginning to form in uncomfortable places as he bounced wildly up and down.

As they cantered across the grass of the Plains, he

slowly began to relax, unconsciously falling into the steady rhythm of the beast under him. His mind drifted back to his grandfather and his farm and he spent some time reminiscing, even going so far as to share his memories with Sirroya. She was an avid listener and kept asking him keen questions about his grandparents and the extended family. It made him realise how little he'd actually been told about them or their background.

That evening, as they continued with the combat and magic training, he realised how stiff and sore he was from being on the beast all day. Despite Sirroya's assurances that it would get better if he left it alone, he judiciously used some magic to ease most of the pain. Camping out under the large, beautiful, starlit sky was a new experience after the time spent in the Great Forest of Spidral or the Darken Hills. Here there were no caves or crevices, no bushes or trees to block the sky, just endless grass on either side of them and the great, open, starry sky overhead. It was warm with a light breeze blowing gently across the plains, bringing the smell of earth and a faint hint of rain. Climbing into the tent he drifted off into a deep, deep sleep, dreaming about farming, his grandfather and the stupidity of bront's.

In the morning Darjoon crawled out of the tent into brilliant sunlight. The wind had picked up overnight and although the morning air felt crisp, he could sense it was going to be another hot day. Sirroya was standing staring fixedly towards the north horizon. He was about to ask her what she was looking at when she spoke without turning her head.

"Well, that's not good. See that red haze just above the horizon there? And then above that, can you see what appear to be some large, white clouds? I think we've miscalculated slightly, Darjoon. That's a sign that the Dragon Breath is about to blow across the Plains. And can you see the herd?", she turned and pointed at the animals milling around beside them.

"They're looking very restless. I'm barely controlling them through the leaders for now, but that's hard work because they just want to run and keep running. I think we'll have to hop up and eat breakfast on the run today. I'm going to do what Y'sarryn recommended and give them their heads, let's see where they take us. This herd still has some really old mares in it, and they'll have seen a few Dragon Breaths in their time and lived to neigh about it", her laughter filled the morning air, belying the seriousness of her tone.

Now that she had pointed it out, Darjoon could see the red-orange mist on the horizon and the billowing white clouds that roiled above it. He winced at the thought of another day on the beast, especially as they'd be running all day.

"Oh well big man, nothing for it but grit your teeth and hang on for dear life", he told himself as he climbed up and took the reins.

Sirroya let out a yell and took off, dust trailing behind her, Darjoon found himself cantering in the middle of the herd, his beast happy to be with others of its own kind. After an initial discomfort where he bobbed up and down at the same time the creature went down and up, he soon rediscovered the rhythm of the day before and lowered his head, urging the big beast up towards the front where Sirroya cantered easily.

They'd been running all that morning, Sirroya in the lead next to what must have been the herd leaders with himself slightly back on the left flank when he noticed her gesturing towards him. Getting used to the animal now, he spoke to it briefly and encouraged it to head over to her. Once alongside he fell into the the rhythm again. She looked at him and winked audaciously.

"Well, you've become quite the rider, young raven-born. Who said you can't teach a mighty mage new tricks, eh? Actually, Darjoon, I've been holding the leaders back for a while now but I think we're going to have to pick up our pace. Wherever they're going is still somewhere ahead of us, and they're getting even more skittish. I don't know what you've been told about the Dragon Breath, if anything? Obviously it has nothing to do with dragons. It's a large volcano to the far north of the Plains, somewhere in or near the Desert of Thoth. Fairly regularly, the volcano blows off steam and when it does, a current of hot air sweeps through the Plains, in turn becoming super-heated as it's picked up by strong winds from the desert. It then blows down the length of the Plains which themselves form a natural funnel to speed it up, compress it and increase the heat even further. When that is combined with the regular southerly winds that usually blow at this time of year it gets even worse. Y'sarryn wasn't joking when he said it could just about melt the skin off our bodies. Most animals that live out here, especially the reptiles, have developed special abilities in order to survive. In fact...", the roykili she was riding tossed its head, snorted and pranced sideways.

"Whoa, big boy, easy now. Let's just stop here and have a quick break. I need to check something."

Sirroya slowed and stopped the leaders that in turn caused the entire herd to stop. The big animals took the opportunity to catch their breath and graze but snorted and tossed their manes. She vaulted off her mount and walked over to some scrubby plants growing near a solitary rock. Bending down, she sniffed the plant and then looked closely at it while rubbing the leaves. Darjoon dismounted gingerly, grimacing and then waddled over to her, feeling the effect of the hard riding they'd been doing all morning.

"See here, Darjoon? That sticky white substance on the leaves as I rub them? That's a natural defence mechanism of these plants. Being inflammable, it will coat and protect them for the duration of the Breath. It means the desert is getting ready for it soon. I wish we had something like that, although I'm not sure it would help."

"Why not?", Darjoon asked.

"Because our skin would survive, but our lungs wouldn't. This plant has water stored in large bulbous roots underground and doesn't need to breath for a few days. It'll probably fade in colour, but it'll survive. We, however, do need to breath and when you breath in super-heated air you'll just cook your lungs. It'll be like drowning, only you're not underwater. We better get moving if we're going to let those animals help us find shelter. Come on, let's go!"

As they turned, Darjoon's and then Sirroya's animals began to run, followed by other members of the herd.

"Darjoon! Quickly grab him before... Nooooo! Stop, come back you silly beasts"

They watched the rapidly disappearing dust cloud as the entire herd ran off away from them across the plains. Sirroya stared in despair, her brow furrowed in concentration.

"It's no use, I can't get them to come back. It looks like we overstayed our welcome with the herd. I don't blame them for running off as it's already feeling a bit warmer. Well, that's us done for, there's no way we'll survive out here with no protection. Look at that horizon, Darjoon, see how red it's become and how high and close those clouds are now? I think the Breath might already be on its way towards us."

Darjoon stared around at the bleak grasslands that stretched away into the distance on all sides. Desperate, he looked for large rocks or anything that might provide some form of shelter. In despair, he watched a small furry creature hopping madly through the grass right past them. It didn't even seem to notice them, or if it did it didn't care. Of course! Was he stupid? He calmed himself, then sent out his senses, carefully listening with his magic for any large collection of animals. Immediately, he sensed a large gathering to the north-west. Grabbing Sirroya, he began to run in the direction he saw the small animal was heading in.

"We've got to follow that little creature, Sirroya. It knows where it's going and I sensed a gathering of animals somewhere ahead of us in this direction. They must know something we don't."

"Wait, what? There's nothing that way! It's just the same everywhere else, grass and more grass. Are you sure, Darjoon? I mean the roykili seemed to go the other way, did you see? Okay, okay, stop pulling. I'll trust you, look I'm right behind you. I, hey, aaaaaaahhh..."

Darjoon had stopped suddenly, exploring a small opening into which the animal had hopped. Sirroya, not realising he had stopped and busy looking in vain for the herd that had disappeared by now, barged into him from behind. The ground suddenly gave way under their feet and they both plunged down an incline in a shower of dirt, grass and small stones, sliding and tumbling until they fetched up on a hard, rocky surface. Darjoon lay flat on his back, gingerly feeling his temple, then looked at the blood on his hands. That explained the dizziness. He slowly sat up, feeling a throbbing begin behind his temple. Sirroya was sitting up and staring around them in awe as the dust slowly settled.

"Darjoon, would you look at this, it is enormous! I think we solved our problem of surviving the Breath. I don't see it coming all the way down here, do you? This is just incredible. Where is all that light coming from? Oh gods help us, would you look at that? I've never seen anything like it before, this is incredible!"

Darjoon grimaced in pain and frustration. All his training on the art of silence was obviously lost on Sirroya. She was jerking her head around like a manic puppet and babbling away at the top of her voice. As he looked around, he had to admit that it was very impressive. They were in an enormous underground cavern, with a high ceiling that stretched up into darkness. The walls of the grotto were covered with an algae or fungus that gave off an eerie blue glow, reminiscent of that from a full Tregora moon. Not far from where they had landed was the large sandy beach of a massive lake that stretched off into the gloom as far as he could see. What Sirroya had just spotted were some subterranean grasses among which were lying an odd assortment of creatures. The large truktari of the plains were there, light-brown and faster even than the roykili, especially over short distances. They practically lay on top of small furry creatures that looked like the one they'd followed in here. There was no attacking, no ripping and rending of small bodies that he'd have expected. Instead they all lay placidly beside each other, even hopping or walking over their neighbours. He got up and walked towards them, while Sirroya hissed at him and plucked at his sleeve, trying to pull him back.

"What are you doing? You don't know what they'll do to you? You're not small and furry are you, so be careful."

He looked at her and laughed, despite himself. She'd been so loud just now and yet here she was whispering at him. He shook his head and continued walking down towards the creatures. She reluctantly followed him as he walked between them, most of whom calmly moved out of their way. There was no timidity, just calm acceptance. Darjoon walked down to the water, feeling thirsty after all their riding of that day and wanting to wash his head. He mopped at the gash on his head, then took a long, cool drink. The water was refreshing, with a slight tang to it, not unpleasant, just different. He yawned widely and laid out his cloak on a soft patch of grass between two animals, who both made room for him while Sirroya satisfied her thirst and filled up their water-skins.

"Well", he yawned again, his jaw cracking, "might as well catch up on some shut-eye. There's nothing happening here and all we have to do is just wait for the Breath to pass."

She yawned too, feeling very sleepy.

"Hey, move over, you little ball of fluff, that grass you're on looks nice and soft", she muttered at one of the small creatures.

"Well, if I must, but I was quite fond of that spot, you know. Still, I can see how you're bigger than I am, so I'll just take this one next to you. Mind if I cuddle up? It gets a bit cool down here by the water and you feel warm", the creature moved over and then snuggled up to Sirroya as she lay down.

"S'fine by me, whatever. Just need to close my eyes a bit", Sirroya mumbled back at it.

Darjoon stared in fascination as Sirroya continued her conversation with the little creature, who was quite happily telling her its life story in between yawns. Not a very long one from the sound of it. He was just about to ask the animal what it meant by saying to her that she'd feel better in the morning, when it dawned on him that he could hear other conversations too. He listened in fascination as two of the truktari discussed their respective litters, and how one of them had lost two small one's the year before. Something didn't seem right here. His head felt fuzzy, and he was struggling to focus his eyes. Was it the blow he'd taken earlier? He yawned again, watching as a new arrival looked around warily at everyone and lapped up water from the lake. After a little while it blinked its eyes blearily, then ambled over to a patch of grass and stretched out between a big truktari and a small creature, snuggling in between them.

Darjoon sat bolt upright, now fighting the lethargy he felt. Chanting under his breath, he extracted the toxins out of his body, watching in sick fascination as a sticky blue jelly dripped off his fingertips onto the grass. Sirroya had stopped nattering with the little animal and was snoring gently. He watched her, loathe to disturb her peaceful sleep. Looking around, he marvelled how these animals had discovered this lake and the effects it had. By some strange co-incidence it allowed them all to survive the dreaded Breath without killing one another. He really began to understand Y'sarryn, who had painstakingly shown him not just the village where the free-folk lived, but how everyone there lived in harmony with nature. They used what was available without abusing the precious cycle of life that went on continually all around them. In fact, they became part of that cycle, not fighting it, but embracing it. He shook his head as if to clear the last vestiges of toxin from his body, then walked over to Sirroya and shook her shoulder.

"Come on sleepy-head, wake up. Hey, Sirroya, can you hear me? Good. The water we've been drinking has some drug in it that makes everyone tired. It seems to calm all these animals down, allowing them to co-exist without any killing. I don't want to lose control though, so do you want to carry on sleeping or shall I get it out of you? ", he laughed at her frantic attempts to scrape it off her tongue, "Okay, okay, calm down, it's not like you've been poisoned, it's just a mild hallucinogenic and won't do us any lasting harm. You'll be fine, just sit still and stop fidgeting and I'll have it out of you in no time!"

Darjoon carefully drew the poison out of her as he had done his own body, and Sirroya dry-heaved as she saw the blue jelly drip down her fingers and onto the grass. She rustled around in her pack and drew out a small glass vial which she used to collect some of it. Darjoon looked at her quizzically.

"Disgusting, I know, but we might have a use for this at some point, you never know. I can't believe we were poisoned by a lake. I did wonder how I was hearing that little guy speak to me, it didn't seem natural but I was so relaxed it didn't matter. We should get out of here now", she looked at the glowing water and shivered.

"No, no, relax. I think the effects will last quite a while. My magic tells me this is pretty potent, and anyway, they'll keep drinking from the lake when they wake up, won't they. If we see the effects wearing off on the animals, then we'll head out, but don't forget that the Breath is still out there. Hand me that water-skin and I'll remove the toxin from it and we can get fresh water that way."

Settling down again, Darjoon dozed off, relaxed and sleepy despite not having the toxin in his blood stream. Sirroya settled down next to him, watching the animals carefully and occasionally looking out over the lake. The illumination provided by the algae was unvarying, giving no indication of day or night. The entrance they'd fallen through was high up and partly obscured, so she couldn't determine the time of day from that either. She wondered how they would know when to leave, guessing that somehow the animals would guide them again, as they'd led them here. Yawning, she snuggled closer to Darjoon who grunted and rolled over, muttering in his sleep. She shook her head slightly, pursing her lips in recognition of how important this young man was, and how little he knew of his true significance. Falling asleep, she dreamt about flights of Dremrel that swooped overhead, hundreds of them filling the sky with their red, glowing eyes, sinister black wings and sharp, foul teeth. She could smell them, a warm, sulphurous breath that was filled with decay and she shivered in her sleep as they grabbed hold of her and shook her.

Waking up, she felt someone shaking her and looked up at Darjoon, whose eyes were fixed on something across the lake. She sat up and noticed all the animals had their heads lifted, looking in the same direction as Darjoon. She looked out across the lake and stared at the steam coiling on the far side. It seemed to be alive, growing in size every second. At the edge of the lake, large fish were starting to slither out the water, standing up on four short legs that they had grown in place of fins. Walking out of the water, they began to burrow into the mud along the shoreline.

Darjoon stood up and wandered down to the water. Putting his hand in, he turned to Sirroya, "This is so warm, you could bathe in here. Smells funny though. What do you think is happening?"

Sirroya wandered down to the shore, "I think the

Breath is out there heating the river. It might even be boiling it, depending on the temperature. That would explain the steam on the far side, it's probably where the water flows into the lake from above ground. What's that there?"

Further down the beach was a large lizard in the shallows, catching some of the fish as they emerged from the water. Further in the lake, some dark shadows showed there were a few more of the scaly creatures.

"Well, they seem to like it in there. No surprise as they're cold-blooded. Here, that gives me an idea. Help me catch one of these fish, will you. Well, don't just stand there, tell me if you think they're edible? You are a master mage, aren't you? I would hope you could tell the difference between what's edible and what's not?"

Darjoon blushed, remembering his brush with death from eating the blue poison berries in the Darken Hills.

"Of course I can, and yes, they are edible. I just need to extract the toxin like I did with the water. Here, let me help you catch some more."

They caught a few fish and then moved further back in the cave, away from the other animals just in case. After grilling the fish over a small fire, they ate their meal and drank the water that Darjoon had cleansed, then settled down to watch the lake below. More and more fish were leaving the water now and burrowing into the mud. Apart from a few that went down to get water, the animals were just lying around and not moving. The blue algae seemed to be glowing a lot brighter than before, glinting off the scaly hides of the reptiles in the shallows. Even they were starting to climb out of the water as the steam at the far end continued to billow and stretch across the lake, hanging just above the water.

"Sirroya, how is it that you seem to know so much, about almost everything? It's so easy to forget how young you are, because you seem to be so much older and have so much knowledge. You've learnt magic, you know how to ride and you even know how the Spidral assassins operate. Are you sure you've not been to Spidral before? Some of the people, well, it almost seemed as if they recognised you", Darjoon looked over at her quizzically.

"Well, it's not that hard to understand, if you just listened to what I told you, oh great and mighty mage. As I said before, my mother gave me a lot of books to read, and I grew up on a farm, so of course I can ride and through reading I know what roykili are. Any self-respecting Empire youngster knows how to ride, by the way, not like you silly raven-born who are so scared of their own shadows. But of course, you're not part of the Empire, are you, so what would you know? Maybe if you lot joined us instead of fighting all the time you'd know better. Now I'm tired after you woke me from my beauty sleep so I think we should both just get some shut-eye and then wait to see when this lake cools down. That and the animals starting to leave should give us fair warning", she raised her hand as he opened his mouth, "No, Darjoon, no more questions. I'm really tired."

He watched her turn over and listened as her breathing slowed and she began to snore lightly again. He couldn't put his finger on it and not for the first time just wished she wasn't so evasive. It's true that everything she said made sense. The Empire often had explorers who documented what they found, so it was quite feasible that she'd read everything in a book. It was just that she did everything with such easy grace as if she'd done it all before, not like someone new to it. Sometimes in their combat training she'd performed some moves that took him by surprise, because it was nothing he'd ever taught her. She said she'd learnt that from the young men and her brothers in the tavern near where she lived, part of the skill of just surviving, but he couldn't be sure. He was still wondering about it when he drifted off to sleep.

They spent a few days in the cave, eating fish and drinking water and watching the lake, chatting about what they'd both read and Sirroya gave him more information about the Empire. He realised again how little the raven-born were taught about the world outside their borders, how ignorant they'd become. The steam had eventually covered the entire lake and then slowly started receding. They also noticed that the blue algae on the walls was fading as if in tandem with the diminished steam. A day later and they realised the animals were getting restless and starting to move together, the cats in pairs and the smaller animals in little groups. The algae was just a dull blue glow now and the steam was all but gone. When Sirroya collected more water, she noticed it was decidedly cooler and some of the fish were emerging from the mud and heading back into the water, evading the lizards that had returned to the shallows to feed. Soon, some of the animals started to drift off towards the side of the cave. Darjoon and Sirroya, along with the smaller animals, waited for the large cats to go and then started to follow. After a scramble up a relatively steep incline, they emerged from under a rocky overhang, blinking in the sunlight of mid-morning. There was a faint, burnt odour in the warm air and they could see the ground was scorched for miles in every direction. Amazingly though, there were already green shoots appearing among the blackened grasses. Trudging up an incline and down into a grassy bowl that seemed to have already turned back to green, they were pleasantly surprised to find the same herd of roykili that had been their companions previously. The two they'd been riding still had their harnesses on and Sirroya quickly snared them with her illusion magic. Darjoon groaned out loud at the thought of sitting bare-back again, but at a sharp look from Sirroya he reluctantly clambered onto the animal. They set off at a trot, heading towards the Desert they knew lay to the north-west.

After a few days of travelling, they noticed the roykili herd becoming skittish and edgy. Cresting a rise and trotting down into a shallow bowl, they saw a herd of what looked like domestic turmisra on the ridge in front of them. Turmisra were a highlands animal very similar to the goat and were known to be docile, gentle creatures who would eat anything that was given to them, including the scraps off the table. They were prized for their hardiness, but also their milk and meat. Darjoon recalled how his grandfather had always kept a small herd around the farm because they were so effective at garbage disposal. He'd often played with the young kids in among the herd and they'd accepted him as one of their own. Sirroya leaned over and called to Darjoon, "Fancy a bit of milk? We might be able to find one with young that are still suckling. I could make us some porridge for breakfast again. Wait, what? I can't hear you, hang on, let me ride over. They've got what? Sharp teeth?"

Darjoon was frantically signalling Sirroya as he watched the turmisra look-alikes start to charge down the opposite slope. She hadn't seen the sharp horns and the wicked looking teeth. These were definitely not the docile turmisra he was used to. Despite their obvious size advantage, the herd of roykili wheeled as one and charged back up the slope they'd just ridden down. By this time Sirroya was angling towards Darjoon, her hair flying in the wind as the animals gathered speed. He stared, incredulous, as he saw she was laughing, then he burst out laughing himself.

"Turmisra! Can you believe it, fierce turmisra! With teeth like Dremrel. They looked so cute, too. To think I wanted to milk them", she laughed even harder and almost fell off.

"Well, they're gaining on us, so we better pick up the pace", Darjoon flattened himself against the mane of his roykili, his cloak flying out behind him.

The initial momentum gained by the fake turmisra as they charged downhill faded as the roykili herd crested the rise and gathered themselves, leaping forward on the open plain. One of the animals faltered as it bounded over the ridge, catching a hoof on a rock and sprawling, it crashed down on its side. It was up in an instant, leaping forward but all too late. Darjoon stared back in sick fascination as the leading turmisra jumped on it from behind, their sharp teeth ripping into the animal's rump and dragging it down. It jumped up again but another turmisra grabbed a mouthful of leg, bringing the creature down in a cloud of dust. They could see the others ripping chunks out of it as it lay kicking and squealing. The whole roykili herd redoubled their efforts as if they too had seen the slaughter. Veering west they thundered along in a cloud of dust and ash, slowly pulling away from the evil creatures but not before another animal stumbled and fell. Again it was ripped apart by the handful of turmisra still following after the herd. Soon, the turmisra fell back, slowing then stopping and returning back to the feasting behind them, kicking and fighting among themselves. The herd didn't lessen their pace but at Sirroya's command wheeled around in a big arc, heading north-west in the original direction they'd been travelling. They kept up the pace, then slowed to a canter and finally a trot. There was no sign of the carnivorous turmisra, nor did they see them again in the days that followed as they continued their journey towards the desert.

One morning, just as Darjoon felt his body was finally getting used to the relentless daily ride, they crested a steep rise onto a narrow ridge and saw laid out below them an endless sea of sand. Great cliffs stretched out to the east as far as he could see. They dismounted, feeling the heat wafted up by the warm air from the desert below. Sirroya removed the harness from both roykili, and after a quick hug of the beast she'd been riding, let them rejoin the herd which wheeled and headed off into the plains.

She turned back to the desert and swept out her arm, "Well, this is it, Darjoon! Welcome to the Desert of Thoth. A nastier, more desolate place I don't think you'll find anywhere else. There are some very strange creatures in this desert and not all of them on four legs. It's not just the lizard-men that are slimy and dangerous, let me tell you."

Sirroya glanced over at Darjoon as she caught the appraising look he gave her.

"Well, so I've read in books, anyway", she shrugged and Darjoon turned and looked out over the desert.

"Well, somewhere in that place is a warrior called Turmoos and I have to find him. Why do I feel like it'll be searching for a needle in a haystack? Did your precious books tell you anything about him? No, I didn't think so. I don't even know which tribe he's from. Hey, what's that glittering down there? There, over on the left, can you see it? That trail just down there to the left, the one leading into the desert, are those people and wagons on it?"

"Yes! Yes, they are!", Sirroya clapped her hands, "Well done, Darjoon. That's a trade caravan, I'm sure of it. We might be able to join up with them and travel together. It'll be a lot safer than being out there on our own and they might even know about this warrior you're looking for. Oh, this is lucky. Come on, let's go catch up with them before they get past us."

Sirroya flung herself down the trail leading into the desert with Darjoon in hot pursuit. His legs ached, feeling stiff and sore after all the riding, but they soon warmed to the task. He was sweating freely as they burst out onto the desert trail. The caravan wasn't far away, and two outriders pulled their mounts round and cantered back towards them. Darjoon smiled, in spite of himself. This could work out well. Maybe their luck was still with them. It had been going their way so far, why should it change now.

9 DESERT GUARDS

"So, young people, you want to travel with us?",
Droikin was the overseer the guards had taken them to.
He was big and fat and his robe was open in front,
showing a solid chest above his bloated stomach, all
covered in thick, coarse, curly black hair. A large, round
medallion hung on a gold chain from his neck. It was
inscribed with letters in a language that Darjoon didn't
recognise.

He twirled his curly, black moustache in his left hand,
while his right hand hovered over an ornate hilt in a
curved scabbard. His maroon robe swirled in the breeze,
the colour being a symbol of his rank, at least according to
Sirroya who claimed she'd read it in her books again.

"Do you have coin?", he asked them, "I don't offer my
protection for free you know. This is a profitable
enterprise, not a charitable mission for stray orphans". He
sniffed loudly and looked down at them as he sat on his
large horse.

"Actually, we thought we could help you with that.
Protection, I mean. We're both warriors you know",
Sirroya batted her eyelids at him.

"Ha! Warriors, they say. Haha!", he turned to his

guards who laughed with him, "Really? Just because you've got some swords strapped to your belt, you youngsters think you're warriors, eh? Grufti, see what they're made of?"

He leaned forward and leered at them, "If you can last one round with my guard and he thinks you can fight then you can sign on. But I'm not paying you what I'd pay professional guards. You get water, food and the protection of the caravan. In return, you give your life for this"

Droikin swept his hand around indicating the various wagons and beasts. A tall, hooded figure stepped away from the group of people who had come to see what was going on. He stripped off his sandy robes, revealing a muscular, solid body with numerous white scars criss-crossing his chest and a stern face with a large flat nose below piercing brown-black eyes. Twin curved swords rested on either hip and he took a fighting stance, calmly balanced on his feet with his knees slightly bent and his hands resting lightly above the well-worn hilts. Looking over at Sirroya, he beckoned her towards him with his finger while looking her up and down. Darjoon made to stop her and offer himself, but Droikin waggled his finger at him to stop him and so he stepped back and let Sirroya advance. As she passed him, Darjoon whispered in her ear, "He's big, yes, but you're fast although not experienced. Use your speed against him and tire him out. Stay out of range for as long as you can and don't let him grapple with you."

She nodded, walked over and stopped in front of the big man, saluting him before dropping into a half-crouch, her sword held above her head as Darjoon had taught her. They circled each other warily, waiting for an opening. Suddenly, the man lunged forward, whipping out both swords and whirling them around his head in a dizzying blur. Sirroya sank low and ducked to the side as a blade whirled over her head, then tucked and rolled just as the second blade whistled down and thudded into the sand where she'd been standing. She flung out her blade as she regained her feet just in time to meet the other sword striking down at her, the sharp squealing of metal on metal telling the crowd how hard the big man had struck. She was forced to tuck and roll again as the second sword cut her shoulder, drawing blood through her tunic. As it whistled past her Darjoon shook his head in appreciation. For a big man the guard was surprisingly quick, in fact he was very quick. Sirroya had yet to launch a single strike at him and was ducking and rolling, desperately trying to evade the blurred swords that cut to either side of her. The man backed off, letting her get to her feet. A trickle of blood ran down her arm but Darjoon could see it was a small cut, not enough to slow her down. The guard lunged again, and this time she didn't roll away but simply slid sideways with her foot outstretched, catching him and thrusting her elbow hard into his abdomen as he stumbled over her foot. His explosive cough turned into a laugh as he whirled to face her with a grin on his face and his swords raised.

"Oho, so the young lioness does have teeth after all. Good, good, I was beginning to get bored. This could be fun after all."

Once again, he advanced with the swords whirling in front of him. This time, she stood her ground and as he chopped down, she parried and ducked under the swing of his second sword, beginning to read his movements. She flashed out her own sword and it pricked him just above the knee, forcing him back. Sirroya was grinning, starting to enjoy herself now and she bounced on her feet, waiting for his next move. He advanced slower this time without whirling the swords and Sirroya took the advantage, stepping forward and lunging with her sword in an attempt to force him back for the first time. Darjoon hissed a warning through his teeth as she did so, watching in horror as the big man countered with both blades, catching her sword and twisting it to the side. He reached down and almost lazily flung her sword a short way away while at the same time twisting around and bringing him closer to her. As she went to grab the sword his elbow caught her nose, knocking her back and down. At the same time he stepped forward and dug his sword-point into her throat, pricking it just enough to draw blood. She glared at him as she lay in the sand with blood trickling from her nose and a thin line running down her neck.

"I think you are not yet familiar with that blade, young one, and you are overconfident too. Certainly not experienced and definitely no warrior. I can't say I'm too impressed, but let's see how your friend does first, before I pass my final judgement. Right now it isn't looking good for either of you."

Withdrawing the sword, he reached out a hand and heaved a disgruntled, bloodied Sirroya to her feet. She stumbled past Darjoon with her head lowered as he walked forward. The guard turned to face him and stepped back, brandishing a sword in front of his nose in a mock gesture of respect.

"Aha, I think we have a raven-born here, eh? Now this, this is more like it. None of that Empire softness but hopefully a real challenge. So, young raven-born, maybe they threw you from the nest because you were useless at this, eh? Hahaha, let's find out shall we."

Darjoon stood still and silent, his eyes fixed on his opponent and his knees bent while he balanced on his feet. He was breathing slowly and evenly and hadn't even taken off his cloak as had Sirroya and Grufti. He simply stood calmly looking at the guard without even a weapon in hand. Grufti looked at him quizzically for a while, then advanced slowly, not whirling his swords but holding them balanced and ready. He circled around Darjoon, who had still made no move, until he was standing right behind the raven-born. Without warning he stepped forward and whirled one sword from the side at Darjoon's head and at the same time struck down at his unprotected legs. Darjoon vaulted in almost slow-motion back and to the right over the sword below, while the sword above flew past his head, not even grazing the cloak he wore which had flown up as he'd jumped back. Sweeping round, he landed on his knees next to the guard and his hands shot out in two blurs, hitting the guard once in the abdomen and once in the kidneys. Grunting in spectacular fashion, Grufti folded in half and collapsed in a heap on the floor. Darjoon picked up the two swords and held them on either side of the guard's neck. As he watched the guard fighting to get his breath back, he addressed Sirroya as if he were in a training session.

"Remember this, Sirroya. When they're big, they're often slow. A man with two swords is almost always confident and this can be a weakness. Don't fight them with the same weapon, as you may well be outmatched, instead use speed and agility to hit them hard."

The guard wheezed as he struggled to get his breath back and then looked up at Darjoon, who was watching him carefully without removing the swords from his neck..

"Well, huuuuh, raven-born, huuuuuuh, you were as expected. I, huuuuh, can see you've been, huuuh, trained and trained well. Welcome aboard, we'll be happy to have you."

Darjoon reached out his hand and helped the guard to his feet while the big man leaned on him, his breath coming easier now. Droikin was beaming as he walked over to them.

"You were right, Grufti. He didn't disappoint at all. I can't remember that I ever saw you taken down so quickly before, not even by that crazy woman, what was her name? That raven-born mage that we had here all those years ago. You even cut her twice before she had you, don't you remember? You must be getting old, Grufti, or maybe this one is really that good. Okay, okay, everyone, nothing to see here. Go and get back to your wagons, the caravan is moving out", he rubbed his hands together, "You'll all be much safer from now on, a genuine raven-born is a rare guard to have. Mind you, young raven, don't think our deal is any different. I'm not paying you any more than I agreed to up front. Here, shake on it."

"I'll shake with you, Droikin, but you need to know that I work as part of a team. She signs on as a guard as well as I", Darjoon gestured towards Sirroya.

"Oh, fine, fine, it's still worth it to have you along, even if she is useless. Well come on, shake already and we can head off."

Spitting in his palm and shaking hands with Droikin, Darjoon walked over to Sirroya. Grufti had recovered from being winded and was applying an ointment to Sirroya and her various cuts as well as a wrapping over her shoulder.

"I assume you both know how to ride?", he chuckled then started as Darjoon nodded, "Really, raven-born? You can actually ride? On a horse? Well, that's surprising but good, good. See those two mounts over there, they're yours. I want you both at the rear of the convoy, where all the dust is and where all the newbies like you go. Make sure you keep your mouths closed and your noses covered or you won't be hungry by the time dinner comes around. You'll be amazed how filling sand can be. Ahahaha!", Grufti stalked off as Darjoon groaned. He was still aching from the roykili and didn't fancy any more riding.

"Oh, cheer up, Darjoon!", Sirroya slapped him on the back, "These have actually got saddles and they're well trained caravan horses. It'll be much better, you'll see!"

Her face fell as she looked at Darjoon sheepishly.

"I'm sorry, I'm afraid I didn't do so well back there. Grufti was right, I was, well, I was overconfident. Sometimes all the book knowledge in the world doesn't stand up to real life, eh?"

Darjoon smiled at her, "Actually, Sirroya, you weren't too bad. He's a very experienced warrior and knows his trade well. In fact, I thought at one point you might have him. You're definitely getting better but you should never, ever be too confident. Anyone can surprise you. Anyway, I suppose I don't have a choice on the riding, so let's go do this again."

They rode for the rest of the day behind the caravan in a cloud of dust, keeping a sharp lookout as Grufti had commanded. Occasionally he would fall back and ride with them, but never for very long. Covered in sand and spitting it out for the hundredth time, Darjoon rinsed out his mouth again, realising why Grufti never stayed with them at the back of the caravan. He wasn't relishing the thought of another day there. It wasn't only the sand but the smell was truly awful. Towards the back of the caravan were a couple of wagons that belonged to some gypsies and he was pretty sure they'd been cooking their dinner while riding. It hadn't smelt good at all, especially mixed with the smells of horse and bront dung and probably the latrines on the wagons too. Towards nightfall, the caravan stopped to pitch camp, the wagons all drawing into a large circle for protection. Sirroya and Darjoon were shown a spot under one of the wagons where they would spend the night.

Darjoon finished unrolling his bedding then walked over to where Sirroya was chatting and laughing with one of the gypsy ladies. The lady glanced suspiciously at Darjoon, muttering something under her breath and forming a sign with her hands before quickly leaving. He was used to that sort of behaviour as it had been the same in Spidral. People were naturally wary of the raven-born, many believing them to be an incarnation of some evil. Sirroya smiled at him in greeting.

"Apparently we've been invited to join the gypsies for dinner this evening. Better get yourself smartened up, Darjoon, there's going to be dancing as well. Do you know how to dance? No? Funny that, I didn't think so. Well, that's easy, I can teach you. Oh stop frowning like that, we might as well enjoy ourselves while we're here. We'll ask for information and go around to the other wagons as well. Maybe someone in the caravan knows about this tribal warrior you're looking for."

Later that evening Darjoon stood just outside the firelight in the darkness, watching the other people . Most of them were gypsies but a few were from the other wagons, drawn to the sound of a party. They were pretty much all Empire folk, probably traders, with a few obvious desert people in their typical, brightly coloured robes. Every time someone looked at him they'd mutter under their breaths and a few had gone so far as to actually spit on the ground in front of him. He'd simply ignored them, remaining aloof and standing off to the side. Sirroya wandered over to him.

"Okaaay, young raven. You're doing the 'leave me alone' act a little too well. That's not exactly going to help your case, is it? I've been telling them that you were kicked out of the nest because you're too fat, I mean, you are bigger than the average raven-born", Sirroya quickly continued as Darjoon began to protest, "Yes, yes, I know, I know, all muscle and bone, not fat, but it looks like you're on the large side and so we'll use it. All you have to do is be the jolly fat man, show them a few tricks, and they'll warm up to you in no time."

Grinning at him, she saw the look on his face and pre-empted his questions, "Why? Because, young mage, if we want to get any information out of them then we need them to like you, okay? Come on, you can do a few magic tricks, you did them for Lord Gromtag back in Spidral. Something like that would be fine."

Darjoon spluttered and tried to get a word in, but she continued relentlessly.

"Oh please, hardly trivial, it's for a purpose. I don't want to be in this desert or this caravan for any longer than you do, so the sooner you get them on our side the sooner we can get the information we need and get out of this dust-bowl", she put her hands on her hips and glared at him.

Darjoon just stared at her. She had a way of relentlessly beating down every argument he came up with and now she even knew what they were before he voiced them. He sighed, knowing she was right and followed her back towards the fire, trying to smile at all the unfriendly faces. One of the lesser known facts about the raven-born was that they actually did do so-called 'magic tricks'. In reality it was almost all sleight of hand and not magic at all as they disdained the use of magic for such trivial pursuits. It was partly a hobby for them and partly used to train them in dexterity, which was useful when wielding smaller knives and other objects. So it wasn't surprising he had a small bag with a collection of cards, paper and exploding powder. It was the same collection he'd used for the nobleman in Spidral.

The crowd oohed and aahed as the small, fiery bird darted over and around them, then dove into the fire and exploded, showering them with harmless sparks. Darjoon had entertained them with card tricks, pulled coins out of ears and various other assorted illusions. He'd left the best for last and smiled as the crowd applauded in obvious appreciation. As they drifted off to the various cooking pots and wagons, Sirroya took his arm.

"Well, young raven, that was impressive, I really didn't know you had it in you. I mean I hardly got to see you in Spidral as I was busy, ah, collecting things. What a real little entertainer you are. Did you know you were acting like a real clown? If they were scared of you before, they certainly won't be now. Well done, Darjoon, you even had me convinced that you weren't the deadly great mage I knew you to be. We got a good haul out of this one, don't you worry, it was well worth it", Sirroya was beaming.

"Good haul? What do you mean, good haul? Were you taking money from these people? Please tell me you weren't stealing from them!", Darjoon stared at her.

"Let's just say that I made sure the, uh, hat was passed around. Oh, don't look like that, just a bit of harmless commerce. This is a trading caravan, after all, and these are gypsies, so I'm just fitting in. Come on, let's grab a bite to eat, I'm famished and that food looks, well, actually it looks more interesting than good. Personally, I hope we can keep it down."

Grabbing a plate of what they hoped was stew, they sat down and Darjoon began eating while Sirroya counted the coins that she'd collected. They were finishing their dinner when one of the scowling gypsies wandered over and addressed them, "Look, uh, not like we didn't enjoy the show or anything, but really, we're normally the one's doing the entertaining. You're not going to be doing that every night, are you? Because that's not good for business, ours or yours, if you understand me, yeah? We wouldn't want your magic act with the daggers to, uh, backfire, if you know what I mean?"

Sirroya put her arm on Darjoon's arm to stop him from standing up or doing anything they might regret later.

"Oh no! In fact, that was strictly a one-off. We're guards, not entertainers at all. Here, Darjoon will show you how, won't you Darjoon? Well, don't just sit and glare at me, get up and show the kind man how you did that trick. They are feeding us, after all."

Darjoon shook his head, then stood up, looking at the gypsy. He reached over and pulled a coin from his ear.

"Well, sure, anyone can do that. What about that one where you..."

Sirroya left them discussing various tricks and went looking for information. She'd seen a few of the older gypsy crones huddled by a particular wagon and wandered over there. As she got closer, one of them made a peculiar sign with her fingers, touching the tip of her index and other fingers to the tip of her thumb, while she held her pinkie straight up. For good measure, she also spat in the dirt in the direction of Sirroya. Changing her mind about talking to the crones, Sirroya veered away and started heading back towards the fire. A hand touched her elbow, causing her to stop and turn around.

"Listen young lady, don't you mind that old goat. She's not been right in the head for a few years now. She keeps thinking she's seeing bats instead of people. Bats that look like men, would you believe. It seems that she thinks you're someone she knew long, long ago, but given how old our Fitrilla is, I know that's impossible. She's just spooked, babbling on about how young you still are and how you must be evil. Just silly stuff, really. Were you looking to get your fortune told, dearie?"

"Sorry! I, she, what? Fitri... Young... She... I, I mean not really, actually I was looking for someone else."

"Oho, a special someone is it? Well, we can certainly help you there. I have many potions that can help you find someone and even get them to like you, and my friend has many that will even help you keep them for as long as you like. Or until you get bored of them. Ahahahahaaa", the crone cackled to herself.

"No, actually, yes, that's right. A desert warrior I once met who took my breath away. That's why I'm here in the desert again, I'm looking for him because I think he is the one. His name is Turmoos. Can you help me find him?", Sirroya had made up her lie on the spot but at the mention of his name saw the crone's face turn paper-white and she bustled off.

"Hello, old lady wait, what did I say? Please, come back", she called after her in vain.

The crone continued to walk away, ignoring Sirroya and muttering and mumbling under her breath. Sirroya ran after her and grabbed her elbow to turn her around. Turning, the crone bared her teeth and hissed at Sirroya, causing her to stumble back.

"Get away from me! Are you mad, naming him like that? Listen and listen well, my dear. Don't be fooling with me or it'll be the last practical joke you ever play on anyone, I'm warning you. I don't know who you think you are, but I'll not be trifled with", shaking free of Sirroya's hand she marched off.

Sirroya let the old lady go, shaking her head. What did she mean? Who was this warrior that his name put such fear in an old gypsy? It was obvious the crone was really scared as she'd gone deathly pale when she heard his name. She went back to Darjoon, where he had just finishing explaining to the eager gypsy the secret of his dragon fire spell, a combination of very little magic and a lot of black and white powder. Enthralled, the man was clapping his hands with delight.

"Come, come", he said, "this will make us good coin in the years ahead. Now it is time for you young one's to dance, yes? Come and join us in celebration tonight. The Tregora moon is not far off and so we dance to bring her closer to us and so ensure the gods do not forget us."

Reluctantly they let themselves be dragged into the firelight among a group of young people who were already dancing. As they started dancing together, the music changed to a much slower tempo and some of the couples started holding each other close. The gypsy and now his wife were pushing the two of them together with knowing winks and sly smiles. Sirroya looked up at Darjoon, seeing how warm and brown his eyes became in the firelight. His black hair had grown out a bit and the length suited his broad face. The sun had darkened his complexion and brought out smile wrinkles in the corners of his wide, clear eyes. His full, red lips were not far from her own and she felt her heart beat faster as he breathed on her, his calm, gentle face looking down in rapt concentration as he focused on the dance steps, oblivious to how she was staring at him.

Darjoon stumbled and stood on one of Sirroya's delicate feet. She fell back with a gasp, and he looked up to find her staring at him wide-eyed. He looked at the old couple obviously watching them, then turned to Sirroya.

"Well, why didn't you watch your feet? I've been telling you to be more graceful for weeks, Sirroya. You stomp around like one of those hefty bronts. You need to practice the exercises I gave you so that you move on the balls of your feet, not your heels. It'll give you a lot more poise and grace. Wait, where are you going now? Hey, Sirroya, wait up! Oh, come now, we can't all be naturally nimble. Sirroya!", Darjoon sighed in exasperation.

Sirroya stormed off out of the firelight and into the night as he stood there puzzled and watching her retreating back. Wait, what was that look on her face? It was almost as if, as if she was... "No!", Darjoon thought and shook his head, "that can't be possible."

There's no way she would feel about him as he was beginning to feel about her. Was there? He looked around as he realised some of the gypsies were laughing at him.

"What? What's so funny?", he demanded and blushed when they laughed even louder.

"You are, young raven-born. You and your woman having a lover's quarrel over dancing. You must dance from the heart, big man, not from the head. You were only focused on your feet, but she was focused on you. You should have been looking at her instead. Don't you know the way of a woman?", the gypsy's wife answered him.

"What? Lovers! Who, us? Oh, don't be silly, you've been drinking too much. We're not lovers.", he snorted.

The gypsy woman threw back her head and laughed at him, "Drink? We don't drink, raven-born. Do you see any fermented drink? No, obviously you are blind as well as clumsy. Stop looking at your clumsy feet, young man, and look at her heart for a change."

A chill spread over Darjoon and he shivered. They were right, she had been looking at him in a certain way. All he could do was moan at her when he was the one being clumsy.

"You idiot, Darjoon!", he thought angrily to himself. "Idiot, idiot, idiot!"

Blushing furiously he rushed away from the firelight and into the night, eager to get away from the well-deserved laughter. What had he been thinking and what was he supposed to do now? This changed their relationship completely, didn't it? Had he really fallen for her, or worse still, had she fallen for him? Could it all be true? Wouldn't that be wonderful. The thoughts whirled around furiously in his head, screaming at him in opposition.

Suddenly he stopped and turned his head, listening intently. There it was again, someone screaming, and this time not in his head. The shrill, sharp scream suddenly cut off but not before he recognised that voice. It was Sirroya. Plunging wildly through the desert darkness he ran towards where he'd heard the sound last. As he rushed over a dune, he saw Sirroya being bundled over the shoulder of a tall man flanked by two companions. Without thinking, Darjoon charged towards them angrily and the two companions turned towards him. They were only wearing a simple loin-cloth and their skin had a strange scaling all over. One of the creatures flicked out his tongue, licking his lips and as Darjoon closed with them he saw a forked tongue and bright green eyes above slitted nostrils. Without blinking Darjoon sent a blast of magic at the two creatures and immediately felt himself hurled forcefully backwards, flying back and thudding into the dune behind him. As the darkness closed in, he heard a final, muffled scream from Sirroya and then spiralled down, down, down into a pitch black night.

In his dream he is riding across the desert, chasing after Sirroya who sits balanced on a wild turmisra that is trying to tear her with sharp horns as she rides it. He can't catch her, but he can hear his metal harness jingling and can feel the dust blowing into his open mouth as he spits out endless sand. The creaking and clinking noise of the harness was becoming as irritating as his dry, dusty throat and he coughed and spluttered, trying to sit up and failing.

Looking around at the brightly painted ceiling and walls, Darjoon reeled and then, as reality rushed in, realized he was lying on a bunk in an old gypsy wagon. Pots and kettles were clinking against each other overhead as the wagon rolled from side to side on its way through the desert. The sun streamed in through the glass windows along with the odd puff of dust that seemed to filter in through the very fibres of the wooden beams above him. He struggled to sit up and an old lady sitting in a chair beside him stirred and laid the back of her hand on his brow.

"There, there, don't fret, dearie. You'll get used to it soon enough. How are you feeling this morning? That was quite a blow you took", the crone fluffed up his pillow then pushed him back down.

"No, no, I think you should just sleep a little more, you've taken a nasty tumble and a blow to the head and you've had a bad brain fever because of it."

"Please! Tell me what happened! Where is Sirroya? Where?", Darjoon fought the blackness that threatened to engulf him, "Tell me now, where is she?"

"Hush raven-born, hush. You must relax or you'll open that gash on your head again. We are all sorry for your loss", the crone had her hand on his chest as he struggled feebly to sit up.

"What? What loss? You mean... No...", the impact staggered Darjoon and he sank back down on the pillows under the feeble weight of the old lady's hand, "How... How do you know that she... that she's gone?"

"Because it was the Y'rdirak, raven-born. The evil lizard-men have taken her and you will never see her again. I'm sorry, but they are cruel and brutal and they always abuse their prisoners. They use them like slaves and then, when they are all used up, they eat them. I'm sorry, but it is better you hear the truth, young one. Every year, the caravans lose a few people to them", the crone shrugged her shoulders, "It is just a fact of life, and like so much else, a stark consequence of trading in the desert."

Darjoon rolled over with his face to the wall and wept, surprised at his own reaction. He'd known for some time now that his feelings for Sirroya had been growing, but hadn't realised just how much. The crone patted him on his shoulder and started crooning to him and he stiffened, insulted that she would treat him like a baby. But as she continued, he slowly relaxed as her strangely soothing voice lulled him into darkness.

The dreams came again and in the dream the tall lizard-men attacked him with teeth and claws, ripping and rending. Sirroya hung suspended in a cage and was surrounded as they danced around her in glee. They poked her with long sticks and she cried out, calling his name over and over. Waking up sweaty and crying out in despair, he realised the wagon had stopped moving and the blue glow of the Tregora Moon was streaming in through the open windows. The crone rose from beside him and mopped his brow with a cool cloth then used a spoon to feed him a dribble of some salty broth. He swallowed it eagerly, hungry for more and soon finished the bowl. She fluffed his pillows and then tucked him into the bed like a baby. Once she started singing again, he soon fell asleep, lulled by the latent magic in her voice.

Darjoon yawned, stretched and raised his arms. His knuckles scraped against wood and he started, then looked up at the wooden ceiling with its patterned skylight. He was lying in a bunk bed in the gypsy wagon and it was festooned inside with brightly-coloured cloths. This time it was swaying from side to side and he could feel they were moving along at a fairly brisk pace. What looked like late afternoon sunshine streamed in through the coloured windows on the side, creating a myriad coloured patterns on the blankets on his bed and the wall opposite. There was a faint tinkling from the pots and pans hanging from the ceiling. Sniffing himself, he realised he was overdue a good scrubbing. Come to think of it, he was thirsty as well as ravenous. Flinging off the blankets he swung his feet over the edge of the bed and stood up in one smooth movement. Immediately he staggered and threw out a hand to steady himself. What was wrong with him, he felt so giddy, drunk even? Waiting for the dizziness to pass, he put a hand to his head which felt like it wanted to explode. Feeling a cloth tied around his head, he stumbled to the wash-stand above which hung a large, ornate steel mirror. The stranger in the reflection stared back and for a moment he wondered who it was. It was a gaunt, hollow face with stubbly beard on chin and jowls. Dried blood in the one ear must have trickled down from under a bloody rag that was wrapped neatly around his head. His hair on top was matted with blood, although he could see someone had tried to sponge it out. There were dark rings under his eyes, one of which was still a little red and puffy and the surrounding area was bruised green-blue. Touching his eye socket gingerly, he winced at the pain. Well, at least he knew what to do with that. Summoning up some simple healing magic, he continued until the swelling and bruising slowly disappeared. With the redness in his eye gone, he began to unwrap the bandage from around his head, whistling as he saw the deep gash just above his right eye that ran diagonally up into his hairline and ended above his ear. As he finished the healing on that, he smiled, wondering where Sirroya was. A bit of help from her would have been useful, as he was feeling quite drained from the use of all the magic. Realising that if he'd been hungry before, his stomach was growling ravenously now he thought of asking her if she had any chranth left in her pack.

Sirroya! Suddenly it all came back to him in a rush of images and emotions. Darjoon staggered and putting out his hand knocked the empty wash-bowl to the floor. The wagon door at the front flung open and the crone came bustling in from her seat beside the driver.

"Sit, young raven-born, sit down before you fall down.

You know... What, how, how did you do that? You, your, the wounds you had, they are all gone? Let me have a look, young one. Hush, hush, easy now. There, it's okay, I won't hurt you. Here, sit down on the bed."

She guided him back to the bunk bed, pushing him down gently but firmly, then traced the location of his wounds with her fingers, drawing them lightly across his head and face.

"Yes, yes, very good, very good indeed. That is a fine job of healing, young one. Very fine. You are more powerful than you seem, yes? Are you not hungry now? Wait, there is chranth bread here that will help revive you. Yes, we know about your beloved chranth bread, raven-born. We travel here, there and everywhere and we pick up many secrets about many things", she smiled down at him as he wolfed down the bread.

"If you know so much then tell me gypsy, tell me the secret of the Y'rdirak. Tell me where I can find them and how I can kill them all", Darjoon snarled and spat out the last words.

"Ah, vengeance, is that what you want, young one? No, no, raven-born, that is not your way or the way of your people. Why would you dishonour the memory of your beautiful young lady in that way? No! It is better by far to live with a free heart, living with the world and not against it, living in balance. You are young and your wounds inside will heal slower than those outside, but they will heal in time. There is no magic to heal a broken heart, raven-born, but in time even that will pass."

"Vengeance, gypsy? No, I'm not talking about vengeance, that is for the dead. I'm talking about rescue. I am going to go and fetch her back because I know she is alive. I would know if it was any different, if she was truly gone. I must rescue her before it's too late. I... I dreamt about her last night. She was calling me and asking me to save her", Darjoon's eyes took on a far-away look.

The crone grabbed his hands, holding them tightly as

he tried to resist and turned them both palm up. She stared down at them intently, reading the lines and muttering under her breath. Looking up at his face, her breathing heavy and her eyes slightly glazed, she said to him in a breathless whisper, "Yes, you are very powerful, young mage. But your power is not so strong as the love you bear. Love will save you in the end and not your power. You are right, I can see that. I believe you are connected to her, but maybe not in the way you think. Not all love is the same, even though it may feel that way. Yes, yes, I too believe she is alive. I can read the connection, it is very faint but it is there. You have a slim chance of saving her I think."

The crone blinked, letting go of his hands and looking piercingly at Darjoon, "We are stopping for the evening soon and there is much you must know if you are to attempt this, although I still think it is foolish. None that find the Y'rdirak ever return to tell of it. There has never been a single prisoner that has escaped alive in over two hundred years. I do not think much of your chances, young raven-born, but I will grant you that yours are better than most", she smiled grimly at him.

That evening, as Darjoon sat around the fire, the gypsies all argued with him, trying to dissuade him from what they saw as a suicide mission. None of them were willing to go with him, and they weren't really willing to tell him anything, either. They'd all come to respect this big, gentle young man who had treated them with courtesy and kindness, when they were so used to being disrespected. He'd even been willing to show them his tricks and magic. Darjoon argued back and finally an old man agreed to give him the information he was so desperate for.

"Yes, I will tell you, young raven-born. But Y'rdirak?", the old man turned and spat on the ground then drew thoughtfully on his pipe as he turned back to Darjoon, "Beasts and worse than beasts, they are killers with no conscience and no honour. They kill without thinking, even killing their own kind just for sport. Your magic won't help you, young raven-born, powerful as you might be, because they are shielded against all forms of magic and worse than that, the shielding they have will reverse the spell on the caster. This is what happened to you the night they took your friend. You were lucky, young one, very lucky because they thought they had killed you afterwards, with that tremendous blow to the head. They obviously wanted to finish you off but they underestimated what a thick skull you have, eh. Although maybe not how thick you truly are!"

The gypsies laughed out loud at that and the old man grinned, happy to have a captive audience.

"Nasty beasts, they learn combat from before they can walk, as soon as they are out of the egg. Oho, I see that sounds familiar to you? Let me tell you a little secret, raven-born, they have some of the best warriors in the Old Lands, even better than the best among your own people."

As the old man warmed to his task, the young gypsies leaned forward to better hear what he was saying. Coughing, he cleared his throat and spat, then took a few more puffs of his pipe and continued.

"As you know, back in the mists of time the Great Raven laid her eggs in a nest high above the Darken Hills. It was a small clutch of just two eggs that she laid and then nurtured, spending time sitting on them in her warm, woollen nest and singing to them the knowledge of the ages. In one of those eggs were your ancestors, the father and mother of the raven-born. But the other egg was misshapen and discoloured and as time went by it became covered in grey scales. So the Great Raven kicked that egg from her nest, where it bounced off the Darken Hills and rolled across the Plains of Breath", he puffed on his pipe and sent mysterious smoke signals floating into the smoke above the fire.

"As it rolled across the Plains the egg fell down through a crack in the ground and rolled into a massive underground lake. The Great Lizard found this egg there and because it had scales like itself took pity on it. The egg was infertile, but the Great Lizard inseminated the egg and this caused it to develop and grow and so he built a warm nest from old leaves and thick mud and spent much time lying near the egg and teaching it his dark, evil ways", the youngsters leaned in even closer as his voice dropped to a whisper during the last sentence.

"When the egg finally hatched, out came a male and female Y'rdirak, the lizard people, who after some time in the cavern eventually left their father behind and swam out through an underground stream that emerged onto the Plains near this desert. They lived there just outside the desert in peace, even catching and training the roykili that they tamed and rode, becoming fierce and joyful hunters. Living as one with the land, they drank the milk and ate the meat of the roykili that they loved which gave them all they needed. But the Great Lizard grew angry with them because he felt they had abandoned him down in his underground lair, and so while they laughed and basked in the sun of the Plains, he asked the Old Dragon to breathe on them and drive them back underground so he could be with his children again. This is how the Dragon Breath came to the Plains, burning everything before it and driving all creatures underground to escape the scorching heat.

"Now the Y'rdirak feared their evil father which is why they had left in the first place. So knowing it was he who had brought the Breath and instead of returning to the underground cavern and lake with all the other animals, they drove their roykili forward until they found a secret place of hiding. This secret place is where the roykili shelter from the Breath to this day, away from the other animals that go underground and still none know where it is. It was not a large place and soon there was no room for both the roykili and the Y'rdirak and so it was that the large, beloved herd turned on their few, weak masters and drove them back out into the awful heat of the cruel Breath from which they fled. Many Y'rdirak were burnt alive during that awful journey until finally they stumbled into the Desert of Thoth where they live to this day. It is said that the betrayal of the roykili and the heat of the Dragon Breath drove the remaining lizard-men mad and this is how they became the twisted, brute beasts and cannibals they are today, eating the flesh of their own kind as well as of those who fall into their hands or who they take for their cruel pleasure", he took a deep breath and spat vehemently into the ground.

The young gypsies let out a collective sigh and then applauded quietly and politely, enjoying a tale they had probably heard many times before. Darjoon realised with a start that the underground lake Sirroya and himself had stumbled into must be the one mentioned in the old man's tale. Thank Zukar, the warrior goddess, they had not come across any Great Lizard, only the smaller ones that had hunted in the shallows. Was there some truth to his tale? He looked at the old man who had relit his pipe and was now puffing away peacefully.

"But if what you say is true then the Y'rdirak and the raven-born are related? They would be like, like... Well, they would be our cousins? Surely, if that is the case then they can reason and think like we do?"

"Cousins? Ahahahahaha!", the old man's laughter became a fit of coughing and Darjoon waited politely for him to catch his breath so he could speak.

"No, raven-born, they are no more cousins to you than the bront is a cousin to us. They are wild, brute beasts that do not take time to think, all they can do is kill, kill, kill. It is suicide to think about tracking them down. They only ever allow one desert tribe to contact them and then only one spirit from within that tribe. If it is not the great Turmoos who contacts them then it is no-one. He is the only one who knows where they are and if you can find him then you have a chance of finding them. But who can know where the spirit of Turmoos is? Ah, that is a hard question that none here have the answer to", he fixed his piercing eyes on Darjoon with a glowing intensity.

"Why not? Isn't this caravan heading to a meeting of the tribes? Surely he will be there with them, won't he?", Darjoon asked politely.

"Oh certainly, young raven-born, he may well be there. But what if he is? Who here knows what the great Turmoos looks like? None of us have ever laid eyes on him, that is for certain, and some of us have met these tribes a dozen times over. No, he is the elite of the elite, the warrior of warriors, a living legend among all the tribes. Maybe he is no longer alive? If he were, then he must be very old by now, far older than I am. But for you, young raven-born, we will try. Oh yes, if only so that the great Turmoos can speak sense into you, we will try to find him", the old man turned back the fire, shaking his head.

"Good! And I thank you, old one. I'll ask around when we get there, I'm sure they'll tell me...", Darjoon trailed off as almost every gypsy burst into laughter. The old man was practically crying from laughing so hard and then promptly dissolved into another coughing fit.

"What? What now? What are you lot laughing at this time?", Darjoon was indignant.

"Forgive us, young one, please. You do not understand how it is. The tribes will most likely kill you on sight. Even I can see you are not entirely raven-born, but to them you will certainly look like one and they hate your kind with an unbridled passion. I thought you knew because their hatred for the raven-born is legendary. No offence intended, but face it, your people are not truly welcome anywhere. Among the tribes it is a great and important honour to take the breath of a raven-born. In fact, many of the elite warriors have killed your kind, certainly almost all of those who make it this far. I believe there is only one of your people, a woman, that has ever won the tribes over. Perhaps you knew of her as she was here not so long ago. Her name was Ma, no, what was it, Mee-something, no, ah, yes, I remember now, she was called Misroan. What? What is it, young one? Have you heard the name yourself? Do you know of this raven-born woman?"

Darjoon stared at the old gypsy with his mouth open. His own mother had come here, of course, it made sense now. Darjoon's head was whirling with questions. How had she won the tribes over? Had she met with Turmoos, or the Y'rdirak? Had she travelled with the caravan as he had done? But when he asked the gypsies, no-one seemed to know, only that everyone had been in awe of her and her strange companion. Could the companion have been his father? Had the two of them met with the legendary warrior, Turmoos? That must be why he had to come out here to find him, because his parents had been here before. Darjoon gratefully accepted the drink that the old crone gave him, not realising she'd slipped a little potion into it. Once he drifted off to sleep beside the camp-fire, they carried him into his wagon and laid him in the bunk-bed. She smoothed his brow, smiling down at him. So young and passionate, so innocent and powerful. Could he really be the one she'd seen in her dreams, the one who would save them all? In disbelief, she'd felt his great power when she'd read his palms and seen something of his destiny. Let him sleep for now, tomorrow would come soon enough and even powerful mages had to rest.

Darjoon woke up and stretched, his bones and sinews cracking as he watched the sunlight streaming into the wagon, shining on the ever-present, dancing dust motes. He yawned and stretched again, feeling refreshed and rested, better than he'd felt for a while now. The magic was stirring in his bones and he could feel it was fully replenished, ready and waiting to be used. Frowning suddenly, he wondered how he was going to free Sirroya when he couldn't use any of that powerful magic against the Y'rdirak. He shook his head in annoyance. There must be a way past their defences. Realising the wagon had stopped he lay awhile and listened to the hustle and bustle outside. Finally stretching one last time, he got up, splashed his face with water from the bowl and stepped outside into the heat of the day and the noisy, brightly-coloured chaos that was trading with the tribes.

10 TRIBAL WARRIOR

Darjoon could see that the caravan had arranged itself into a semi-circle, with the opening facing towards an impressive array of coloured tents scattered over a large area. The tents were made of leather, tanned and cured, and in some cases had great white bone-like posts and what looked like curved ribs that acted as tent-poles. Flying above almost every tent were brightly coloured flags that fluttered in the light breeze. The entire camp-site resided in a large depression with an enormous dune on one side and small hills on the other. This shielded the tents from the constant wind, and provided some shade and shelter in the afternoon. Nearby was a relatively small oasis surrounded by palms that in turn was fed by a stream that trickled out of the hills. Many of the tents had a long folded skin that wound round the lower ridge, designed to trap the morning and evening dew that ran off the roof and funnel it into gourds hanging on the sides of the tents.

The people themselves were burnt dark by the sun, the males predominantly black-haired and brown-eyed, with a scattering of blonde hair and blue-eyes here and there primarily among the women. The men wore breeches of leather, but were naked from the waist up and adorned themselves with pieces of bone tied into leather thongs that hung from their necks and large bone earrings that were thrust through their ear-lobes. They all carried one or more large and small curved knives, some having a bow and quiver slung over their shoulders as well.

Darjoon immediately attracted aggressive stares and loud, hostile comments uttered in a strange language, all of which he ignored as he was so used to it by now. The gypsies were sitting at a makeshift table and were bartering with several tribes-folk. They all fell silent and stared at him as he walked over to the old man who had been telling the story last night. The old man turned, and then called out to him.

"Young one, these people believe you to be an entertainer and one who has been rejected by his own people. It is why they are not even now spilling your blood on the sands. Perhaps in order to avoid that for as long as possible, you might deign to perform a few simple tricks for them. No magic mind you, as that will likely trigger an attack. They are not fond of magic here, even if they occasionally use it themselves. I warn you, be very careful, young one. They believe you are 'fat' and therefore useless. It is not a characteristic that they prize, and I have told them there will be no pride in killing one such as yourself, especially because you are not fully raven-born."

At the last word, some of the tribes-folk started to mutter, looking across at the warriors standing on the other side. Darjoon frowned, but at a warning glance from the old man began to do his usual pattern of prancing and waddling. Stumbling over to one of the warriors he took a coin from the tall man's ear, spinning it so it flashed in the sunlight and then tossed it to a young boy who caught it eagerly and ran away. The tribes-folk laughed and the warriors began to relax. Dancing away lightly, he pretended to trip over his own feet. Not wanting to get his robes full of sand, he tucked and rolled as he landed, easily regaining his feet and stumbling forward. They laughed again at his silly antics and soon the hum of conversation and business continued as before. Darjoon did a few more simple party tricks for the young children, carefully making sure he used no magic and continuing to stumble and waddle around to show off his fat uselessness. He didn't notice that one of the warriors was watching him intently, especially every time he fell. Having taken a few swigs from his water-skin, Darjoon headed over to the communal latrines to relieve himself. Feeling better, he started back to the gypsy camp, not noticing the same warrior lounging beside some of the tents.

The warrior casually and quietly drew a small dagger from his belt. He balanced it expertly on his fingertips and then, pinching it in his fingers, threw it hard at Darjoon, who without thinking simply plucked it out of the air, dropped to a crouch and flicked it back in one smooth movement, magically maintaining and increasing the momentum of the blade. The warrior ducked as it thudded into the tent post behind his head. Darjoon readied himself as the warrior lunged forward and attempted to grapple with him.

Slipping to the side before the man got near him, Darjoon tucked and rolled, coming up with a blade in his hand. The other warrior had already unsheathed his short, curved sword and they circled each other warily. Feinting and lunging, using kicks and jabs, the two fought furiously for what seemed like ages to Darjoon. He was careful not to use any more magic and matched the warrior blow for blow while at the same time being careful not to use the few opportunities he got to end the fight for good, which he felt he could have done at any time. However he was not able to land a crippling blow which would stop the fight without death and he could see the crowd around them was growing all the time, both tribes-folk and gypsies. No-one had intervened so far and he was frantically trying to think what else he could do when the warrior stepped back, stuck his sword in the sand and threw his arms in the air laughing uproariously and looking around at the crowd. He received more than a few grins and other warriors laughed as well. He turned and faced Darjoon, who was still crouched ready to continue the fight.

"A clown is no clown who can fight like you do. I saw you were more than the fat clown you pretended to be and I was right. Well done, young man, you have done me great honour in battle. I am Nasrindo and you are welcome in my tent", the warrior touched the knuckle of his bent forefinger to his forehead as he said the last.

Darjoon, not knowing what to do, straightened and mumbled the same words back at him while performing the same gesture. The warrior smiled at him, nodded in approval and continued speaking.

"You are not the first raven-born warrior I have encountered but you were wise to conceal your true abilities at first. It is death to any raven-born who comes here unannounced. I can see though that you are not a true raven-born although I mean you no disrespect. You remind me of those who have been here before, in fact you have something of both of them in you. I have been waiting for you for some time now, wondering if you would ever come. Welcome, Darjoon, we have much to speak of, you and I. The one who came before you was an extremely powerful mage and warrior and so I think you are too. That is who you are really looking for, isn't it?"

Darjoon stared at him. He must be speaking of his father and mother. But who was this warrior? His mother's letter had mentioned someone called Turmoos, not Nasrindo. He would have to ask the man if he knew Turmoos or could find him for Darjoon. But first, before anything he had to get Sirroya free. That was his top priority.

"Watch out, raven-born!", in a heart-beat Nasrindo dived across in front of Darjoon and then slumped to the ground. Darjoon stared at the dart embedded in his back.

Out of the corner of his eye he saw one of the gypsy traders diving towards him with a knife in hand. Pivoting on the ball of his foot, he ducked and kicked as the man flew past and sent him crashing to the ground. Jumping to his feet, the gypsy threw off his robes, revealing the black leather outfit of a Spidralite assassin. He slipped a long blade from his harness and closed on Darjoon with the blade whirling and stabbing in a frenzied blur. It was clear the man wanted to finish him off quickly and Darjoon did his best to counter with the small, inadequate blade that was still in his hand. Realising he would be outmatched, he rolled forwards and ripped Nasrindo's short, curved sword out of the sand where he had planted it just moments before. The desperate clash of metal on metal rang out as the two met in a flurry of sword-blows. No-one dared intervene, but watched in fascination as two obviously talented fighters whirled, kicked, punched, slashed and stabbed at each other. Darjoon fought desperately and this time held nothing back in trying to land a killing blow. Relentlessly, step by step, he felt the assassin forcing him further and further back. Renewing his attack he felt his strength draining away, and realised he was still tired from the earlier bout. Still he refused to use any magic, knowing that to do so would simply mean the tribes-folk would finish what the assassin had started. As he watched the man closely, he saw a slight dip in his left shoulder just before he tried another overhead stab. Waiting for it again, Darjoon reacted milliseconds before the assassin, stepping to the right and forcing the downward sweep to one side with his blade. Turning, he let the man's momentum carry him past Darjoon while at the same time he reversed his blade and let it slide into the man's chest, the assassin's own weight being used to drive it deep into him. Jumping back, he watched as the assassin slumped to the ground, blood pumping from the wound and trickling out of his nose and mouth. Rushing over, he kicked away the assassin's dropped blade before dropping to his knees next to him. Seeing the man's mouth moving, Darjoon lowered his head so he could hear what he was saying.

"You, huuuh, fought, huuuh, well, raven-born. I, huuuh, salute you", the assassin coughed, his bright blood flecking the desert sand, "you may ask and I will answer. This is now your right."

"Who sent you and how many are there", Darjoon asked urgently, knowing the man was close to death.

"One of us is sent by the raven-born, and one of us by a nobleman in Spidral. There are only two of us. One was meant to kill you but the other was meant to take you alive", the colour was slowly fading from the man's face, his breathing ragged and Darjoon had to put his ear against the man's mouth to hear him.

"I, huuuh, I, huuuh, aaaaaahhh", with a final rattling gasp, the assassin slumped back, dead. Darjoon stood up and ran over to Nasrindo who was lying stiffly on the ground. The warriors around him respectfully stood out of the young man's way, making space for him to kneel next to the body. Darjoon explored the man's torso, feeling the muscles tightening already. He'd suspected the assassin's blade was poisoned and realised Nasrindo would be paralysed and probably die soon if he wasn't healed. Calling to two of the gypsies he knew, he had him carried to his wagon as quickly as possible.

Barring anyone from entering except the old crone, Darjoon raised a shield-spell around the wagon, hoping it would remain undetected and prevent the tribes-folk from sensing the magic he would have to use. The crone started back at his first use of power, muttering under her breath and making signs with her fingers, then seemed to recover as she helped him remove the dart from the man's back.

She sniffed it and exclaimed in disgust, "This is a bad poison, raven-born. He may not die from it directly, but it will damage his mind if left for long. In fact, too long, and his body will begin to rot from the inside and that will kill him. I do not think even your powerful magic can cure him now, see how the poison has travelled swiftly through his body? Look there, do you see how his toes are already changing colour? That is a sign of how far and fast the poison has spread. Perhaps we should let his people have this body before he worsens or they may think we killed him. That will not be good for either of us"

The crone made another sign in the air with one hand, warding off death. Darjoon ignored her and focused on Nasrindo's body. He could sense how the poison had penetrated deep into Nasrindo's body and was biting into his internal organs. Slowly, he began to move it out, watching as small drops ran down the man's out-flung arm and dripped onto the floor. The crone grabbed a bowl and placed it under his hand to catch the drops, shrugging when Darjoon looked at her questioningly.

"We collect everything, raven-born, it is our way. This may be of use to both of us someday."

His throat tightened as he remembered Sirroya collecting the blue drug from the lake. Hours later, he straightened his aching back, confident that almost all the poison had been removed from the warrior's body. Staggering in exhaustion, he would have fallen but the crone steadied him, guiding him to the bunk bed on the opposite side. He lay down and she forced some gruel past his lips even as he feebly tried to push her away.

"Easy, young one, easy. Your body needs this to recover. That was strong magic you were using and I must confess I didn't think it possible to heal him, but truly you are a powerful mage. Eat now and then sleep, you will feel better soon."

He nodded gratefully and mumbled his thanks, having barely the energy to speak. Once he'd finished the bowl of food he drifted off, falling into a deep sleep that he'd not experienced before. The crone looked at the young man lying there, then glanced across at the warrior. His previously rigid form was relaxed, the breathing easy and full and he just looked like any tired man having a nap. She applied a small dab of ointment to his back on the entry wound the dart had made, smiling to herself in the knowledge that Darjoon had missed that little thing in his focus on the poison. She looked across at the exhausted young man in wonder.

"We should never be alone, young mage as even the best of us can miss the obvious. Sleep now, for you have certainly earned it this day", she whispered to him as she drew the curtains and stepped out of the wagon.

Assuring all the people gathered outside that both men were fine, but that under no circumstances was she letting anyone disturb them, she folded her arms and sat down pointedly on the steps, daring anyone to cross her path. The gypsy folk went back to their tables and the warriors, after eyeing her warily, wandered back to their tents. Throughout the night, she kept watch over the wagon, making sure no-one approached it.

Darjoon yawned, opening his sticky eyelids and blearily looked around the by now familiar wagon. Recognising the reflected, coloured light on the walls, he looked towards the window and blinked in the bright morning sunshine. The bed opposite him was empty and he wondered if the warrior had survived the night or would he find a lynch mob outside. Finding a water-skin next to the bed, he thirstily gulped down most of it and staggered to his feet. Emptying the rest of the water into the bowl, he splashed his face and wiped his eyes clean. Gingerly he stepped outside the wagon and found the old crone sitting on the steps sewing some skins together.

"Morning, young raven-born, you look terrible. You're just skin and bone inside that robe now. Come, there is porridge over there on the fire. Feel free to have as much as you like, you'll need it I think. The milk is in that skin hanging next to the fire, be careful it can be quite warm. Yes, I see your question", she put up her hand at Darjoon's expression and answered his unspoken question, "Don't worry, young one, the warrior is fine. He has gone to speak with his people now. After all, he wasn't the only one who needed to sleep for two days to recover."

Two days! Darjoon stared around the camp-site noting that even though all the wagons were still there, a lot of the tent-city that had been the tribes' living quarters were all gone. His heart contracted as he thought of Sirroya still in the clutches of those evil beasts. He was just about to whirl around and ask the crone whether Nasrindo was coming back when he saw the big warrior walking towards him.

"Morning, raven-born, how are you this morning? You look terrible by the way. Come, you should immediately eat something warm and sticky. Come here, sit down and eat this good porridge for there is much we must discuss", the warrior sat down next to the fire and beckoned to Darjoon.

While Darjoon wolfed down the porridge, hungrier than he'd ever thought he could be, Nasrindo watched him and smiled. Having woken up the morning after Darjoon had healed him, he'd thanked the crone and told her to take good care of the young mage, while he returned to his own tent where his friends and family were already mourning his death. They had been overjoyed to see him return and in such good health but had asked many questions. He had told them that Darjoon knew the art of making poultices, not wanting them to know it was magic that had cured him. He told Darjoon all of this while he was eating.

"You see Darjoon, not to boast too loudly but what you see before you is not just any warrior. Among the tribes there are a few of us who are the elite warriors, a small group who in times of need will band together and fight for the good of all the tribes-folk. It is the best weapon we have and more because it creates unity among us all. It is also an incentive for warriors to push themselves and so prove they are worthy of one day joining this elite band.

"You now have the gratitude and respect of all the tribes because not only did you fight with an elite warrior and survive, but you have saved him from a cowardly murderer as well. My spirit would not have survived such a miserable death and I would not have enriched my tribe for the future. Now I still have the chance to die an honourable death and bring them much joy and satisfaction in this life and the next. Ha!", he slapped his knees, smiling and barked once, a loud and joyous sound.

"The old crone has told me about your missing friend and I must warn you, as the gypsies did, this rescue will likely mean death for both of us. Yes, yes, don't worry, I will go with you and my tribe will provide everything we need. But I do not hold much hope that we will succeed", the warrior looked into the cooking fire as he spoke.

"The Y'rdirak do not easily give up what they have taken, that is for sure. But come now, put away that frown, raven-born. We will fight together with honour and who knows, perhaps one day they will sing our names in the songs of both our tribes. Now if you've finally finished stuffing yourself with all that porridge can we go and get ready? Really? You want more? Well, I will wait for you to finish eating. After all, fat man, I suppose you do have a reputation to uphold", the warrior laughed as Darjoon refilled his bowl and gulped down more of the hot porridge.

Just as Nasrindo had said, the tribe was grateful and everyone gave them supplies and provisions to survive in the desert for a number of weeks. Darjoon thanked them, knowing full well what a sacrifice it was. He then went and said goodbye to the gypsies, the old crone slipping him a few small bags of herbs and medicines in the skin bag she'd made for him. Leaving them behind, Nasrindo confidently led the way into the desert while telling Darjoon the tribe had sent a pre-arranged smoke signal the day before and he believed the lizard-men would meet them at the usual rendezvous.

"It feels good to be be walking instead of riding and I was getting pretty tired of being in bed all the time", Darjoon remarked as he marched along purposefully, filling his lungs with the clean desert air.

He could feel the magic inside him was growing and also changing somehow and he sensed that he too was growing and adapting, his body accommodating the increase in power and shaping itself from all the exercise he'd been doing.

Nasrindo glanced across at the young mage, his steps light and sure across the desert sand. He could see the young man drinking in the sunlight, as if it was filling him with magic and he was sure he could see a faint glow around the raven-born mage. The warrior thought back to how he'd made his vow to Darjoon's parents, swearing on his ancestors that he would take care of the young mage when he came. They'd asked for nothing more than his life, that he would promise to take care of him for the rest of his natural days, or until Darjoon no longer needed or wanted him. He'd given it freely when they told him of the prophecy related to the young mage and in return for the gift of magical long life that Darjoon's father had given him.

One day he'd gone out into the desert as Turmoos, the man whose grey-bearded friends were ageing and dying, and then some years later he'd returned to another tribe as a warrior called Nasrindo. No-one had questioned him, especially not after they tested him and found him worthy of the elite band. It was true that young warriors would sometimes leave their tribes and wander in the desert before joining themselves to another tribe. It was simply their way and no doubt he would be doing that again in the future, if Darjoon ever let him go and he returned to the tribes-folk.

Camping at night, they sparred and exchanged fighting lore, testing the raven-born ways against the elite warrior tricks and techniques. Nasrindo was again impressed at how the young raven-born handled himself, at how quick and agile he was for such a big man. He realised that Darjoon had been toying with him when they'd fought before. He was a formidable opponent for anyone, especially if he were to use his magic in combat as well. He shook his head in awe, no wonder he'd beaten a Spidralite assassin.

In this way they travelled for a few more days until finally they arrived at a cluster of small hills where the arranged meetings with the lizard-men usually took place.

"Okay Darjoon, this is it! Now remember what we discussed. I'll be going in first, all alone. You cannot come with me. If they see you or smell you for an instant, then it will be all over. They'll either kill both of us or they'll just disappear and we won't get this chance again. I will find out what I can about your friend and whether they still have her. If she's still alive then I will barter for her life. My tribes-folk and I have provided gold and other ornaments, things which the lizard-men value."

He grinned at Darjoon's frown.

"Don't worry about it, my trinkets were given me by women who desired me for a husband. It is our way. Unfortunately it looks like I'll have to disappoint them again."

"Those poor ladies, Nasrindo, how you toy with their hearts."

Darjoon relaxed and grinned back at him. There was something about the warrior's confidence that gave him assurance and filled his mind with peace. He'd come to like this warrior over the days they'd spent together and if anyone could make this work, it would be Nasrindo.

"Now you remember what I said, Nasrindo, even if you don't like it. If it looks like your plan is not working, then you must offer magic to them and call me in. As the gypsies and tribes-folk have all told me, magic is even more valuable to them than gold. You will signal me down and introduce me and I will teach them whatever it takes to get her free. Whatever it takes to free Sirroya, Nasrindo, understand? No matter what!", Darjoon looked at him earnestly.

"Yes, Darjoon, I understand but I don't have to like it. I will bring you in only if I must. I am used to bartering with tight-fisted traders, although this is not so easy. I must tell you honestly that you should not get your hopes up. They may not have her any more and even if they do...", he lowered his eyes and looked at his feet, not able to look at him.

Darjoon just looked straight ahead and didn't respond, his face grim. Shaking his head, Nasrindo walked over the crest and down into the narrow ravine. Darjoon crawled forward until he had a view directly in front of him without exposing himself. When the two of them had arrived they'd positioned themselves downwind of the meeting place, hoping that the lizard-men, who had a keen sense of smell, would not pick up Darjoon's scent. As Nasrindo entered the meeting-place and made a strange guttural noise, two lizard-men came out of a cleft off to the side of the trail and stepped in front of the burly warrior. Although he was not short, they easily over-shadowed him as each creature was around eight feet tall and massively broad across the shoulders, with large muscles on their arms and chests. They never stopped moving, their eyes darting about and they were constantly flexing legs and arms, their muscles and limbs like writhing snakes. Their heads turned from side to side, and their eyes constantly roved the horizon while their forked tongues flickered in and out, no doubt testing the air for scent. After a brief, guttural conversation, one of them gestured suddenly at the warrior. Nasrindo took the gold and trinkets out of his bag, laying it on a flat rock in front of him. The lizard-men began shaking their heads and then gesticulated at each other, grunting in their harsh voices while the warrior stepped back respectfully and bowed his head, waiting for them to finalise their discussion.

The argument seemed to continue for ages until finally one of the lizard-men put out his hand towards the warrior, palm flat and claws pointing down. Darjoon guessed that meant their refusal of the bargain. There was more conversation from Nasrindo but once again, the creature gestured a refusal. Finally, Nasrindo gave a glance back up the trail and spoke to them briefly and this time the lizard-men looked very excited, their heads darting around furiously at the rocks and dunes. Nasrindo raised his arm and waved in the pre-arranged signal for Darjoon to come down. He breathed deeply, then got up and walked down the trail slowly with his hands out in front of him, not wanting to alarm them. As he got closer, he could smell a putrid, fishy, swamp-like odour and realised it came from the creatures in front of him. Their glittering black eyes had gold slit pupils with a membrane that swept in from both sides whenever they blinked. They had small slit nostrils that were moving and wrinkling and their tongues flickered out constantly as they sampled his scent. They blinked at him in consternation and then one of them started back slightly, turning his body as if to ready itself for an attack.

"What, do I smell bad to you too? I hope so, you freak. I hope you can't stand the stench of me", Darjoon muttered angrily under his breath.

Nasrindo turned and looked at him, his frowning eyes and pursed lips signalling the need for caution.

"Darjoon, they say that she is alive and they still have her and are willing to trade. But they are not interested in the gold or trinkets I have brought. I believe they have sensed some great magic nearby and that's what they are holding out for. I tried to convince them otherwise, but nothing else will do except they have this magic. It may be they already sensed you while you were waiting, even if they could not smell you, although I don't know how that's possible."

Darjoon smiled grimly, then took out the staff from

behind his back where he had tied it. At once one of the creatures drew back and hissed a warning, lips wrinkling over sharp, yellow teeth. Then the same lizard stepped forward and jerked its head at the staff, rasping out a single guttural sound. Pulling its lips back over its teeth and wrinkling the nose-slits above its mouth, it hissed then turned to its companion and began a guttural speech.

"I think it is saying this is a very powerful magic. It seems it is trying to convince the other one that they should accept the staff. I think it is their shaman, a magic user and not just a warrior. Are you sure about this, Darjoon? That staff looks very valuable and magical, and we don't know what they might do with it", Nasrindo shook his head as he looked at the staff.

"There is nothing I have of more value than Sirroya's life, Nasrindo. Yes, I am sure. Tell them I want to see her before they can have the staff. I want to make sure she is still alive."

Nasrindo grunted at the lizard-men, and the one standing next to the shaman headed back up the trail. A while later, it came back, pushing someone ahead of it. Darjoon gasped as he saw the state of Sirroya, her unkempt hair blowing around her muddy, tear-streaked face. There were blotches and bruises on her face and arms along with crusted blood on a nasty wound on her neck. One of her arms was hanging limply at her side and he saw that she was gagged and her eyes were almost swollen shut. Nasrindo rushed over and took her from the creature, bringing her over to where Darjoon was standing, his face red with rage.

Spitting on the ground as Nasrindo led Sirroya past it, the shaman grunted a single word, "Ssraknim!"

Nasrindo recoiled, looking visibly shocked and after attending to Sirroya, turned and stared up at Darjoon, his eyes wide open.

"Look what they've done to her", Darjoon said, aghast, "What did that shaman say? What does that word mean?"

But before Nasrindo could answer, the shaman walked over and grabbed the staff from Darjoon. Shrieking in pain, it threw the staff to the ground and nursed the hand that was still smoking. The Y'rdirak warrior stepped forward and raised his spear, holding the point at Sirroya's throat. Darjoon's blade materialised in his hand in a single fluid motion and Nasrindo rose to his feet, his legs planted and his curved sword out and ready, facing the creatures. No-one moved for a space and then Sirroya moaned as the Y'rdirak warrior poked her again with the spear, teeth bared angrily. The shaman began grunting at Nasrindo who grunted back in response.

"What's it saying? What's the problem?", Darjoon asked, eyeing the lizard with the spear.

"The lizard says the staff is cursed and they cannot touch it until you lift the curse. If you do that we can still have the girl otherwise we will all die here. You must lift the protection, Darjoon."

"Protection? What protection? I haven't done anything to that staff. I can't even use it myself! My mother left it for me back in Spidral and that was the first time I ever saw it."

Nasrindo bent down and tried to lift the staff from where it had fallen but quickly dropped it as his hand began smoking. Licking his fingers, he turned to Darjoon.

"This has definitely got some magical protection, Darjoon, I could feel it through the heat. I'm sorry to do this to you, but you must try to remove the protection from the staff or none of us will get out of here alive. The rest of the creatures are just behind that ridge there, and even if we kill these two, they will surely come and kill us long before we can escape. Remember that your magic is of no use against these creatures", Nasrindo looked at him seriously.

Darjoon picked up the staff and held it in front of him, trying to sense any magical protection. As before, he could easily sense the strange magic that twisted inside the gem but he couldn't get a sense of any protection. He glanced aside at Nasrindo who was staring intently into the gem, seemingly captivated by what he was seeing. The gem began to pulsate softly, a faint green light coming from deep within its depths, similar to what Sirroya had seen previously. The Y'rdirak began grunting nervously among themselves and the warrior turned and grunted in a whisper to the shaman. Holding Sirroya, they began to back slowly down the trail, the warrior keeping the spear pointed at her neck.

Darjoon tensed, angry and frustrated as he saw Sirroya slowly slipping out of his reach. In desperation he reached inside for his magic and felt his subconscious slide into his conscious mind, only this time it felt very different. He staggered as a tremendous force roared out of the staff he was holding and the few large rocks that were scattered nearby suddenly and dramatically floated up into the sky as he felt himself rising in the air along with them. Darjoon twisted and turned as he slowly rose, desperately holding on to the staff and trying hard to get a sense of what was going on. He could see the others were also rising slowly and all he was able to sense was the odd, powerful magic that emanated from the staff in his hand. As they hung suspended he began to recognise key components of the strange magic and sensed in them a connection to the lizard-men who were writhing nearby. Reaching in with his mind, he touched a part of the magic, nudging it in the same way he used to control animals. How had he known to do that? With barely time to register the question, he instantly felt like he was being twisted painfully inside out and almost as if it were in the far distance, heard a muffled thump as he spiralled down into complete and utter darkness.

Time passed as Darjoon lay there until finally he awoke, rubbed his gritty, gummy eyes and then looked around. Dust was still swirling and slowly settling to the ground and seeing movement nearby he glanced over at

Nasrindo and saw he was slowly shaking his head as he feebly brushed sand and debris off himself. Jumping up, Darjoon reeled and dropped to his knee, putting a hand to the ground to steady himself. Moving more slowly this time, he tried again and then hurried over to where Sirroya lay, still and unmoving. He reached for her with magic and could feel she was alive but unconscious. Rapidly untying the ropes binding her wrists and removing the gag he looked around for the lizard-men, but there were no Y'rdirak to be seen. Just a spear, some ornaments, and a few scattered clothes lying in the dust among fragments of shattered rocks.

11 THE LOST TRIBE

Nasrindo shook his head and coughed, clearing his mouth and throat of dust and trying unsuccessfully to sit up. Slumping back, he waited for the dizziness to pass and then propped himself up on his elbow, shaking his head to clear it. His cloak was full of sand and debris and he shook his head as he brushed it off. What had happened? Watching groggily, he saw Darjoon frantically untie Sirroya and attend to her. At least she seemed to be alive. Turning his head and surveying the broken rocks and scattered debris, he could see there were sandals lying not far from him along with some necklaces and other ornaments. There were no footprints to indicate which way the Y'rdirak had left, which was strange. Feeling pain on the side of his head, he rubbed it then pulled his hand away as it felt sticky and saw blood on his fingers. That explained why he was so dizzy. Moving carefully this time he managed to sit up slowly.

The dizziness swept over him again and he gratefully accepted the water-skin Darjoon offered him. He looked around, noting Sirroya's still form lying where Darjoon had untied her.

"How is she?", he asked, seeing the look on Darjoon's

face.

"She's breathing, but she's taken a beating from those evil beasts! Zukar knows what they did to her. Or what's happened to them? I can't detect them, nor can I see any traces of them. Can you see where they went?", Darjoon looked around.

"I'll have a closer look but I don't see any obvious footprints. I don't see why they would have left their clothing or ornaments behind. They were here one second and gone the next, just vanished into thin air. Ow! It's okay, I think, just a scrape on the head but you don't have to press so hard though. Owww, okay, okay, that hurts. Seriously, do you have to push quite so hard?", he grimaced in pain.

"I think your head is fractured. Now sit still and don't be such a baby", Darjoon took Nasrindo's head in his hands and quietly muttered a spell.

Nasrindo smiled to himself as he felt a gentle tingling across his scalp. It was handy having a mage that could heal your broken bones. He shook his head again and this time there was no dizziness at all. Feeling the area where it had been fractured, there was no pain either.

"That's great. I can see you'll definitely come in handy. Where've you been all my long life", Nasrindo stood up and stretched, "What about Sirroya, did you heal her too?"

Darjoon sighed, "Well she's bruised and beaten but from what I sensed her body is holding up fine. I'll go do that now but she's going to need far more healing than you did. I didn't want to be interrupted in the middle of it by those disgusting reptiles coming back, so you'll need to keep an eye out for me."

They scoured the area to see if it was safe but could find no footprints nor even a trail or any other sign of the lizard-men. Even after they climbed a dune and looked around from a higher vantage point, there was still nothing. The creatures had literally vanished out of their clothes and into thin air. Returning to where Sirroya was lying, Nasrindo bent down and felt her pulse.

"Hey, Darjoon? I don't think this feels too good. Unless I'm wrong, her pulse is weak and erratic. You better do that healing right now. We seem to be safe for the moment and I'll keep watch while you're busy", he picked up his spear and sat on a fallen rock nearby, scanning the horizon.

Darjoon rushed over and knelt beside Sirroya, taking her hand and feeling her pulse. Nasrindo watched as Darjoon took both her hands in his, and he heard him muttering under his breath, just catching the words, "strange magic". Looking around again and then back at them, he saw Sirroya's eyelids suddenly start fluttering and watched as her cheeks slowly became pale, all the colour draining away while her lips turned blue. Stepping forward in alarm he reached out to Darjoon, whose eyes were closed, to warn him of Sirroya's change in complexion. Just before his hand closed on his shoulder, Darjoon turned around to face him and opened his eyes, his face perspiring freely and his eyes wide and staring as he let out a long, low groan. Nasrindo watched in horror as the young mage's eyes rolled up into his head and he slumped to the floor, clearly unconscious. Sirroya gave a last rattling, wheezing cough, and then lay still and breathless.

Looking at one and then the other, he had no idea what to do. Kneeling down he shook Darjoon frantically but there was no response. Feeling for his pulse, it was there but like Sirroya's earlier was weak and erratic. Stepping over to Sirroya, he took her hand and could feel she had no pulse at all. Her lips were now bright blue, etched starkly against her snow-white face. Something must've gone wrong with Darjoon's magic. He stepped back in sudden realisation, staring around him out of instinct. Of course! The lizard-men had used magic of their own on Sirroya, most likely to set a trap for anyone who tried to heal her and Darjoon had fallen for it. It had worked perfectly and now having taken the bait on a hook he couldn't refuse, Sirroya was dead and Darjoon was dying. Nasrindo sat back on his haunches, his head bowed for a while in silence. Then he got up slowly and began digging methodically, the ground hard and unyielding.

After a long while, he placed some of the more meaningful ornaments on the large rock at the head of the stony grave and looked up as the sun slowly sank down toward the desert. He took his bearings then picked Darjoon up, grunting at the effort of lifting the heavy man. All his attempts to revive him had been futile and his pulse was as weak and thready as ever. Staggering under the weight, he put him down again and shook his head. There was no way he could carry the heavy young mage across the desert. He looked around at the debris lying scattered in the sand and started to pick up one or two bits and pieces that looked likely. Much later as the sun finally sank below the horizon and night closed in, he finished tying off the last shredded piece of clothing around the cursed staff. It had now become part of a make-shift litter he'd built using what little he had. Grunting with the effort, he rolled Darjoon onto the mage's large grey cloak in the middle of the litter and picked up the two ends of the frame. He stumbled into the desert and headed in what he hoped was the direction to a cool oasis he'd visited once before. Late that night he staggered to a halt and after making sure Darjoon was comfortable, wrapped himself in his cloak and fell into a deep sleep where the lizard-men chased him through the desert and the lovely Sirroya, now blue-lipped, snow-white and with dead eyes, reached out from the sands and implored him to help her. Waking early in the cold morning shivering, he stood up and stretched, then made sure Darjoon was still alive. After a sparse breakfast, he picked up the litter and trudged on through the soft sand and up into the unforgiving desert dunes.

He'd lost track of how far he'd come and although he tried, he just couldn't remember how long he'd been walking under the burning sun, forcing his way through the hot, soft sand underfoot. Was it actually the same day, or were the many days and nights blurring into one long, excruciating day of torment. Was this in punishment because he'd stolen the amulet from that girl? It had been so long ago and he'd been sure no-one would've missed it. He'd only realised later it was a charm of sorts and suspiciously threw it away, then found the girl distraught and in tears because it had been a gift from her grandmother. It was meant to have been a lure, to entice a fine, young man into her bed and into her life for good. Now she lamented that she would die alone. He'd tried to comfort her, but to no avail and then he'd finally left her alone as she sobbed her heart out. When he went back to her house the next day, he'd discovered her hanging from the rafters. Everyone had said she was a bit crazy and they weren't surprised, but he'd blamed himself for her death and waited for the gods to punish him. Now it seemed they had finally done so, waiting patiently to strike him down. He didn't understand what had happened. He'd been sure they were headed in the right direction and he knew the desert well, but somehow he was still lost.

Staggering, he fell to one knee, then struggled to his feet and took another step forward. In the distance he saw what he thought was a woman walking towards him. Ah, perhaps it was her at last, the young lady he'd stolen from. She had finally come to torment him. Or was he already in the afterlife and this was his reward? The woman was carrying a large waterskin and she came up and held it out. As the cool mirage slid down his throat his knees buckled and, seeing the shape of a hangman's noose, the blackness swept over him and carried him under.

The fluttering noise persisted, pushing at him through his ears. His eyelids, grimy and sandy, flickered with the light streaming into the tent through flapping cloth. Opening them carefully, he looked around in wonder. The tent poles above him were draped in brightly coloured silks, floating and snapping in the warm breeze blowing through the tent. He managed to prop himself up on an elbow and look around, staring at the strange swords hanging on the opposite wall. They were like snakes, their sinuous curves crossing over each other, and the hilts had backward pointing fangs that curled in over the hand-grip. He froze in fearful memory, knowing there was only one tribe in all the Desert that had swords like that. Had he really stumbled on the Lost Tribe, or was this the afterlife? He remembered the stories his grandmother had told him, about the Lost Tribe and how they'd been just like their own so very long ago. When some people from the Old Lands had fled the violent birthing of the Empire and the endless wars, they had gathered in the Desert of Thoth and formed tribes and alliances. The tribes had migrated to the coast, living in an uneasy partnership while feeding on the little that the harsh land provided. They survived relatively peacefully with just the occasional skirmish over resources or the odd power struggle. Most of the tribes were made up of specific nations, like Spidralites, or Srinthians or Klarandians, but one of the tribes had been an almost equal mix of different nationalities. Keeping very much to themselves and preferring to live further inland, they still gathered annually at the Great Meeting of the Tribes, until one year they never showed up nor in all the years that followed. No-one had ever seen them since or knew what had really happened to them. Many rumours and legends persisted over the years but no facts emerged. Some said they'd turned to cannibalism and eaten each other while others held they'd used magic to excess and destroyed themselves, or had mysterious powers and lived half in this world and half in the underworld. Still others maintained they bred with lizard-men and coveted their scaly females, hatching their offspring from eggs. Now here he was, in one of their tents. He smiled ruefully to himself, perhaps he would learn if the cannibalism part was really true.

He turned as a short, dusky woman entered his tent

quietly and smiled in greeting when she saw he was awake. She had long, brown hair, with deep, green eyes that crinkled at the corners when she smiled. A strong, straight nose rose above full, red lips and separated her high cheekbones above soft cheeks that dimpled sweetly at him. The innocence of her features was lost however, once you looked into her eyes and saw the experience and hard determination that burned there.

"It is good to see you are awake, warrior. May the desert bring you peace for all your days, and may the rain fall in kindness on your head. You were in the sun for a long time and I'm surprised that one such as you didn't know better?", those eyes were piercing him now.

So, he thought, she's direct and to the point and not the innocent she appears. He answered her carefully.

"Thank you for your kindness, maiden. May your friends be at your back and never eat with your enemies, and may your trades always be profitable. I would not normally walk in the sun, but my friend was in a bad way and I had to get him help as soon as I could. It is unfortunate that towards the end I had indeed lost my way."

"No, warrior, I disagree. I do not think it is unfortunate at all. Providence has brought you here and so you see, you must have been on the right path all along. I hear an old greeting from you and from that I gather you must be from the R'kadizi tribe?"

Nasrindo simply nodded in agreement, waiting for her to continue.

She looked at him quizzically for a moment then continued speaking, "You are welcome here among us until you have recovered. Then I'm afraid you will have to leave as we offer little in the way of community for outsiders, unless you choose to renounce your former and future life and all it holds for you, including your family and friends. I do not apologise for this is our way and always will be", she bowed as she said this, obviously used to reciting this for others.

He smiled dangerously, "I understand what you say, noble lady and I will leave here just as soon as I am able, but I must tell you that I cannot and will not leave without my friend. How is he?"

She started in surprise, then exclaimed, "Your friend? That is a strange thing you say, as he is not of your tribe or even of your people. We can see he is one of the accursed ancestors, in particular that evil nation of raven-born. He has gone to a place well away from the tribe and yourself and I'm afraid this is not a trail that you can use. You will have to leave without him."

The last she said with an imperious finality..

"What?", Nasrindo gasped, "You mean he's dead? No, this, this... It cannot be! Must not! It is impossible, he must not die, don't you understand? It would be a disaster for all of us, for all the Old Lands. Please, let me at least see his body!"

Nasrindo struggled to sit up but the lady held out her hand to stop him.

"Wait! Lie back, warrior, he is not dead. He is simply resting in a place where his strange magic is unable to do himself or us any harm. It will take much power to heal him. He has been deeply bitten by the scaled one's dark ways and their poison burns hot inside his body. We have a duty not just to protect him but ourselves as well. Once we are sure everyone is safe, then we may attempt the healing. I warn you this is not often or easily done, and we must take time to achieve our full power and focus for it to be effective."

Seeing Nasrindo was ready to object, she forestalled him, "No, don't even ask me, wariror. You will not go there now or ever. It is utterly forbidden. If you are healed before him, then you will have to leave, if by some strange miracle of fate he recovers before you, then he may accompany you. It is our way and has been thus for centuries. Do not believe that you can hinder your recovery as I will be directly responsible for your welfare and aside from taking your own life, there is nothing you can do that will prevent me from healing you. No, I think you must accept that you will leave here alone."

She was no longer listening to his desperate entreaties, but simply handed him a skin of water and left. The next day he tried again to reason with her but to no avail. This time she simply intoned the standard greeting, checked to see that he was okay, left a new water-skin and walked out. After that day, food was brought in by others who did not even greet him but simply worked around him quickly and quietly while occasionally the lady would bring him water and run her hands lightly over him. He could get no news of Darjoon no matter what he said. After his third attempt at speaking to the lady failed and he got upset with her, she no longer came, leaving it to another quiet one to bring him the water-skin and check on his health. This went on for some time as he lay healing from the sunstroke that had almost killed him and as he recovered he started his daily exercise routine, determined to be fit for when the time came to rescue Darjoon.

Stretching, he could at last feel the strength returning in his arms and especially his legs. He'd lost track of how many days he'd been confined to the tent, forced to do all his exercise routines in the small space next to his bed. As his strength had returned, he'd tried to leave the tent but every time there was someone outside and they easily manhandled him back into bed. Looking outside he could sense it was still early in the morning, just before the sun began to sail back up into the sky. Stepping quietly to the tent entrance, he quickly looked out to see if anyone was guarding him. Surprisingly, this time there was no-one just outside or anywhere that he could see from the tent opening. One morning just before they'd pushed him back into bed, he'd seen the lady disappearing over a set of dunes to the west, following a trail leading out of the oasis that they were camped in.

Slipping quietly along the same trail, he revelled in the freedom of the desert again, the sounds of slithering snakes and insects and once, an owl flying overhead, hunting the nocturnal mammals that were now heading home to their burrows. Realising he might bump into someone coming back along the trail, he veered away, angling to the side of the dune as he carefully made his way down. Crawling over a rise and seeing a small stand of trees surrounded by what appeared to be a faintly glowing mist, he ducked quickly then raised his head carefully and looked again. In the middle of the trees he saw a tent, and in the quiet, desert air could hear what sounded like low chanting sounds. As he started to slide down the sand and head to the side of the trees, he felt his arm being caught and held fast by someone. Jerking back, startled, he swung around and stepped back but there was no-one there. Now he felt his legs being caught and he thrashed, trying to free them from the invisible web. What was going on? He felt it tightening as he thrashed, and now the other arm was caught too. Taking a deep breath, he frantically pulled his body back and tried to shake loose the invisible, sticky web but with no luck. He was able to move a bit, but he couldn't break free. The little strength he'd built up over the last couple of days slowly ebbed as he thrashed and fought and finally he slumped back, watching as the sky lightened and the sun finally came up. In desperation he'd even tried biting the air, in case there were real threads that somehow he just couldn't see, but nothing had worked and eventually he hung his head in despair, wondering how long he would have to hang here in mid-air and if they'd even bother looking for him. They might think he'd headed back out into the desert.

The sun was already high up in the sky when he suddenly slumped to the ground, free of the web. Not trusting his tired muscles, he shuffled round and shaded his eyes, looking up at the lady who stood with her hands on her hips and glared at him. To either side of her were two burly guards and each had a spear leaning on their shoulders. She turned to them and issued commands in a language he didn't understand, then retraced her steps carefully and joined the trail, headed towards the stand of trees. Two other guards came plodding through the heat-haze over the rise and took up positions further down the trail, obviously guarding anyone from following. As one of his captors lowered their spear and attempted to prod him with it, he climbed quickly to his feet and followed the big man while the other walked closely behind. At his tent they left him inside and headed off without saying a word. Later in the afternoon, the lady appeared in the tent doorway, still frowning. She looked at him intently for a moment, then came over to the bed where he was reclining. Running her hands lightly over his brow, his chest and then his belly, she grunted to herself as if agreeing with something someone had said. As she turned to leave, he tried to reason with her again.

"Wait! Please let me see my friend. It is very important that I get to speak with him. You don't seem to understand", he pleaded.

"No, you are the one who doesn't understand. Did I not tell you that it is unlikely you would ever see him. I have already made it clear that you cannot enter the sacred place, maybe now you believe me? Don't try again, you foolish warrior. This time you were lucky but we might not have seen you for days and in that case you would have simply died, trapped in the web as you were. There is only one entrance and as you have seen it is well guarded. Tomorrow you will have to leave here because you are now well enough to survive your journey home. We will give you everything you need to make it back. This is goodbye, warrior, and good hunting."

She walked out the door, ignoring his protests. Late that evening, after his daily exercises he lounged at his tent door and watched the camp activities. Seeing that everyone had gone down to a large tent in the middle of the encampment and no-one was watching, he sneaked across to what he believed was some sort of food preparation area. Searching quickly he grabbed a long knife and slipped behind the tents, quietly heading out on the trail to the sacred place. As he came over the rise and headed down the dune, he noticed there were still two warriors guarding the trail. They watched him intently as he approached and one of them casually stepped forward, his legs slightly apart and knees bent. Nasrindo knew that fighting stance from long experience and could see they were obviously confident, as the other guard didn't move but just looked on, feigning boredom and ignoring him. Realising there was no point in talking to them, he immediately went on the offensive by launching a vicious attack designed to overwhelm an enemy quickly. The guard simply swayed and ducked and moved back from every strike, toying with him. The other guard smiled now, showing his teeth and evidently enjoying the show. Nasrindo changed to a fighting style that had always served him well in the past by switching the blade to his left hand and holding it over his head. Pushing forward with his palm held up in front of him, he looked to distract his opponent and create an opening. As he pretended to strike with his left hand he pulled it back at the last minute and flipped his right hand around, extending his fingers and making a blade of his hand, punching up towards the guards throat. His opponent didn't blink but simply swung his hands around in front of his face in a blur of movement, twisted to the side and grabbed Nasrindo's arm, his elbow connecting and driving deep into the solar plexus, winding him and dropping him to the ground. The guard followed through by grabbing his left arm and jarring his elbow, causing him to drop the knife in his hand. Gasping in pain and trying to get his breath back, he lay on the desert trail in the sand holding his injured arm. The guard picked up the knife, flipped it round and tucked it into his belt while making a comment to his friend and laughing. Nasrindo knew a lot about fighting and he knew a lot of tricks that the other tribes used, but he'd never seen anyone do what the guard had just done, or seen any other tribesman move so fast. No wonder the other guard had just lounged there. He shuddered to think what a powerful army these warriors would make. After a muttered conversation with his friend, the guard who had disarmed him pulled him to his feet, and pointing with his spear, showed him that he needed to walk ahead.

Back in the camp the people were going about their regular business, as whatever meeting had taken place was obviously over. The guard marched him through the curious stares and into the large, central, communal tent of meeting. Inside, a number of old men were sitting on large wooden chairs that had been intricately engraved with curious markings. The markings included bats, snakes and some sort of strange-looking cat. They all looked up in surprise as the guard brought him in and pushed him down into a kneeling position in the middle of the tent. Out of the corner of his eye, he saw the lady enter and take a seat on a large, wooden chair with ornate carvings of leaves and what looked like large flowers. She looked across at him, her lips pursing while she shook her head in mute disapproval.

The guard and the old men entered into an animated conversation and he could tell from the guards gestures that he was simply relaying what had happened on the trail. One of the elders laughed out loud, the others smiled and then what appeared to be the oldest gave some sort of salute to the guard who returned it and left. The elders all looked at him in stony silence as he squirmed, his knees uncomfortable on the hard, gravelly floor. Trying to rise, he noticed the old man who was obviously the leader holding out his hand, palm forward. He sank back to the floor again and glared at them.

"So you would scorn our hospitality and attack us. Is that how you repay your debts, tribesman? What is the meaning of this behaviour? Have the collective lost their way and are now without honour? You may speak, you who are of the elite."

"I must see my friend. I...", Nasrindo spluttered indignantly.

"No! No, you must not see your friend but you must leave us, as we have asked of you already. Did our healer not make it clear to you? We are not like your blood-thirsty collective, we do not harm for the sake of it, and we do not leave someone to suffer. We are peaceful healers who live as one with the land around us. All we ask in return is that we too are left in peace. You will not accept our ways, that is obvious and so you must leave."

The old man swung his palm towards the door with finality, then turned away, preparing to speak to the man on his left.

"Please!", Nasrindo pleaded, "Wait! You do not understand. I have a blood oath with the man you are holding prisoner."

"What! Explain yourself at once", the elders all turned to face him as one, the leader rising and the lady leaning forward in her chair, gripping the arms tightly.

"I have sworn blood oath with this man's parents to take care of him forever. His father was a great mage from across the sea and his mother was raven-born. They believe this child has a unique destiny and they made me swear on my ancestors with my own blood that I would protect him at all costs. I cannot leave here without him. Even you and your people must honour a covenant of blood", Nasrindo looked at each of them in turn.

There were shocked gasps and then grumbling among the old men. The lady just stared at him, her mouth open in wonder and her eyes narrowed.

"You... You made blood oath with... with... with outsiders", the word was spat venomously by one of the old men.

"How dare you do that? With someone not even from

the Old Lands? It is unheard of! This has never happened in all our history and for good reason", the old man had stood up as he spoke, saliva collecting in the corners of his mouth as he hurled the words at him in anger.

"Guards! Take him out of our sight and deep into the desert. Give him no sandals and no provisions", the leader looked at the guards as he coldly gave his command then turned to Nasrindo, "May your soul fly free, warrior, and may you return to the bosom of she who gives life. It is done! This is the worst sentence we will give but you have deserved it with your unrighteous act and your crime against the collective."

Nasrindo stood up as the large guard came in, resigned now to his fate. It was the same in any of the tribes, this death sentence, and no condemned man was ever killed at the hands of the tribes-people but rather they let the desert do it for them. The guard lifted Nasrindo to his feet and turned him towards the door, then stopped, looking over his shoulder. Nasrindo turned to see the lady standing up and walking towards him. She looked at him with narrowed eyes, shaking her head slightly to warn him that he should not speak.

"Wait, old one's. I have something to say on this matter", she said.

The old man in the middle stood up at her approach and bowed graciously, "Very well, great healer, you have the floor. But I cannot see what you have to say that will change our decision."

She began debating with the elders in their own tongue, and Nasrindo could not follow it. The guard stood next to him, his drawn sword and massive body a powerful incentive to remain still. Just then, he noticed an old crone wander in from outside. She walked up to Nasrindo and as she did the guard respectfully sheathed his sword and stepped out of the way, letting her sniff him which she did loudly. Wandering over to one of the big, younger men sitting on the floor at the back of the tent, Nasrindo watched in fascination as she sat down in the man's lap. She was chuckling to herself and played with the man's long hair, pulling at it. Suddenly, she reached down and ripped clear the young man's knife, holding it to his throat and pressing down. Nasrindo realised the debate between the elders and the lady had stopped, and everyone in the tent was breathlessly waiting to see what the crone would do. Turning suddenly, she pointed the knife at Nasrindo and began speaking in a strong, clear voice that he could understand.

"Tears! Your journey will end in tears, warrior. Go back, foolish one, go back through the desert to your tribe, to your home and never look back, not if you want a happy life."

Nasrindo shook his head in denial. He would never go back, no matter the cost. The crone shrieked with laughter, then carried on speaking in the same calm voice, "Before you die, and you will die, you will have a brother and a sister. Oh yes, a family of death and not-death."

Nasrindo stared at her in shock. It was not possible to have siblings as his parents had died long ago when he was still young. His father had run out on them when he was just a baby and had never been heard from again and his mother had brought him up by herself, having never taken another man. She died of fever not long after he came of age. The crone let out a blood-curdling wail and then started sobbing wildly. Suddenly she stopped and in the same strong voice as before, she spoke calmly to him, "The creator of life and destroyer of worlds is with us now. The blood of the old ones has not been burnt away, but this blood will save us all in the end. That's if we can save it first!"

She suddenly began laughing again, throwing her head back and showing her blackened, rotted teeth. As a yellow stain appeared on the young man's lap, followed by the acrid stench of an old woman's urine, she gave a satisfied sigh and rose, stumbling out into the night while still laughing hysterically. The lady and the old men turned away and continued their debate, the lady by her gestures obviously referring to what the crone had just said. Finally, the leader gave a grunted command to the guard. The big man prodded Nasrindo, who had sat down and waited through the discussion, and when he got to his feet he shoved him towards the door and then escorted him back to his tent.

Nasrindo watched the guard stalk off, then lay down wearily, wondering what the crone had been talking about. He also wondered if they were going to take him into the desert in the morning, to begin the march of death? He was just wondering how he would survive, when the lady entered through the doorway and came over to stand next to him, looking down at him with her penetrating gaze.

"Did you understand what the old lady was saying?", she demanded.

"Understand her? That old crone... Phwah! I mean I could hear and recognise the words but she's crazy, she...", he began to say.

"That old woman is a great and respected seer", the lady interrupted him, "She has never been wrong, even now in the last years of her life during the decline of her mind. Whatever she has said, it is all true. You would do well to respect her and pay attention to what she said. I ask you again, did any of it mean anything to you? Don't lie to me, warrior, I will know."

He numbly shook his head, trying to unscramble his brain and think about what the old woman had really been saying. The lady continued.

"The 'creator of life and destroyer of worlds' refers to those who come from the place over the sea. You probably know it as the Sorcerer's Isle or the Glass Isle. During the Great Fire, we could all see the smoke rising and we knew at that moment the island was destroyed and had became the Glass Isle of today. It is thought that all the people of the island perished in that awful destruction.

We do not believe they ever left their island, so there was no reason to think any of them escaped. Tell me now, who were your parents?", she snapped out the last question the way a man threw out a whip. He sat up and looked at her warily, then answered slowly.

"My parents were tribes-folk, like yours. I never knew my father or anything about him. He disappeared when I was still very young and was never heard from again. My mother was the kindest woman you could ever meet and her parents were our Lead Hunter and Great Healer respectively, both of whom were honoured and revered in our tribe. There were rumours that the man she had taken for a husband was actually an outsider, and it was only because of her parents that she was safe. For that matter I too was spared because of my grandparents. In time, I was able to win respect for her and for myself through my own acts of valour."

The lady nodded, then bowed her head as she thought it through. Nasrindo waited patiently until her head snapped up and she barked out more questions.

"And the young man lying in the sacred place? What do you know of him and his parents?"

Nasrindo looked surprised, expecting further questions about himself. He almost breathed a sigh of relief, hoping she didn't press him regarding his age. But then he stiffened, realising that this could be a difficult answer as it was important to conceal Darjoon's true identity and purpose.

"Darjoon? Well, he is raven-born just as you said. His parents were, uh, well, quite obviously they were also raven-born, although maybe the, um, the father, he might have come from Klarand, from the Empire. This is why Darjoon looks slightly different."

The lady stared at him for a while, looking deep into his eyes and saying nothing. Finally, she blinked and barked at him again. He almost started back at the controlled ferocity in her voice.

"If you want your friend to live, warrior, then you should think very carefully about the price of truth", turning, she stalked out of the tent, leaving him lying there in confusion. Nasrindo stared at her retreating back, wondering how he could conceal Darjoon's true identity. He spent the night tossing and turning, trying to think of ways he could get Darjoon and himself out of the clutches of the Lost Tribe.

The next morning, as Nasrindo finished his breakfast, she marched back into the tent. Putting her hands on her hips and without greeting or preamble, she began barking questions at him again.

"So, warrior, have you considered the price of truth? Are you willing to save the life of your friend, or is the truth itself too high a price? Don't think you can fool me for that will be a mistake you will live to regret."

Nasrindo looked up at her, suddenly realising it was foolish to pretend he didn't know. There was little to no risk any more and he had no other realistic options. If Darjoon wasn't already dead, then he was probably close to it. He himself had at most a day to live, after which this Lost Tribe would ensure that he was forever lost in the harsh desert outside. He sighed.

"Fine, Great Healer. I will gladly pay the price of truth and tell you what little I know. Darjoon's father was not from the Empire but from over the sea, from Sorcerer's Island. He was a very powerful mage, one of the strongest I've ever met apart from Darjoon himself. He had been visiting the raven-born when he fell in love with one of the council-members, she who was Darjoon's mother. Somehow their High Sorcerer suspected them of having more than a professional relationship and once they realised this they fled in fear of their lives before he could report them to the Council. They had arranged it so it would appear the mage had kidnapped her, allowing her the opportunity to return one day and protest her innocence", Nasrindo had lowered his head while speaking, shaking it slightly at the end.

"I'm not sure why they came to the desert tribes, but it seemed that the mage had business here. It was clear that he knew the ways of the tribes and that he even knew some of the elders. While they were with us, one of the seers from another tribe prophesied that his child would save the Old Lands", Nasrindo looked up at the woman, but she showed no reaction.

"It was about this time that our chief's son got very ill. All the powers of the local shamans had done nothing to stem the fever that burnt his body and he was slowly fading away. The lady stepped in, and using a powerful magic healed the boy so that within half an hour he was sitting up, eating and talking as if nothing had been wrong. The chief, and indeed the whole tribe, were very grateful as it was his only son and the chief was too old to have another. In gratitude they promised them whatever they asked for", again Nasrindo lowered his head and shook it.

"Finally, there came a time when the powerful mage had to return to his own land, and it seemed the raven-born lady was intent on returning to hers. Before they went their separate ways, they asked the tribe for the favour that was their due. They had the tribe call in the mightiest warrior they had, and they made him swear a blood oath, that until the end of his days he would care for the child that she would bear. Of course, they all thought it was easy to promise this, as they knew the couple were leaving and would probably never be back, and the woman wasn't even pregnant. But before they left, the couple spoke to this warrior alone and told him that the child would definitely return one day. So this warrior, who had become very fond of both of them, swore a blood oath to protect the child for the rest of his days", Nasrindo lowered his eyes and stilled his heart, breathing in deeply to calm himself and looked away from the lady for a moment, then stared straight into her eyes.

"When that warrior passed on he needed a successor,

and so I was the one chosen and now I carry that oath myself. That warrior was related to me and so the original blood spilt for the oath remains pure and undefiled. There is no breaking of the original vow", Nasrindo continued to look up at the lady who stood there looking at him, a half-smile on her face.

"That was well told, warrior. It seems you are willing to pay the price after all. Well, almost, but never mind, that other piece of truth that you have concealed will remain with you. It is not so important, not for now at least."

She turned to leave, and Nasrindo sat up, calling after her, "Great Healer, wait! What about Darjoon? Will you save him, now that you know the truth about him and that he is very much an outsider, half Old Lands and half Sorcerer's Isle? He must be saved, Great Healer, the prophecy is true, I know it."

"What do you take us for, tribesman, do you think we are the Y'rdirak and care so little for life? He is already safe. Did you think we would stand by and watch while the one who would save us all passed from this life?", she laughed at Nasrindo's expression.

"What? Did you imagine we were unaware of the prophecy? You have told me a fine story, so let me tell you one in return", she turned back and came to stand near him, looking down with her piercing eyes.

"Long ago there was a prophecy by one of our seers that the Old Lands would be under threat from flying demons. These demons would feed on the people themselves, destroying their minds and sucking out their life-blood. None can stand before them, as they will have the power and strength of ten warriors and healers. But a young mage would be born who would not only destroy the demons, but would overthrow the Empire itself and put an end to the evil forever", her face was flushed and her eyes were sparkling.

"Based on what the old seer had said and this story you told me, I believe Darjoon is that young mage. I can certainly sense his great power, and as you said it is unlike anything I have ever experienced. It is a unique blend of magic, probably as a result of the union you spoke of. From all I have heard in this world, and believe me tribesman, we are not as cut off as you might believe, there is no-one else alive in all of the Old Lands who has that kind of power. To have wielded that staff he had to... well, he... well, it's just staggering. I don't think he realised at the time what he was doing but the sheer power of the staff would kill me if I dared so much as brush the surface of the magic it contains inside", she shook her head.

"You can be grateful of that power he possesses, warrior, as the two of you could easily have been destroyed along with the lizard-men. Now listen carefully to me and remember what I am about to tell you. Your blood-debt requires much from you", she narrowed her eyes and leaned in towards Nasrindo.

"To properly harness the power that he needs, he must travel to the mist-lands of Fr'bazim, as this is where the staff came from originally. There he will learn not only to use the staff correctly but to harness part of the magic that is in his blood. His father must have gone there and absorbed it, because I can sense the frost-magic inside him. We healers have a saying regarding magic, 'As it is in the parent, so in the child'. Children of mages absorb all the magic their parents have learnt at the time of their conception. It is why Great Healers are allowed just the one child", her eyes took on a pained look, she paused, and then she continued.

"To get to those lands, he will have to travel through a magic portal. The knowledge of that portal is beyond me, or for that matter any Great Healer in any of the tribes. Nor is it a raven-born, Spidralite or Empire secret. In fact, it is not in the Old Lands that he will find the knowledge he needs. I believe that he must now travel to his father's home. He must go to the Sorcerer's Isle to find what he needs, and you must go with him. What say you?", she leaned back and folded her arms, waiting for his response.

Nasrindo had listened to all that she said with growing alarm. Now that she had finished he stood up quickly and angrily, pushing back his chair and starting to pace up and down in the tent, speaking as he walked.

"Do you... Have you... How... Do you have any idea what you are asking? The mist-lands? Magic portals? Travelling to the Sorcerer's Isle? You know that they call it the Glass Isle now because there is nothing but melted rock on that accursed island. What will he find there other than his reflection? This is insane, he must return to the raven-born lands with the knowledge he has of his father and the prophecy. The raven-born will know what to do with it and they will have the power to help him, not some crazy legend about snow cats that run with wolves. Yes, I have heard those wild tales around the camp-fire at night. They are just legends and stories, none of it is true", Nasrindo turned and faced her angrily, standing tall and straight as his frustration boiled over. He couldn't believe that any of this was real. It was a child's fairy-tale and she was mocking him with her stories. He lifted his chin in defiance, not caring now if they killed him. She narrowed her eyes and stared him down, radiating power and self-control. Her chest heaved with emotion and barely repressed anger.

"Listen carefully, tribesman, as I do not waste my time on trivial fancies or idle speculation let alone camp-fire stories. The Glass Isle is known as that because, indeed, most ship captain's are simply scared of their own reflection in the shiny mass and never venture close. But there were extensive underground structures that may have survived the destruction, even if the people did not. The knowledge he needs, that we all need, may be buried there under the melted rock. If not, then the only alternative would be asking the Circle of True Ones, and I don't need to tell you what a suicidal venture that would be. The only way one lives to see the Circle is if you are invited, and my sources inform me there hasn't been a new invitation for over fifty years, unless you or your raven-born friend received one recently? No, then those wolves must be our last resort.", she arched an eyebrow as she looked at him. He shrugged his shoulders, still fuming.

"Obviously I haven't, but I'd have to ask Darjoon as it's possible he has. He's certainly had quite some adventure already and when it comes to him, nothing would surprise me. I'm not sure which is the worse evil, the Glass Isle or the Circle. When can I see him? Has he asked for me? Don't you realise that he's all alone and needs a friend?", Nasrindo was pleading again.

For the first time, he saw real emotion in the lady's eyes as they flickered and opened wide, but then they narrowed and her mouth pursed. She looked down briefly at the floor, then into his eyes.

"Yes, warrior, I believe it is time you did see him. In fact, I am now convinced that it is very necessary, but I must warn you first! The rebound of the healing spell he performed has changed him significantly. Not in any physical sense, but... You will have to be patient with him. I'm afraid your friend cannot remember his past, especially not his recent past. At this moment, he believes that he is in the raven-born college and it is quite likely that he will not even recognise you. I am hoping that by bringing you to him, we might begin the process of restoring his memory. If that doesn't work, then... Well... Perhaps it would have been better that he died. You see, warrior, it seems that with his damaged and failing memory, all his magic is failing too. At least if he was dead, we would simply have no hope at all, rather than this meagre thread that is rapidly dwindling to nothing."

THE END

ABOUT THE AUTHOR

Growing up in the sugar cane farms of the Natal midlands in South Africa, and later enjoying the wild outdoors of what was then the Eastern Transvaal, Jackson always had a love of open spaces. He now enjoys living in the tamer countryside of southern England. Being an avid reader from a young age, he eagerly devoured J.R.R. Tolkien, C.S. Lewis, Edgar Rice Burroughs, and later Raymond E. Feist, among others. Daydreaming out in the country was always second nature to him and a means of escape from the confines of modern living. This escapism resulted in many untold stories, but now they fight their way free, released into the world as words on a page.